**To The I
Bruce W.**

Text copyright © 2018 Bruce W. Perry

All Rights Reserved

9781718199576

Email the author: bruce.perry.author@gmail.com

All characters in this publication are fictitious and any resemblance to real persons, living or dead, is purely coincidental.

To The North

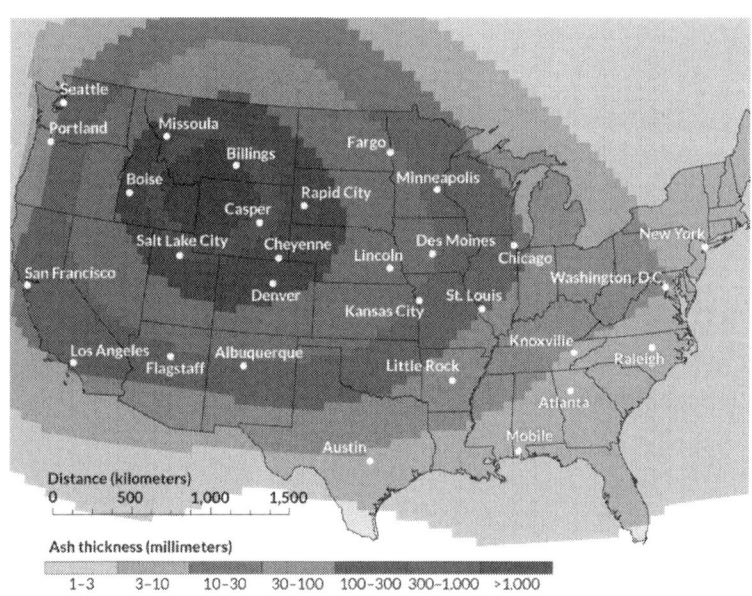

Image credit: Science News;
https://www.sciencenews.org/article/supervolcano-blast-would-blanket-us-ash

More Fiction by Bruce W. Perry:

Accidental Exiles (**A young Iraq veteran flees the Middle Eastern wars to Europe**–available in paperback and ebook. "**A genuine pleasure to read. It is hard not to respect any author who is able to capture the terror and heartbreaking nature of war, while also detailing the delicate heartbreak of missed chances and lost love**, and Perry achieves both with a deftly-subtle hand. The tone is consistent, the pacing is perfect, and the plot is striking in a way that fiction often lacks." *Self Publishing Review*, 2017)

Barbarous Coasts (**The first book in the Karl Standt crime thriller series**)

Gone On Kauai (**The second book in the Karl Standt crime thriller series**–Hawaii noir. "The plot...eventually provides a thrilling revelation." *Kirkus Reviews*, 2013)

Compulsion (**The third book in the Karl Standt series**. Two detectives pursue a serial killer working through a dating agency. "The book's great strength is its characters." *Crime Fiction Lover*)

Journey By Fire (Armed with a crossbow, Mike Wade roams the dystopian USA deserts in search of his captive daughter Kara. This "tautly told tale turns out to be a vibrant addition to the genre... **an effective odyssey through a burned, blighted future America**." *Kirkus Reviews*, 2017)

Guilt, A Novella (A sinister mystique seems to haunt three American businessmen when they hire a guide to take them into the Swiss Alps. "**A fast-paced and engaging novella with an intriguingly dramatic twist**." *Self Publishing Review*, 2017)

Devastated Lands (Young people fight to survive an eruption of Mt. Rainier. "A thrilling story set in an unforgiving landscape, as well as a personal drama of Shane Cooper, who is torn between his purely selfish need for survival and equally strong need to help others...**an entertaining post-apocalyptic adventure pitting man versus nature**." *IndieReader review*, 2017)

Lost Young Love (Coming back from a devastating injury, **a man reflects back on the peaks and troughs of his young affairs with women**. "This uniquely themed work will make you blush, laugh, and … remember your own early stumbles and triumphs in the realm of young love." *Self Publishing Review*, Aug. 2017)

The light shines in the darkness, and the darkness has not overcome it.
John 1:5

We live as we dream—alone.
Joseph Conrad, *Heart Of Darkness*

To The North

CHAPTER 1: NOVEMBER 2025

The ash gathered on an empty road that ran through the desert. It fell silently, with a muffling effect like heavy, dense snowstorms. They did their best to plow and shovel it to the side of the road in gray, sooty piles. The men and women wore masks and the dust filled the sky and choked out the sunlight. Then after days and days, the storm finally stopped.

The ash covered the mountains, too, like an ungodly layer of gray dirt. On account of what it did to engines and machinery, even a centimeter of it was enough to shut everything down, including the airports, factories, farms, utilities, and most of the major highways.

Brad Garner had crashed in a roadside motel called La Casa Grande just south of Las Cruces, New Mexico, outside the boundary of the worst ash deposition. He'd sleep on the narrow hard bed, fitfully, then wake up with the pale sun gushing through a tawdry set of shades. He'd been there for a couple of weeks. He hadn't bothered fleeing farther south into Mexico, or still deeper into Latin America. He couldn't force himself to take that last step. His family was still somewhere in America. They, like millions of others, were presumed dead. He had friends who had left, anyone with means, after the eruption. They went to places like Costa Rica, Australia, New Zealand, South Africa, and Terra Del Fuego.

Those were presumptuous moves; few regions were expected to escape the fierce winter, of the nature of an impending ice age, or the destruction and disruption caused by vast amounts of piled-up volcanic debris.

Garner would throw his shade open, make two cups of watery Mr. Coffee, and stand outside in the parking lot watching the pink light gather in the desert. There would always be one or two other people in the motel, but he hardly ever saw them.

In the distance were dim outlines of grayish brown mountains, an empty highway, and a desert that was like a lunar landscape.

He'd go back inside his threadbare room where a stuffed backpack and a duffel bag lay on the floor, grab his keys, and walk down the road to the Raw Frontier diner. It was a merciful place, an always-open, familiar spot where he could get breakfast and talk. He didn't mind the walk; it was long but calmed him. He wore a yellow kerchief over his face to prevent the ash from getting into his nose and lungs, when it was still carried in the wind.

A pickup truck would stop once in a while, he knew he appeared desolate and anonymous to other people. Most of the time, save one when it rained sulfurous mud, he would wave it on.

The diner was all but run by Julie, who was the only waitress. She lived in a trailer out nearby in the desert. It had an old black horse tied in the back of it; she drove a banged-up Ford Bronco. He was curious but not altogether unbelieving about why she still lived alone. He found her friendly, kind, and cute. Like him, she had sailed up to the line of middle age, and what had happened before spoke in the lines on her face.

He didn't ask her yet about her alone status or brought it up in a flirtatious way, because everyone's situation was skewed or warped back then.

"Hey Brad," she'd say when he walked in, the diner usually empty. "Hungry?"

"As a horse. What'd you got?"

"I have fresh eggs today, grapefruit, rye toast…"

"Any hash?"

"You know I have corn beef hash. You don't have to ask."

"Okay, I'll have eggs, hash, fruit with coffee. Say, can you put cheese on the eggs?"

"Of course."

"Whatever cheese there is. How was last night? Quiet?" he said.

She'd been complaining of coyotes. Packs of them feeding off the animal carcasses that littered the still polluted desert. Her family had stayed in eastern Idaho, near the Tetons, on the same ranch as her parents. They were all gone now, like his.

"It was a full moon. For a moment, I saw the stars… I didn't hear a thing. No coyotes."

"Good. The mangy dogs forgot about you."

Garner settled onto an old swivel stool at the counter. He could taste the bourbon whiskey from the night before, a coarse patch on the top of his mouth. A couple of guys who drove cattle trucks took up another booth. They wore wide-brimmed hats but set the hats on the table. They had dirt and ash on their leather boots.

Another man walked in as Julie set a cup of coffee in front of Garner. He sat at the counter and took his own hat off.

"Got any jobs for me?" Garner asked her.

"A screen door in back needs fixing, and the Bronco is making another sound. A new one. There's always pots and pans."

"I can't make any promises about the Bronco, but the rest of that stuff is done."

She continued wiping the counter. He thought she had really black, beautiful hair, like a bear's fur. But longer of course. She looked up at him, smiled.

"Wonderful. Thanks."

The old man who did the cooking, Ross, moved around silently in the back. He had white grizzle on his cheeks, looked like he shaved about once per month, and wore a cooking smock over a yellowed t-shirt. He was always there, starting before 5 a.m., and Garner would see him drive away in a pickup after the diner closed at 8 p.m.

Garner thought of working at the diner, but he didn't want to do any cooking and he didn't want to make a commitment. He'd have to do it, or something else, if he encountered problems paying his motel bill.

He smelled the aromatic cooking–eggs, butter, bacon and sausage. He heard the old man scraping at the griddle with a spatula. Garner sipped his coffee. The two guys in the booth seemed deep in conversation. The man at the end of the counter took out a cell phone and placed it on the counter.

Then Garner's food arrived. He dived into the pile of eggs first. Julie lingered for a moment.

"This is delicious. Thanks so much." People used that expression all the time–Thanks so much–but in his case the gratefulness was genuine.

"I'll give you seconds. There's plenty left over."

He'd only known her for a few weeks, and had begun to wonder why they couldn't have dinner at her trailer. He hadn't even seen it yet. Then again, he was no different than

To The North

anyone else; not really making plans. Living hour by hour.

"All I do is work," she said, looking away, in a making conversation kind of way. She left the comment out there dangling.

"Why don't we have dinner some time?"

"Really? I don't know."

"Have a whiskey. There's still some around. Watch that sunset."

"When you put it that way…"

She was real pretty, Garner thought, and the way the world and the years had put some miles on her had made her more attractive. It was okay to have friends, in his circumstance. That was called survival.

"I don't want to drink alone. I don't want to start in on that."

"I know what you mean. You still staying at La Casa?"

"Yeah," he said, a bit embarrassed. "Temporarily…"

"I used to like the pub they had, when it was still open."

"I wouldn't know." She'd known that part of New Mexico longer than he had. She'd lived in Tucson and her husband and kids had been on a holiday in Idaho, at the parent's ranch, when it had happened. When she'd heard, she had just gotten in her car and driven with desperation across Arizona, with no destination in mind. The area was familiar to her because she was New Mexican born.

The old man put two plates of ready food up on the counter for her. He scowled at her from the kitchen, then went on with the cooking.

"I better go," she said. "I'll let you know, though."

It gave him some hopefulness. Yet she was right; he wouldn't want them to drift into a misery-loves-company type situation. Two lonely hearts getting sloshed on pointless evenings and cheaper whiskey, talking about their

5

misfortunes.

When he scraped his plate clean, he turned to the man next to him.

"What are you doing with a cell phone these days? I thought there was no service."

"I went down to southern Texas, got service, and called some relatives back east."

"Did you get good reception?"

"Fine. The east is getting ash storms, but they're holding up. I got some news about what's happening up north. What the military and the feds are planning to do. They're sending a bunch of probes up there. This shit is for real; it's like a dead planet up north."

Everyone in the diner was listening, including the cook, who stepped out of the kitchen wiping his hands with a towel.

"They're putting things in the region that don't have to breath, like drones. They want to find out how things are, beyond flying jets overhead, which of course they did."

Only the planes originating from airports that weren't choked with ash, Garner thought. He was quiet for a minute, taking it all in.

"Any reports yet, of what they found?"

"No. Don't know whether it's started yet. They don't tell the public anything; this is all leaked stuff that finds its way on Twitter and Facebook." The internet was agile enough to survive a calamity that affected two-thirds of the country. In New Mexico, a web connection came and went.

The man started to chew on a piece of toast. "They expect to find nothing alive, maybe a peep here and there, in the worst hit states. Wyoming, Montana, Idaho, most parts of Colorado, Utah, Iowa, Nebraska, North Dakota. Eastern Washington and Oregon. Places that got really buried with ash…and still are…"

The diner went silent.

"These drones and probes will be taking readings and gathering data and stuff," the man added.

"Good that'll do," grunted one of the two men in the booth. "These places got three, six, even 10 feet of ash. Won't be able to live, grow anything, find clean water, for 10, maybe 20 years. 'Data and readings.' I could'a told 'em that. Don't bother. Over 13 million lived in those states—no one knows how many are dead."

"Could you be quiet *please*? Please!" someone cried out. They all looked up. At the end of the diner, sitting in one of the booths, was a younger woman, a little girl, and a grandmother type. They'd been eating quietly up till now.

"You're scaring our daughter. We don't need to hear anymore of this! Isn't it bad enough?" The young lady fought back tears. "Look what we've already gone through! How many of you, with all your flippant comments and tough talk, lost family members?"

"Why, we all sure did, Ma'm," the man in the booth said. "Everyone knows someone."

"We have to leave. C'mon Becca. Willie. The bill?" Flustered, she stepped out of the booth and hurriedly gathered her things.

"The meal's on us today," Julie said, not moving from the counter.

"No, I insist," the woman said, reaching into her purse. It seemed to be a point of pride.

"You can get us next time," Julie said.

"Oh alright." She took the hand of the young girl, and looked up at the men. "You'd think you'd have…more restraint, or respect! We're just the fortunate ones, that's it! Let's go."

Then the three of them left the diner, the screen door closing hard behind them.

There was only about 20 seconds of silence, before the men spoke up again.

CHAPTER 2

"They won't know anything until something, or somebody, a kind of team, goes in there to see what the real damage is."

"All them bodies up there," the second booth occupant said. "It's just awful. Tragic. No one's comin' out; that's what I hear. That didn't escape the ash clouds and pyroclastic flows, right away. Can't wrap my head around more than a million dead. It's like those historical reports you read about. Extinctions, and things."

"Well, we're still here," Garner said. "And billions more of us."

The other man in the booth was looking down and pushing his coffee cup across the formica of the table.

"Air's not breathable up there. You have to wear a hazmat mask. It'll be like that until the eruption's completely stopped, and it hasn't."

They were about 1,100 miles, depending on the route, from Yellowstone Park, the epicenter of the super volcano.

Yet it seemed much closer, since it influenced everything, and every life, in one way or another.

Julie wandered around refilling people's coffee cups.

"People in underground bunkers could survive," she commented. "With weeks worth of food and water."

"And a fresh source of oxygen, as in oxygen tanks," the first booth guy said. "You'd have to be seriously prepped. I suppose, the best prepared could survive. Time's runnin' out even for them."

"Ought to send an Army of masked suited men in there, pronto," his partner said. "An Army of HazMat responders."

"I heard they were planning something like that," the man at the counter said. "But they're starting with the drones and the robotics."

"Goddammed Mars Explorers," one of the booth guys said. "Only the machines can cope. Drones and 'bots. Otherwise, you'd have to send 100,000 men or more in there with space suits."

"Bet they have the equipment," the man across from him said. "The government? They stockpile all kinds of survival gear and technology, vast warehouses full of it. In secret. For themselves and their families, only. You'll see, the ones who survive this will be all them down in Washington."

"Hell," his friend said. "Look what we're going through after just a dusting of that shit. We're gonna run out of bottled water, unless they ship some up from Mexico. No airports or shipping going on, anywhere. You can't plan for a catastrophe like this. FEMA–are you kidding me? I'll tell you what I'm going to do; head for Argentina, Chile."

"They won't take you," the other man said. "Millions of American refugees? Nah! It's already causing a problem with the Mexican border. Think you're going to be able to drive across all them borders? And they welcome you with open arms? Forget about it."

"Drive? No way, I'll fly. I'll drive down to Mexico, or Panama, or Nicaragua, and fly south. I'm selling my house."

"Who'll buy it?"

The man at the counter laughed. "I'd say we're all just going to have to sit tight. Clean up the ash, inventory the food and water, and sit tight. Hope we don't get any more ash clouds."

"Hope is cheap," one of the booth men said, bitterly.

Julie and Brad had gone silent, listening to the men trill. Julie dropped a bill on their table.

"When you get a chance…"

"Waiting isn't an option," the man said, reaching into jeans for a bill fold. "We've had massive crop damage. The livestock is all dead, millions of them, lying in the desert and fields out there. And the winter's going to be hell."

"Maybe not as bad here," Garner said. "This is the desert. We're closer to the equator."

"Not close enough. And deserts can get cold, too." They all, by instinct, looked outside, to the Organ Mountains in the distance, with the shimmering heat of the desert and the pallid sun smeared by drifting ash clouds. The mountains looked grayish white now.

All the talk had forced Garner's mind back to October 10, 2025.

CHAPTER 3: OCTOBER 10, 2025

    The scientists knew it was coming, because the three calderas in the Yellowstone region began filling with magma. But only the National Park and the surrounding towns were evacuated, as a precaution. They hadn't been able to predict the exact timing of the super-volcanic eruption, or even if it was going to happen at all. Until it was occurring, and then it was too late.

    Yellowstone had experienced swarms of small earthquakes, which wasn't unusual. They were used to seeing swarms of 1,000 or more per month. But the daily clusters of quakes became more numerous, and each of the quakes was atypically strong.

    The animals—the bison, elk, deer, brown bear, even birds—fled the refuge beforehand, in a determined, en masse manner. The land began to deform, huge swathes of forest and rock-covered ground rippling in the way of fluid, as it held back the profound geologic pressure of gases from below.

Garner was in the airport in Chicago, Illinois, the day it happened. He had just exchanged a text with his wife Kiatsu, who was with her dad and their two kids outside Pocatello, Idaho. Not 100 miles from Yellowstone National Park, they never had a chance. Garner watched the television in the airport terminal and the multiple explosions from Yellowstone, towering shafts of black ash, debris, and fire bulging out and filling the skies around southern Montana, Wyoming, and eastern Idaho.

The networks displayed pictures of chaotic fleeing crowds and bumper-to-bumper traffic jams from places like Butte, Montana, Bozeman, Montana, and Casper, Wyoming, then the terrible darkness that befell the land, the lethal blizzards of ash that suffocated everything that moved within hundreds of miles of the explosion.

Garner spent an hour intermittently on the phone with Kiatsu, begging her to drive as fast as she could with the kids west into Oregon. The southern direction towards Salt Lake was probably out, so all he could implore was "go west." He felt pitiable, standing helplessly in the airport terminal with the phone pressed to his ear; he knew his family couldn't just ride it out in the house.

They couldn't go north toward Canada on interstate highway 15, because that would have brought them laterally along the exploding National Park, with pyroclastic flows that brought instant death.

All planes were grounded. It took just a few millimeters of fine ash to clog and disable engines and close an airport. Garner went out and rented a car. Experts appeared on the terminal TVs and diagrams were displayed showing concentric circles emanating from ground zero (GZ) of the super volcano.

A radius of 250 kilometers or about 150 miles around Yellowstone National Park or GZ would receive in excess of 1,000 mm or one meter (40 inches) of ash, collapsing rooftops, destroying electric utilities, smothering factories, transportation centers, and hospitals, and rendering any kind of motor useless. Any travel through it was impossible.

An area with a radius of about 310 miles from GZ, extending from Boise through Salt Lake City and Denver would receive about one meter of ash, enough to kill thousands and bring cities to a standstill. An area more than 2,000 kilometers (1,240 miles) across most of the west and a large swathe of the midwest would be buried in at least 100 mm or 4 inches.

Exposed to the blinding storm of dense particles, all food cultivation and distribution ground to a halt; hospitals, airports, and military bases partially or completely shut down.

The information coming from the experts the networks trotted out was cold and rational. The volcanic debris would also contain deadly, superheated, particlized magma, they said, since most of the vast amounts of magma in the calderas were blasted into the sky, rather than exiting as lava.

Unable to watch the coverage or catch a plane west, Garner just drove. He tried to drive west to Des Moines, Iowa, but State Police and National Guard, some already wearing HazMat masks, blocked his passage. When Kiatsu stopped answering his cell phone calls from the roadside, he began texting. He filled his gas tank and kept going.

Ultimately, there was no going west towards Kansas City and Denver—where roadblocks and immovable traffic jams also occurred—so he kept driving south. He didn't hear from his family anymore. In Arkansas, there was still gas. Crowds of people wandered the dark streets like zombies in towns he drove through, and he'd join groups of people around flatscreen TVs in franchise gas stations when he filled up.

The extent of the catastrophe became obvious when the reports stopped showing local footage and only large-scale airborne images and video simulations. The president made a somber statement, other world leaders. People openly sobbed, talked in hushed tones about "end of days" and "extinction events." Garner wanted nothing to do with that.

He kept driving, keeping eyes propped open with coffee and cokes and adrenaline. A small army of brave, but ultimately suicidal first responders went into the Montana-Idaho-Wyoming zone and only a few came out.

He drove through Little Rock, Arkansas, and then down into Texas. He went west. The ash was coming, everyone said. Endless, bumper-to-bumper traffic snaked southward, toward Houston and Mexico, going the opposite direction that he was.

He felt like an insane man, with no plan, no rationale for what he was doing. It was a strange sort of primal energy that locked him silently behind the wheel for hours and days along unfamiliar and sprawling highways.

After another day's drive, he reached Las Cruces, New Mexico on a near empty tank. He'd sent about one text to his wife per hour, hundreds of them. No answer. The cell phone had finally died. New Mexico was already receiving a dusting of ash, and everyone was urged to stay inside. The ash, even in millimeters, was poison. Breathe it in, and it mixed with moisture in the lungs and became cement-like.

He solemnly placed a credit card on the front desk at La Casa Grande, whose green neon cactus he'd spotted from a few miles away. Then he collapsed on his stomach on the bed in the small room and slept a form of death.

CHAPTER 4

He met Julie at dusk. He brought a pizza and a bottle of Jack Daniels. He hitchhiked, catching a ride with a guy in a pickup, who dropped him off at the end of her dirt road. You could see the weak flickering lights of her trailer nestled several hundred yards away. The dwelling fronted a large space of scrub desert, with the darkening outline of the Organ Mountains in the distance.

When he strolled up the road, carrying only a paper bag with the food and whiskey, she opened her screen door and stepped down into the dried grass and sand.

The light had begun to fail above the Organs, the edge of whose peaks glowed pink. The ash fall had diminished; a normal sky returned gradually, yet he could still sense a coating of luminescent dust out on the desert. Most of the west, however, was reduced to a wasteland.

They put two folding chairs on the front lawn facing the mountains. It was quiet; only a buffeting, intermittent wind, crickets, and the occasional squawk from a crow. Julie brought out two ordinary kitchen glasses and square-shaped plates for the pizza. Garner twisted the cap off the liquor bottle and poured them each three fingers. A slight breeze came off the desert, which still radiated the day-time heat.

"Well," Garner said, raising his glass. "Here's to the sunset, and the first nip of good bourbon."

"Cheers," she said, sipping her drink, followed by a grimace.

"It has a bite, doesn't it?" she said. Garner took a big swallow. He could feel the syrupy calm all too well; it moved from his chest to his legs. Julie seemed shaky and tremulous, balancing the glass on her bare thigh.

"Are you cold?" he said. He touched her wrist, which trembled, like a palsy. "I can give you my coat. Here, take it." It was a faded jean coat he'd been wearing for weeks; he draped it around her shoulders.

"Thanks."

"The pizza isn't half bad. Pepperoni." He pealed off a couple of slices and put them on their plates, then they ate quietly for a minute.

"Do you ever go up into those mountains?" he asked, nodding toward the 10,000 foot peaks. "Those fantastic peaks. I can't tell whether it's snow or ash. I think probably snow. Maybe not."

"We went up there just a few days ago. Me and Tanya. It has snow mingled with ash, like a meadow when the wind blows dust on new snow. We drove up that dirt road and hiked around a bit, just for solitude, and the views. I needed evidence that the earth I knew still existed. That not every inch of it was covered with crap."

"And?"

"We saw a beautiful lake; purple and normal looking, the sun's reflections, at least from a distance. We saw some birds, herons and ducks, fly up from the lake. Green forests. Though lots of the trees are grayish brown, now."

"Tanya's your dog, right? Where is he?"

"She. Tied, out back. I can't let her loose in the desert at night, you know. Coyotes, rattlers, everything."

"The horse back there too?"

"Taipei, yeah."

"Taipei? Isn't that in Taiwan?"

She shrugged. "I like the sound of it. It's noble."

"I want to meet Tanya, give her a pet."

"Okay. Hold my drink." She got up and wandered around back, Garner following part of the way. She led the eager dog out from the darkness. Tanya wagged her tail furiously, her taut torso wiggling with excitement. Dogs always acted around Garner as though they'd been abandoned for days, even when it's ten minutes.

He reached out and began to pet her, the dog not timid or snappy at all.

"Wait, is that a Rhodesian…"

"Rhodesian Ridgeback, yeah. Pure bred, I believe." Her voice had a knowledgeable tone.

"I had one for a short time when I was a boy." He pet Tanya's short brown hairs with the bristle that went along the spine and gave the breed its name. She wriggled with excitement, softly whimpering.

"There there, Tanya. How old?"

"Six." It felt good just to pet a friendly, handsome dog, and not think about anything else. The ruins that engulfed the country. The absent people. A part of it seemed like cheap escapism, however.

They returned to their folding chairs facing the desert, with Tanya leashed to one of the seat posts. Garner already felt looped; the Jack went down too easy.

"Do you have any music?"

"The Bronco has a radio. I'm using it to charge my phone. Let's see what I can find."

The vehicle idled at the end of the driveway, like a

small generator. She went over to the Bronco, opened the driver door, and fiddled with the few remaining radio stations. She settled on one playing country ballads, Emmy Lou Harris. She turned it up.

"That's really nice. Really nice," he said, and drained the bottom of his drink. He refilled the glass instantly.

"Want some more yet?" The song was Tulsa Queen, and Harris sang about lonely trains at night.

"You're going much faster than me!"

"What about the lights inside the house?" Electricity was rationed because of the power plant damage.

"Candles. I've got them everywhere. I like candles anyways. They relax me at night. Especially now."

"I know what you mean."

He reached for the dog, stroked her head, settled back in his chair. The breeze was cool, clean for once, and smelled like mesquite.

He refreshed both their glasses, his own for the third time, but he wasn't keeping track.

"I feel like a hobo drinking out of a brown bag." He took the bottle out and placed it on the ground. "But during not the best of times, it works wonders."

"Hittin' it pretty hard lately, huh?"

"I suppose so." He looked at his glass critically, then up into the mountains.

"I'm dulling the pain. I know it doesn't sound very brave. The pizza's good, too." He put his drink down and ravenously bit into another piece.

"How many kids do you have, Brad?"

"Two. Jake and Abby. Eleven and nine."

"I love their names. I can see their faces. That's the way it is with names."

"Now that you mention that…" He took out his wallet, then a small photo.

His voice caught in his throat. "That's my boy, Jake,

in his baseball uniform. He was nine then."

"Jake Garner. Sounds just like a ballplayer. Possibly, a sheriff in a small town. Or a nice dad in a TV show. I can tell you're a nice dad."

"How many kids do you have?"

"I have two daughters, Dakota and Elan." They were going to stick to present tense from now on.

"Totally beautiful names. How did you come to them?"

"They're native American names; Arapahoe."

"Ah."

"You might as well give me some more." She held her glass out; he poured her three more fingers. Emmy Lou's voice, warm, polished, and resonant, rang beautifully over the desert.

"Your kids ride?"

"You bet. Ever since they could stay on a saddle. We had a couple of horses in Phoenix, boarded at some guy's place."

"I always wanted to learn to ride a horse. Maybe you can teach me, on Taipei."

"It would be a pleasure." Then they were silent for a second, sitting in the filtered moonlight and eating and letting the music wash over them.

Maybe I should have brought red wine instead of whiskey, he thought. Then it occurred to him, he was still married. So was she, until they both had firm evidence to the contrary.

"Jesus," he said, guiltily, holding up his empty glass.

"That's alright, Brad. I'm a bit too fond of the alcohol, myself. Half Native American, you know."

"Really?" That would explain the jet black hair, and fine cheekbones. She was a lady of the southwest; he thought they'd be friends for life after this. All those mornings in the diner had rescued him. Talking with Julie.

"Well I'm Irish, so I guess we're both in the same

boat. Prone to the demon drink."

"What does your husband do?" he said.

"He was…is…a carpenter. His company filled up the desert outside Phoenix. Subdivisions. I suppose it's nicer out here. The last time I talked to him, that day, he said he wanted to move to southern Idaho. Nearer the desert. Maybe we'd have a horse farm, breed and board horses. Teach horseback riding, right?

"Good clean country in Idaho. Tommie was all ready to sell the house in Phoenix. Move. I talked to Dakota, on the phone. She told me the Tetons were pretty, the people were nice. She wanted to ski, ride a big black horse. She likes, you know, the dramatic looking steeds."

"You mean like Taipei?"

"Yeah."

"Where did you get that horse?"

"I found it with the house here. The family had run away."

"You're just squatting here?"

"Right. I guess I'm kind of a caretaker. Don't know what happened to the owners. Ross, the cook, said they high tailed it to Mexico, when the eruption started."

Garner looked up at the sky, the stars fighting through a thin ash layer. A shiver went through him. He suddenly felt tight. The whiskey and the song made him sad.

"Why don't you introduce me to Taipei."

"Sure."

She untied the dog's leash and they walked in the dark to the back of the house, where the horse had a large, wooden lean-to for a stall. He could smell moist hay, and hear the horse snort and scrape his hooves as they got closer. It stood in the dark like a huge black shadow.

The music seemed softer and tinnier from a distance. Julie walked up and took Taipei's reins and walked him over. He reached out and stroked the tough, dewy hide of his neck.

The horse shifted around in the darkness.

"Do the coyotes ever bother him?"

"No. I'm afraid of lions, though. One time, I could hear the cough, you know, the roar, from out there. I thought I did. I took him inside the house for the night."

"Funny, he must have taken up all the room!"

"He did." He held both whiskey glasses, as though he was at a party and felt the insecure need to carry his drink around with him.

"Poor thing," she murmured, stroking his mane. "I don't think I feed him enough. Hay's hard to come by. Only desert grasses."

After a minute she tied him back up, turned, and looked up at Garner. Her eyes were bright in the darkness, set off by the long shiny black hair.

"Will you dance with me?" she said.

"Of course I will." He put both drinks down on the desert floor. She came over shyly and placed her arms around his neck. She leaned in and rested her head on his shoulder. He linked his hands around the small of her back, and they swayed back and forth to the music.

"I'm drunk," she murmured, only after a minute.

"Me too."

She lifted her head off his shoulder a minute later, after the good feelings had all settled in. It had been so long for both of them that it felt like a foreign feeling, a long lost trait.

"What is Abby like?" she asked, looking him straight in the eye.

"Serious. Beautiful. Talented."

"She has long dark hair, like me. And she loves to swim."

"How did you know?" He hadn't shown her Abby's picture.

"Lady's intuition."

"She loves to dance too. She has a recital coming up."

"That's wonderful."

"What about that other daughter of yours, Elan? They must be stunning; beautiful women make beautiful daughters."

"You flatter me. I'm going to make you guess what Elan likes."

"Riding ponies, and boys."

"Check and check. The boys more than the ponies. And they, her." She paused a moment. "We are drunk."

"I like it this way."

"Obviously, I'm not driving you back to the motel."

"The Cactus Dive…"

"You're staying here." Then she hesitated and…"The couch folds out." A fleeting moment of awkwardness followed.

"I accept your invitation."

"Thanks for dancing with me." She let go of him and they began to stroll back to the house full of candles.

"It was my pleasure."

"Nope, the pleasure was mine."

Before they turned in she wanted to drive them three miles up into the mountains, where they parked. They had the music on. They got out of the Bronco, then she showed him a small steep cliff where you could look down into a creek below. Almost dry. But the water wound through the desert and flowed and flickered away in the moonlight. They sat on the edge of the knoll and stared down into the water silently. The white-noise flow over rocks was the only sound, and after a few minutes he knew exactly why she took him there.

CHAPTER 5

They drove down to the diner the next morning. He had coffee and breakfast, then he helped Ross clean the kitchen pots, and he took a screwdriver to the loose screen door. He figured he'd start working at the Raw Frontier. Julie had some things that needed fixing around her place, too. He thought about learning to ride the black horse with her in the desert.

In a simple way, the work made him feel useful, with a purpose. He was normally a man of the office, a traveling nine-to-fiver, but he imagined he could become one of these country types, if the soiled and stricken landscape was able to recover.

A hard winter was coming.

These thoughts made him feel guilty. His family was still somewhere out west. The last thing he had said to Kiatsu was, go to Oregon. God speed. I'll meet you in Oregon. Go as fast as you can. This was when they were close, too close, to exploding Yellowstone.

His phone was recharged, but no return messages had come through. He figured any replies must be bottled up in servers somewhere, due to the disabling of all the computer farms. He knew computers and technology, due to his old job.

At the end of the day, he walked back down the road to La Casa Grande. The wind had scoured more of the ash off the desert floor, and as the trucks went by, it accumulated in dirty piles on the sides of the road. He pulled his buff tighter on his face, his hat down lower over his eyes.

He removed his key, an old-fashioned fob, and the first thing he noticed when he walked into the drab room was a half-empty Jack Daniels bottle perched on the bureau of drawers. It gave off an air of dissolution and defeat. He poured the rest of it down the sink and rinsed out the bottle. He could use it for water later.

He face planted on the bed, then woke up after an incalculable number of hours, slowly making his way to the lone window. He lifted up the shade to a glow behind the mountains. He'd secretly been hoping for a knock on his door, but nothing came last night. Julie had to waitress most of the day, but he thought she might stop by his hotel afterward, so they could eat together.

They kept their plans unspoken, but all they had anymore was each other, unless some miracle happened. Maybe Julie was Garner's miracle, but all he felt, when the whiskey hadn't taken hold, was the crushing loss of Kiatsu, Jack, and Abby.

A few hours later, he pulled on his clothes and began to walk toward the diner, along a desert road that had small sand dunes of ash. A pickup with an emergency red light blinking drove fast in the other direction, followed by another pickup close behind. He stood on the side of the road and watched them. The second pickup slowed and stopped; he recognized it. It pulled into the breakdown lane.

Something made him walk fast, then jog to the driver's window, which was rolled down. The driver was Ross, the cook.

"It's Julie," he said. "Get in." Garner hurriedly slipped into the passenger seat and slammed the door. Ross pealed out in the dirt of the breakdown lane and sped off. The engine was loud.

"Julie never showed up at work," he yelled.

"Today?" Garner said incredulously.

"Yeah, today! She never misses a day, too. So we asked a guy going in that direction to check in on her trailer. He called. There's been a fire."

"Is she okay?"

"I don't know. I know you two are friends so..."

"Well, what did the guy say?"

"Nothing! Just come! Do I look like a mind reader?" he croaked over the engine.

Garner saw smoke rising at a place in the desert out his window. They came to Julie's dirt road, turned down it, and Garner saw the burned house, and the truck with its red light going.

He didn't see Julie anywhere.

Two masked men in firefighter's helmets and gear stood in the driveway. Ross slammed on the brakes in the dirt and Garner opened his passenger door and ran down to the pile of smoldering wood and collapsed roof.

He put his hands on his head and turned to the men. "Where is she?"

"You mean the owner?"

"Yeah!"

"Well, we found a lady in the wreckage. Deceased. And a horse."

"Shit! Goddamnit it all to hell! Where is she? Where!"

"Back of the house there. Under a tarp. Sorry. Don't look. Just let that body be."

"Goddammit!" he declared, looking up at the sky, his eyes watering. "Jesus Julie!"

One of the firefighters watched him wordlessly, then said, "It was the candles. We're almost sure of that. She must have fallen asleep, and the horse knocked 'em over. Then the door was locked and, the dog was out back. They didn't hear her. She's quiet now."

The candles, and the horse inside, and the lions, Garner thought.

"Where is the dog?"

"In the back of the house."

He ran back near the empty horse stall, and saw Tanya, crouched down on the ground and whimpering. He ran over to Tanya, then looked up and saw the lump on the ground, under the tarp.

He walked over and squatted down, took off his hat and ran his fingers through his hair. He paused, considered whether to lift a corner of the tarp. He stood up and put his hat over his heart.

"God almighty," he whispered. "Julie. You never saw this coming. I'm gonna miss you so bad. Jesus Christ almighty."

He put his head down and walked back and took the leash and the dog back to the group of men standing on the driveway. He didn't look back out to the mountains on the horizon.

To The North

CHAPTER 6

    They held a small, muted service for Julie in the desert near her house, where they buried her with Taipei put beneath the ground nearby. Present were a minister, Ross, Garner, the local sheriff, a few of the diner regulars who drove trucks, and a few of the local women who worked thereabouts and had quickly gotten to know Julie. She really hadn't lived in Las Cruces very long at all.
    Since no next of kin existed, for the time being, and Garner was willing to take Tanya and needed a vehicle, they let him take the Bronco. The minister said something predictable and automatic about Julie joining her family in heaven, but Garner wasn't so sure her family was all dead, even though it increasingly seemed likely, like his own.
    The minister read a few Bible passages, and a young lady played unbearably sad violin music, which mournfully rang and carried over the desert.
    Afterwards, Garner took the Bronco and Tanya back to the Raw Frontier diner, where he saw the kitchen lights on.

He found Ross mopping the floor. Ross came and opened the screen door when he noticed the Bronco pulling to a stop behind the diner. He put some steak bones and other meat scrap on the floor in a bowl for Tanya, then he sat at the counter with Garner.

"What a damned tragic shame!" Ross muttered. He appeared at a complete loss, like someone who had lost his mother, not just a waitress. "I used to call her Sunshine. She lit this place up. You couldn't stay in a bad mood around Julie. Even a sour old fool like me. She really liked you, you know?"

"I don't know about that. She hardly knew me. It's awful, for sure. I was hoping to get to know her better."

"I didn't think she was going to stick around this dusty outpost much longer. Now I wish she left earlier, so she would still be alive.

"I don't know what I'm going to do now," Ross mumbled, as though he half didn't care. "All the gals in town have left or have jobs elsewhere. You wouldn't want to work here, would you?"

"Nah. A waiter? I'm probably the worst waiter in the world."

"Just thought I'd try. No one will buy this place. I'll probably have to close it."

"The truckers will still come here," Garner said, his voice rising, trying to boost the diner owner's morale. "You'll make a brisk steady business with them, and sooner or later, most likely sooner, a college girl will come around who needs a few extra bucks."

"What are you going to do?"

"I don't know. I'll probably go south. I don't know. It depends."

"On what?"

"On what happens with communications. I've got all these messages out there to my family, and the local hospitals

To The North

in Idaho and Oregon, and FEMA and state police divisions. I can't draw any conclusions until I've heard from them. No final ones, at least."

"Well, I'll keep praying for you."

"Thanks." But the comment went over a little oddly, as though Ross had just discovered religion. Then Ross pulled out an old bottle of bourbon from the kitchen. They'd been drinking coffee.

Ross gripped two glasses and placed them on the table. Garner felt bad turning him down, but the bottle Ross brandished looked circa 1980s, and like he'd been using its contents to loosen hard griddle grease. Also, the idea of returning to his drab room at La Casa Grande under a bourbon haze, given the circumstances, seemed distinctly unappetizing.

Garner stood up to go.

"I'll help you with breakfast tomorrow, if you need it."

"I do. Thank you. Come on over at seven." Then he poured himself a shot of bourbon and paused the bottle in mid air, dangling over Garner's glass.

"For Julie?"

"Oh hell. For Julie." As if she could possibly care, he thought.

He threw down the shot, which burned the back of his throat.

"I'll see you in the morning."

"Have a good night."

"You too."

As he drove back, with Tanya in the front seat, he avoided looking at the Organ Mountains. It was too sad. Even Tanya seemed somber and listless.

"Sorry Tanya," he said. "I know you miss her. I know you know what happened to her. Dogs aren't dumb. No sir."

The bourbon, on a mostly empty stomach, had gone

right to his head. The road was dark, and when he reached the motel with its lonely light on the outskirts of the muted, rationed town, he went into the room with Tanya and sat on the edge of his bed with his palms flat over his face. He wept strenuously. For Jake, Abby, and Kiatsu. And for Julie.

To The North

CHAPTER 7

The next morning, he went once more to the Raw Frontier with Tanya. The dog stayed back in the kitchen, curled up on the floor. She seemed to have accepted Garner as her overseer, with a calm and uncompromising dog wisdom.

Garner helped Ross open the place, and the first person to come in was Ken Wilkinson, the local sheriff who had attended the funeral.

Garner came out gripping a pot of coffee and wearing a t-shirt and an indispensable pair of faded hiking pants he wore most mornings.

"I'll have some of that," Wilkinson said, sliding a white coffee cup across the counter in Garner's direction.

"You'll find the service here has declined in both quality and looks," Garner quipped, filling the cup.

"That's no matter," the sheriff chuckled, then assumed a more serious tone.

"After all that's gone on, we didn't need that to

happen. Julie was the best. Simply an outstanding, remarkable gal."

Garner nodded. "She sure was. Cream and sugar?"

"Just black."

Garner still felt rough and furry around the edges, from the light sleep and slug of bourbon. He was grateful that he'd poured out the Jack that was in the bottle from two nights before.

"Breakfast?"

"Please. Tell Ross to whip up something hearty for me."

"Hear anything about the airport opening?" Garner wanted to mine the sheriff for any news, something positive to hang his hat on.

"No. We've been seeing some messages, though. From afar. My I.T. guy has been monitoring some forums on his own. He saw some messages last night that came from the earthquake zone."

"Really? What kind of messages?"

"Pleas for help. From a hospital, in Idaho. Near Sun Valley. They'd been posted a few weeks ago. I passed them on to FEMA, the Idaho State Police, even the Coast Guard. Good that'll do. I'm surprised that if it's coming from a hospital so close to the epicenter that it would still be standing and functioning. How can anybody be alive?"

"Well, clearly they are. And they had Internet." Garner stood holding the pot, then Ross called out from the kitchen, asking Wilkinson what he wanted.

"Eggs! Two easy up and home fries! And bacon if we're lucky!"

"How old were these messages?"

"The last one was about a week and a half ago."

"What did they say?"

"Well, 'Help us…somebody please…' Along those lines."

"Who were they from? Weren't they signed in any way?"

"No. They were fragmented, interrupted in a way. It was as if they were written in duress."

"How many of them?"

"Many. Several short messages. Then they stop. Kind of Morse Code like, random, such as 'help help please please.' Sad. But at least there was a location. You seem real interested in this. It's Brad, right?"

"Yeah. Brad. My family ended up in that general vicinity."

"And have you heard from them since?"

"No."

"Well, I hope you do. Things are opening up a bit, now that the eruption has stopped."

"You said near Sun Valley. Where, Exactly?"

The sheriff laughed. "Well I can't say exactly, but this particular forum has GPS coordinates attached to some of its messages, which offers a pretty good clue. Now if we only had a helicopter. They ought to drop the Army Rangers in there, poor souls."

"Do you have a copy of the messages?"

"I do. What are you going to do? Go look for them?"

"I don't know."

"It's not survivable up there. The air quality is terrible, and everything's buried under ash. No clean water, no food supply, no electricity. The region's a dead zone. Well, you knew that. It's remarkable anyone survived the explosion in the first place, and were able to get a message out. It's a mystery to me, but if you want, I'll show you the message."

Ross came out and put a breakfast plate in front of Wilkinson, who dug into the eggs and bacon, still shaking his head.

"I wondered whether it was a hoax, to tell you the truth. Some knucklehead playing a very bad joke."

Something about the story had stopped Garner in his tracks—he had no place else to go. He was an empty vessel, scoured clean.

"I'll stop by your office and look at the printout. Can I do that?"

"I think it's some asshole fooling around; I really do. The more I think of it. If I catch him, we'll put him in prison and throw away the key."

"I may be able to analyze the legitimacy of the message. I used to be in I.T. myself. You can contact the moderator and ask them if this is the code or footprint of an actual forum post."

The sheriff raised his eyebrows, then seized the mug of coffee and gulped it.

"I'll get you a copy, young man. As soon as I finish my breakfast. I suppose it's worth getting some feedback on them; a second opinion. I did pass it along to the feds. If the messages were real, by Christ, we owe it to those people."

CHAPTER 8

Garner geared up two nights later. He loaded the Bronco up with full and refillable liters of water, from the restaurant and a nearby convenience store. He had a full gas tank, as well as a full gas can he kept in the cargo area. He had plenty of food, at least for now. He had roadmaps of the U.S. West. He had a kid from the local filling station look over the engine and tighten things up; changed the oil filter and the hoses and cleaned the battery cables; even replaced the starter with a newer, used one.

Wilkinson had given him a HazMat mask. Wilkinson thought Garner was crazy. Stark raving mad, on a suicide mission. He looked at Garner incredulously.

"You're really going ahead with this, aren't you?"

"What's it look like?"

"You know I'm half tempted to put the cuffs on you until you come to your senses."

"But I know you're not going to do that."

"No, I'm not. Not that I condone this behavior one

bit. It's just that I've seen men do some pretty crazy, brave stuff, which didn't make sense on paper. You might be one of those. Or you might just be looking for some kind of way out, a bungy jump without a cord. Something that feels good in your own head."

Garner felt a rush that he hadn't felt since…going to the precipice with Julie. Watching that water swirl around below. Julie would have liked this. She would have condoned it. So would have Kiatsu. He was at least half doing it for them, and his kids.

They'd found another message from the same place the night before. That was the clincher; whoever it was, they were still alive. That made Garner feel alive, outside of that end-of-the-road dead zone which the tiny room at La Casa Grande had become.

Ross gave him a cooler of food, a bro hug, then Garner got ready to part ways with the Raw Frontier. He still had to cover his bill at the motel.

Ross had said he'd take Tanya, who could hang out in the kitchen. Garner had no intention of going with the dog. Where he was going, he didn't want to be responsible for anymore heart beats than his own.

Tanya followed him to the exit door of the diner kitchen, her nose about six inches behind the back of his thigh. He paused, and got down on one knee.

"Listen Tanya, this is when I say goodbye. You're going to stay here with Ross. You're better off here." Tanya licked him in the face.

He looked up at Ross, who looked at him expressionlessly and went back to scraping vengefully at a griddle.

"As long as she behaves herself and doesn't piss on the floor…"

Garner looked at Ross, with his boney, tattooed arms, flushed face, and gaggle of tufty white hair and beard. He whispered to himself:

"That is, I think it's going to be better here." Tanya stood and looked at him expectantly, tail wagging slowly.

Garner opened the screen door, looked outside, then shut it again.

"Oh, alright," he said reluctantly. "Hey Ross, I changed my mind. I'm taking Tanya with me."

Ross looked at him dispassionately.

"Suit yourself. I'll give you some dog food."

"I appreciate that."

Ross set the spatula down for a moment.

"Where are you going again?"

"Idaho."

"So you're just going to start driving north."

"Sure. I'll start going up I-25, see where that gets me. I should hit Albuquerque in a day, unless there's more damage in New Mexico north of there."

"There's nothing up north but destruction, and the farther you go, the more ash you'll find. It's not like this planet, the one we know."

"That's what everyone's been saying, but there are also people alive up there. If there's one, who's sending those messages, then there must be thousands."

"You're either a hero or a fool. Probably both. Listen, I have a feeling I'm going to see you again, soon. Any time you want to come back here, I'll put you up, and you can start eating at the diner again. As long as I can hang on to it. Things have been so damn quiet here without Julie, and now you."

"Thanks, but you won't be seeing me soon. I can guarantee you that. If it gets bad..." He was already feeling guilty about the dog. "...I'll send her back with someone going south, right Tanya?"

Tanya stood at the door, waiting for him to open it. She knew they were leaving.

"Ok, we gotta go. Thanks again for the cooler."

He carried it to the car and put it in the backseat with Tanya. By early the following morning, they were on the road north.

To The North

CHAPTER 9

They only encountered cars going south in the other direction. For 50 miles, they were alone on I-25. He stopped once in a rest area and gave Tanya some water in a bowl, stretched his legs. The roadside was bleak, but largely clear of ash, which had mixed with the desert sands, broken glass, trash, and scrub vegetation. The momentum of vehicles had swept the ash aside, like the densest pile of pollen you'd ever seen.

He knew this wasn't going to last.

They would soon drive into zones that received much higher ash depths. Albuquerque was located on the edge of the zone that had received from one to one and a half inches. A small space between his thumb and forefinger; It didn't sound like much, but it was enough to bring the city to its knees. No motors, aircraft, or generators could run after absorbing this fine, dense grit.

He'd seen no road reports on whether he could even keep driving north of Albuquerque. The only radio station he found was a fuzzy Spanish one that must have been broadcasting from the city. He didn't speak much Spanish, so he couldn't understand the D.J., but the music was upbeat.

They started north again, as the afternoon began to darken. No one appeared in the rearview mirror. He saw few vehicles going south anymore; one of them was a Jeep full of drunken rowdies. "Tequila's the drink of choice around here," he said out loud. He saw an empty bottle hurled in the air as they shot past, and it smashed behind them on the roadside.

No stores or stations were open on the side of the road or in the small towns he passed, at least off the highway. He didn't want to dig into his gas supply, in the cargo area, on his first day. He hoped he'd be lucky, stay closer to big cities, and get away with topping off the tank over and over again. That would be highly fortunate, he thought, if improbable.

Before the eruption, the drive he planned through New Mexico, Arizona, and Utah could have been easily accomplished in three days, even less. It would have been beautiful and scenic, with high desert and national parks along the way. That was his fantasy, that he would be the one to rumble the Bronco through the ash, all the way to the suffering and the bereft. The fact that this was a pipe dream he pushed to the back of his mind.

He glanced at the speedometer.

"Running smoothly, Tanya," he said. "About 60-65." Tanya's nose rested near a window he'd opened a couple of inches for her.

"I'm hoping the highway crews have kept a route open for us north," he continued, thinking out loud. They were going 25 north to 40 west in Albuquerque. The latter route would take them across New Mexico and Northern Arizona. Then they'd catch roads to Utah, and on to Idaho.

"Everything's going to be devoted to clearing the

roads to get society back on its feet. And airborne rescues and food drops. We might get lucky. We just might. I don't like the look of that sky though; too dark. There's still too much ash."

They passed a falling down billboard advertising some desert real estate. *Find The Perfect Desert Home Today!*

Subdivisions in the desert, he thought to himself. *You buy the land, you think you're living in paradise. You can see the Sangre de Cristo mountains. Then you start running out of water…you have to get in the car for everything…your neighbors shoot guns in the air at night and threaten your dog. Suddenly it's not paradise anymore.*

"And now it's covered in ash." He looked back at Tanya. "The mountains are nice, though. Check that out, Tanya, on the western horizon. It's still beautiful. The volcano couldn't destroy that vista." He glanced at his gas gauge.

"But I want to fill up soon. We have to find an open gas station; we're going to the first one we find. There has to be one. We're seeing these cars go by in the other direction. They had to fill up somewhere."

The sun seemed to be going down earlier, but it was the shadow effect of the ash. He wasn't looking forward to the darkness. He wanted to at least get gas before then.

"You know, before I went to Chicago, Jack came up to me and says, 'Daddy, why do you have to travel again? Why do you have to travel so much?' I told him I had to work, I had to pay the bills. I wasn't telling him the whole truth. I didn't say that I liked the travel, liked the job, I wanted more excitement than family life. I didn't come clean with him. Now he's gone. They're all gone…"

A tear streaked down his cheek as he stared through the soiled windshield at the dark, empty highway. A dog makes a good sounding board, he thought. This was universal.

"I didn't think about all that then. I buried it all

inside. It was easy just to live the way I'd always lived. Not spending enough time at home, because I could always use the job as an excuse."

He hit the windshield with a splash of fluid, and the wipers smeared the dirty ash around the glass. It would have been easy to turn the wheel a half circle at 65 mph and aim for a desert culvert or a bunch of trees; shut his eyes. Good thing for the dog. Good thing, that's right. But for Tanya in the back, he might have done it. He was grinding through his memories, feeling gone, way down inside himself.

"Jack told me he had a basketball game, and asked whether I was going. No, I said. Had to work. I didn't see one of his games. Not a one. Selfish fucking bastard…A fucking bastard I was. That's all." He hit the steering wheel repeatedly with the bottom of his hand.

An isolated nest of lights appeared to the northeast. A large neon Texaco sign. They still had over a half a tank but he was going to fill up anyways. "Alright, let's get gas," he said to Tanya. He levered down the directional by habit, then rubbed the tears away with the palm of his hand.

He pulled over and the first pump had a frayed sign taped to it, "Out of gas." He told Tanya to wait in the car, then he got out and walked toward the office. The building sat in a lonely, sallow light. Beyond, the gloomy, impenetrable desert darkness.

A man sat in the open doorway on a stool, elbows on thighs, smoking a cigarette.

Garner waved to him. "Are you completely out?"

"The far pump, over there," the man pointed. He had a beard and thick-lensed glasses that seemed to cover his whole face, greased-stained cuffed pants, and an old baseball cap. "Still got some fuel left, but not much. And I don't expect to get a new delivery soon. This is your lucky day, pard."

"Still taking credit cards?"

To The North

He pointed silently to a hand-written sign pasted to the plate-glass window. It read, "Cash only Whining forbidden."

"How's the road the rest of the way to Albuquerque?"

The man took another drag off his butt, then exhaled and dropped it to the pavement, where he ground it out with his boot heel.

"There isn't one. Not all the way, at least. Most people are going south–but now it's down to a trickle. Those that didn't drive away couldn't. They're still there. Waiting to be rescued; waiting for supplies."

"You're saying there's no way through to 40?"

"I heard at least one overpass came down. The highway's are closed. The ash weighed too much after those thunderstorms we had. You don't want to go into Albuquerque anyways." He nodded just inside the door, where a shotgun leaned against the wall.

"Some of those that stayed in the city hung around for the opportunities."

"I'll take 25 dollars worth at your open tank." Garner had a 20 and a five; he handed it to the guy, who stood up briskly and sauntered over to his gas-pump controls.

Garner walked back to the Bronco, pulled it up to the open pump, got out, removed the cap, and started to fill his tank. He felt a shadow pass over him as clouds drifted over a purple sky, no longer bedecked with stars. He thought of the brief interval with Julie; he was hearing her voice a lot in the background.

Will you dance with me? They'd seen the stars together. *Poor Julie. Poor Brad. I'm one sad bastard.*

The sun had finished setting behind the mountains.

Tanya watched him pump the petrol from behind the open window.

"Maybe east is the way to go after all," Garner said, the gas fumes strong in the air. "Heck, I still have a company, an employer, as far as I know." The company had a New York office, and the means to relocate to Europe. Many other private companies, especially small ones, were no longer viable. They were dead entities, but not his.

It seemed like another attractive option that bloomed in his mind. A way out and a way back.

"We could drive through southern Texas to the Gulf, maybe even take a boat to the east coast. They're likely to get on their feet faster back east." He finished pumping, then he stood for minutes on the pavement, torn in each direction by the landscape. The man sat in the doorway again.

"You're all filled up and ready to go now," he mumbled.

"What do you think is the best way to head east, into Texas?"

"Finally coming to your senses huh?"

"Maybe."

The guy watched him for a moment, with a hint of sympathy.

"What is it, you got family up there? Still alive?"

"Possibly. There are many people who have survived the eruption, and they're not getting any help."

"Best left to the professionals, as far as I'm concerned. There's all kinds of problems up north. With traveling. It's like the moon. Worse."

How could it be worse? Garner thought as he opened the driver door to the Bronco. The air on the moon wasn't breathable, and that's a 100% fact.

He shut the door behind him and reached into the back seat for the roadmap, with an eye for a route east.

With the map was a printed out copy of the final message from Idaho. Wilkinson had given it to him.

To The North

CHAPTER 10

He opened it up and read. It was longer than the others—a line of computer type with the forum heading above it.

"Is someone out there? Anyone? We're in southern Idaho, near Ketchum! Please help! The food is almost gone. I can't move. I'm sorry…if I try to move outside…it's dark…and we'll smother to death! Ash is everywhere. God bless you. If you can help! Please!"

Garner set the message down on the seat next to him. He started up the engine and stared at the dashboard lights. At San Antonio, NM, off Route 25 he could go east on 380; it was probably passable. That route would take them to Roswell and then down into Texas. Then possibly interstate 10 could take them through to the east, if it's clear of ash, to the Gulf and beyond.

He looked at the man, who'd lit another cigarette. He was staring down at his boots. Garner put the Bronco into gear and accelerated out of the gravel of the parking lot.

Darkness had set in. They hit a jagged rut between the pavement and the gravel, then they were back on Route 25 again.

It was a musty blackness, not the clean desert night air he admired. He opened the window, just enough so some cool air blew over his face and kept him awake. He pulled the buff up past his chin.

He was heading north again, toward Route 60 west at Socorro, then through to the Zuni Territory in New Mexico. It was the only thing for him to do. The only thing. He shot a glance back at Tanya, who was passively gazing out at the darkness. Going east appeared...like defeat, he thought. This was the way he could get to Utah, right through the hills and the mountains and the desert, for the long passage north.

#   #   #

The evening was black and moonless, like a purple ocean had poured over them. All he could get on the radio was static, so he shut it off. The festive mariachi tunes that had salved his loneliness had run their course. The roadside was barren and nothing was open on their side of the highway. The engine of Julie's Bronco rattled and shuddered. It was an old, tired, but rugged car, he thought. Julie had no doubt beat it up on her frequent off-road excursions to commune with the desert spirits.

She brought so much beauty, he thought regretfully, imagining her face and the long dark hair and beaded necklace as she held a glass of wine and smiled at the sunset.

It was a mournful notion that doubled in intensity when he thought of Kiatsu.

He prayed under his breathe, *Get us at least as far as the highways are clear of ash*. He figured they'd be lucky to get all the way through Utah–Salt Lake City was devastated by up to a meter of ash–but you just never knew how the all the roads would hold up.

He cast a weary eye to the scrubby roadside, dimly lit

in his headlights. Visions of indistinct forms appeared on the side of the road, mostly mirages. But one time, he saw two cow carcasses, with their dead bulk and sickly luminous forms as he shot past them.

He slowed down, wondering about useful carrion to scavenge. He had a big hunting knife with him.

"Dead cows," he muttered, Tanya staring out the back window. He backed up about 50 yards. They lay in the breakdown lane with their huge distended, ribbed abdomens and tongues lolling out. Beyond the cows was nothing but pitch-darkness. They seemed already bloated and ash saturated. He accelerated away into the empty road.

"We'll be there soon," he said out loud to Tanya, who fidgeted in the backseat and appeared friendly and faintly afraid in the rearview mirror. He had enough gas to go 400 miles, ash-covered roads permitting.

"Socorro's the next town Tanya, then we turn west at 60. I can't miss that turn; make sure I take it. I don't want to waste the gas driving past the turn toward Albuquerque. So just, I don't know, bark if you see the highway 60 sign." His voice carried on in its lonely fashion.

"Socorro's the place where they blew up the first atomic bomb," he said. "They called it Trinity. The test, that is." He tried to picture a massive mushroom cloud blooming above the desert, as blinding as the sun. It was a dreadful image, worse, he figured, than watching a super volcano, which nevertheless gave off thousands of times the energy of Trinity.

"Yellowstone was like a thousand nukes, but nothing really compares to Trinity. They said the sand melted into glass. That was 80 years ago. 1945."

He wound the window down farther to let in more air, which carried a tangy mesquite smell. A faint coolness came from the high plateaus and desert expanses, reviving him.

"That's how populated and cherished Socorro was," he said facetiously. "They thought it was okay to open-air test a nuclear bomb. Like the area was expendable, a throw-away-when-you're-done-with-it land. Zero country. There was no way they were going to do that back east. This was considered a dead land back then, already. Before the explosion.

"Yeah," he shook his head, staring through the windshield to the night. "It sure is empty here. I agree with Julie. The desert has a harsh, pure, rugged beauty. But when they blew that thing up, it was a desert flower from someone's nightmare. Oppenheimer's, that's who. He headed the project."

They reached the turn for Route 60, and Garner watched the sweep of their headlights over the white, luminescent desert.

"He said, 'Now I am become Death, the destroyer of worlds.' Oppenheimer did, after they set that thing off."

When he turned the wheel, he glanced back at Tanya, whose ears were cocked and alert. He was only talking off the top of his head, he thought to himself, still it made him feel better.

"They've got an obelisk erected at the place where the bomb exploded. You can visit it, two Saturdays per year. They call 'em 'atomic tourists.' They leave with tee shirts. Can you imagine that? Look, dear, can you get my picture in front of that nuked sand over there? Then I can put it on Instagram!"

He imagined the obelisk, mute and solitary, standing alone, caked with ash like snow piled against a door.

"Possibly, a bit like going to Auschwitz, but I'm not exactly trying to compare the two events. Only, that you stand in the empty quiet place and only try to imagine the horror that took place there.

"They dropped that awful thing on two Japanese

cities, Hiroshima and Nagasaki. Apparently, the Japanese were ready to surrender anyways. They didn't have to do it. The Russians were pouring down from the north. But they had to make sure of that surrender, and show the Russians what they could do. My dad was in the Navy. He said they were just glad the war was over. They expected a million casualties if they were forced to invade the Japanese mainland. That's what the bombs meant to them."

He shook his head with a silent mixture of regret and disapproval. Finally, he shifted the subject.

"You're probably wondering where we're going." Although Tanya's presence was restful, he wondered whether he should have left her back in the Raw Frontier kitchen. Driving as they were into the zone of an altered planet.

"We're going to pull over in Magdalena," he said. The Magdalena sign appeared, and he began to look for a place to stop. He had some food they could unwrap and eat. He was starved, with little thought about where food was going to come from weeks from now.

CHAPTER 11

He pulled the Bronco off the road and stepped out on to the edge of the desert. He let Tanya out and put her on a leash, then removed his first cloth bag of food, which he'd tied on the top. He had that, and a half dozen other bags, and a cooler.

If forced to go on foot, he could shove some of the bags into his backpack. But he hadn't given that contingency much thought.

"We have to sleep somewhere. It might as well be here." He pulled out a tuna sandwich and two apples, then leaned against the car and took a big bite of one of the sandwiches. He gave Tanya some of the tuna with dog food, which he scooped out into a plastic bowl, set down in the breakdown lane.

He looked at the dark road, no headlights in either direction. "Still got a ways to the Arizona border," he muttered, his voice sounding too loud on the nighttime road. "70 mile or so. We're in the middle of nowhere, yessiree."

He took another ravenous bite of the sandwich, then opened the back door and unfolded the roadmap on the seat, aiming a flashlight at it.

"I wanted to be on 40 going west to Arizona; I didn't want to come into Arizona this far south. In about 50 miles we get to this town Quemado, on Route 60, and then we can go north from there on 491, try to get back on route 40 west." He folded the map up, then closed the back door.

"Let's walk," he said to the dog. "We've been sitting so long. It isn't good to just sit in the car seat all day. It's harder to sleep. I'll be no good, to anyone, if I get sick."

The place they'd pulled over was near a dirt road, which seemingly led to barren desert, and nothing more. But he'd seen a sign for the Very Large Array. It was an installation of 27 satellite dishes run by scientists.

When they were finished eating, he locked the car, sheathed his hunting knife, and took Tanya by the leash. They hiked down the dirt road as a clear evening settled into the desert sky. They both walked quickly. Moonlight cast short shadows on the desert floor. They saw large shadows of the Very Large Array, and eventually heard a thrumming, electronic noise.

They reached a chain-link gate. Beyond the gate was the Array, arranged like huge white mushrooms. The gate was locked, but not far away he spotted a place down by the ground where the fence had been forced up, making a small space. He knelt down and crawled through it, then helped Tanya scrunch beneath the fence on her hindquarters.

"These are some of the most powerful satellites in the world," he said. They wandered across some landscaped grass which had been laid on top of the desert, skirting the satellite dishes, until they were standing beneath one of them.

"They study the sky and space, and try to detect signs of alien life. For all of these scientific marvels, they couldn't figure out what was happening here on earth. Until it was too late. But don't get me wrong…I like them. Something about this array calms me, makes me hopeful. It's something that still works. They must run on generators."

Tanya sat down next to him. "You must think I'm some kind of lunatic," he said.

He got an idea.

"The truck's secure. We can lay down on this grass. Get some sleep. There isn't any other place, except for the backseat. But we're safe here."

He set his coat and hat on the ground, a grassy section in the shadows of one of the huge pylons. The electronic thrum was slightly if not oppressively louder.

"We'll only stay a few hours. It's peaceful. I don't get the impression anyone will bother us." He lay on his back, folded his hands behind his head, and looked up into the sky, through the statuesque mushroom built above them. The stars were like pin pricks on black velvet, some blinking more intensely than others.

"Did I ever tell you how I met Kiatsu? I don't think I did." Tanya lay down from her sitting position, and rested her head on his thigh.

"I was traveling, in Indonesia. In my twenties." He laughed to himself, quietly. "Jesus, it was a bit like this; just stuff some things in a backpack and go. What a time, though. I'd been in Bali, drinking and beaching and crashing in cheap hostels and campsites. Just a young guy, you know, bumming around.

"So I take a plane to Jakarta. The city was densely crowded, crazy busy, fascinating. I wandered the streets, taking pictures, exploring, eating noodles and drinking beer. My tiny room had a wooden window that folded out when you unlatched it; I'd open the window and the humidity, smells, and noise would pour in.

"I'd watch the world go by; cabs and rickety little cars and rickshaws and an endless stream of people.

"I didn't know what I was doing there. I guess I was just soaking in the atmosphere. Trying to find myself. Does that sound stupid, too predictable? Well, I was no different than other guys. I just thought I was unique. So I decided to get out of that giant messy metropolis and see the countryside. I joined a tour of a place called Sentul Hill. It was more like in the jungle; the Indonesian bush. We were crammed into a small crazy bus, bouncing along a rough road, and across the aisle from me was this beautiful Japanese woman.

"She was with a female friend. I thought she was the prettiest girl I'd ever seen. She was shy, demure; she kept her hands in her lap and smiled when I spoke to her. Her English was good. She spoke it eagerly.

"She wore a pretty skirt and a flowered top, and little black boots. I don't know what I first said to her. I think it was 'Look at how green the jungle is.' Something dull and pleasant. Something to break the ice. She was eager to hear about my trip, where'd I'd been, which included Australia. She opened up to me. She didn't view me as some kind of male flirt coming on to her. I wasn't that, of course. I was falling for her."

He laughed, then felt his eyes misting up. Looking up at the sky like that.

"We spent the day together, walking on mountain trails, paying almost no attention to the guides, only to us. She told me about her childhood, which was in Kyoto. She had very conservative parents. She was some kind of secretary in a bank and was traveling for three weeks.

"When I think of that day, I think of Kiatsu with her camera. A flock of pink tropical birds flew over us, like flower petals in the wind. She raised her camera and swept it across the sky, clicking several times, then dropped the camera and gave me a blissful smile. The trail was going up steeply, and she reached out and took my hand and I held her hand to the top of the small mountain.

"We spent that evening in an outdoor cafe high up over Jakarta. Her friend left. We ate, drank a little wine and tea. Everything just flowed like a dream."

"Then the trip was over. I begged for her address. She gave it to me. I began writing her letters, and she was really nice to return them, every one. She had a beautiful writing style; perfect penmanship in blue ink. I was in love with her, but didn't know how it was going to work out. Then she told me she was traveling to San Francisco, and had an opportunity to work there. That was our opening, our opportunity, and I jumped on it. I was there when she stepped off the plane. I was almost dizzy the first time I saw her," he said quietly.

He watched the giant concave saucer against the night sky. It seemed to be moving, but he knew it wasn't. Lying on his back, Garner closed his eyes and fell asleep.

CHAPTER 12

He woke up as the sun crested the mountains in the west. Tanya was curled up with her back against him. He pulled himself into a sitting position, running his hand through his hair, then placed his hat back on and stood up.

He looked around at the desert and at the brightening horizon, towards Texas. He needed a reminder of where they were; he couldn't use booze the night before as an excuse anymore. The Array stood around him like petrified trees. He watched a bird of prey soar majestically past overhead. He was heartened to see something alive. The sky was cottony white, when he thought it should be brilliant blue.

He silently gathered their things. He'd slept pretty good. The threads of dreams lingered like vapors. He'd followed Kiatsu down a forest path. She'd turned around to look at him and smile, but he couldn't overtake her, no matter how fast he strode. Then she was around the corner of the floral path and gone. He never caught up to her, then he woke up.

He and Tanya crawled back through the fence together and wandered down the dirt road, back to the main highway. He felt a strong paranoia and suspicion well up, as if he'd find the Bronco missing or smashed, and that visiting the satellite dishes was a silly, thoughtless mistake.

He breathed a sigh of relief when he came over a rise and saw the car, parked in the sand on the roadside as before. The metal chassis made odd pinging noises as if in greeting. He unlocked it and anxiously started it up. The engine came to life, expelling black exhaust clouds, and soon settled into the arrhythmic rattle of the night before.

The Bronco was just one of those tough old diehard vehicles, he thought. He had three-quarters of a tank left.

With their stuff and Tanya in the back seat, he floored it back out onto the broken highway west in the direction of Datil, Quemado, and the state of Arizona. Quemado was about 60 miles away, and not much more than an intersection. But it offered a route north. New Mexico state road 36 could get them back to U.S. Route 40, and better options for a faster path to Utah.

In between Magdalena and Datil, he saw a bunch of guys on motorcycles on the side of the road, drinking from bottles. They stared blankly, a flat venomous look, as he drove past. They seemed to be going the other way. He stepped on it, flicking his eyes toward the rear-view mirror. He saw nothing but gray road and the off-color desert.

When they reached the outskirts of Quemado, the sky above it was empty but for a string of black smoke and a flock of circling vultures.

He slowed and drew near. He came upon a partly burned filling station combined with a convenience mart. He saw a body crumpled near a large scorch mark on the pavement. He rolled past; the roadside services were partly burned, and he saw no one moving, so he stopped and pulled over. U.S. Route 60 going east was empty.

Someone might be injured inside, he thought, or in one of the empty cars that sat about. He might be able to get some of the gas; the food supplies.

He thought of the motorcycle group. He'd make this visit fast.

"Stay here," he said to Tanya, after parking a short distance from the damaged building. He took along with him a crowbar that he'd placed on the Bronco's floor back in Las Cruces.

First he checked the body, lying face down in a dark sticky pool of blood. No pulse. The dead man had dungarees, sneakers, and a plaid shirt. He clutched a pistol. Garner waited a moment; if he called 911, there'd be no reply. There wouldn't be a phone working anyways. Emergency services were likely tapped out or non-existent. *This was obviously an armed robbery ending in murder*, he thought, as he pried the handgun from the man's stiffened fingers. He pocketed it and moved on. He found red shell casings between the body, which lay near the fuel pumps, and the snack mart.

He went inside. The register was empty, as he'd expected. The refrigerators along the sides were full of food and drink.

Through the window, he could see a vulture sauntering swankily towards the body. He darted outside and hurled a chunk of broken asphalt at it. The bird flapped away with a squawk, settling down insolently nearby.

Going back inside, he thought, if I take provisions it's stealing (but he could leave money on the counter). Would that make him any better than the vultures?

He went back to the vehicle and fetched an empty cloth bag. Returning to the snack mart, he filled it with cheese, milk, salami, chocolate, and mixed Planter's nuts. He didn't take any of the booze.

He left two twenties on the counter by the register, pinioned by an ash tray. He went outside with the bag flung over his back, to inspect the pumps. He couldn't activate them using either his credit card or at the register inside.

He went back outside, and when he looked east down U.S. Route 60, he saw the dust raised from several motorcycles approaching at speed.

He got back into the Bronco, put the bag in the back with Tanya, slammed the door, and raced out of the parking lot back on to 60, planning to quickly turn north on State Road 36. That way would come up about 30 miles down the road in Quemado.

The scorched service station receded in the mirror, but he saw black distant motorcycles in the heat shimmer of the road.

He sped along, going at tops 75 mph, the Bronco's engine making an infernal racket. Within 20 or so minutes, he reached the intersection. He took the turn accelerating north onto New Mexico State Road 36. His heart beat fast and palpably. He glanced in the mirror again. Motorcycles, now closer, took the turn, one by one.

What do they want with me? he thought. Under these circumstances. Everyone's trapped in some sort of mode of escape or survival.

He glanced at the pistol, which he'd set beside him on the front seat. He hadn't even checked it, for a safety, or ammo. He hadn't test shot it. He wasn't much of a handgun guy at all. He'd thought the ash itself was the principle predator.

The mountains filled the western horizon. Ahead was northern New Mexico and Interstate 40 into Arizona. Eventually north to Utah. He didn't want this trouble; he didn't want any confrontations, just to reach Utah in one piece.

A dark brown smudge hovered over the horizon north, like a storm. Yet it wasn't the color of thunder clouds. It appeared volcanic to him; dark brown debris. It billowed

To The North

ominously, like a burgeoning, growing thunderhead.

"Hang on!" he called back to Tanya. He went from 75 mph to 80; the engine sounding high-pitched and complaining harshly. The motorcycles, arrayed across the road, closed on him.

Then his left front tire blew out with a violent shudder. The steering wheel jerked in his hands. "Shit!" he yelled.

Through the front driver's window, he heard the sickening flutter of the shredded tire. He kept on driving but slower, until finally he was sure he was on the rim. He pulled over; the whole vehicle shook violently as he skidded into gravel and dust. The approaching storm had rolled wave-like over the mountains. It looked more like coal-mining pollution than weather.

The motorcyclists stopped in the middle of the highway, about forty yards away. *Second-guessing themselves*, he thought. They weren't blind; they could see what was coming on the horizon. A guy with long black hair sticking out of his helmet angled his Harley across the highway, revving the engine.

Garner pocketed the pistol, got out on the highway, opened the passenger door, removed his backpack. He stuffed water and food into the backpack. He was torn about leaving the sanctuary of the car; they might have to ride out this storm in the Bronco, but not with this gang still around.

Then he saw a figure wander out of the desert beside the highway.

CHAPTER 13

The man stood a short distance away and put his arm in the air, hailing Garner. He had black hair down to his shoulders, a flowered shirt, a wide-brimmed hat with a flat bowl. He was lightly provisioned. In fact, to Garner, he appeared to have shown up out of thin air.

His face was flat and expressionless, at least from a distance. He had intelligent, friendly eyes. He waved to Garner again. The giant storm cloud advanced over the land just to the north–smoky, boiling, and as dark as loam. The wind came up, as if in a prelude. Garner let the dog out. He could see the Bronco was all the way on a rim. The fellow behind him slowly rode his motorcycle their way. He seemed to have smelled an opportunity.

The man out in the desert began walking away. Shouldering the heavy pack, Garner walked quickly around the back of the Bronco, and onto the sandy, gravelly desert with Tanya in front on a leash. The man with the shoulder-length black hair, and now he could see, long necklaces of shells and bones, turned around one more time to see if they were following him.

They were blasted by warm, bitter air pushed ahead by the storm. The weather system moved swiftly. A shadow passed over them; they had less than a minute or so to find shelter.

The man stepped down into a kind of arroyo. Garner was given confidence only by the stranger's assured movements; the first welcoming wave of his hand. He strode past a patch of cactus and yelled ahead to the man, "Hey buddy, where're you going?"

The sun was now completely blotted out.

"To safety. There's a cave over here."

A craggy boulder sat in a chunk of the desert above the arroyo. At the bottom of it was a dark, small opening, just big enough for a medium-sized man. The man lowered his head, crouched down, and vanished into it. Garner looked back toward the vehicle.

It seemed the desert and the ash had been scoured off of the earth and thrown violently into the air, where it swirled in a vortex. The pollution swiftly blizzarded the highway, with a sound like sand hitting a window screen.

He watched the motorcycle gang member struggle to open the Bronco's locked door, then Garner saw the cloud cover him over and the truck and with a sudden desperation he shoved Tanya and his backpack inside the hole and dived into the cave after them.

The mouth of the cave went dark. A fierce wind swept across it. It was pitch black in the cave, then the man, who leaned against a wall, lit a match. His face was grave and still expressionless, but the voice calm.

"We escaped, eh?"

Garner clipped on his flashlight and beamed around the cave, which opened up to about shoulder height. He sat down on his backpack.

"Thanks for helping us." The man nodded silently. His face had flat planes, a strong chin, and eyes that were wise in a weary way.

"The desert is full of caves," he said. "They make good lairs. You just have to know where to find them."

Garner heard the howling of the storm outside, the airborne grit battering their enclosure like hail. The dirt and ash piled up at the cave mouth like snow.

He cleared his throat, then Garner said, "I take it you're from these parts."

The man held out his hand. "My name is Zeke Sanchez." Garner shook it.

"Brad Garner...and Tanya."

"She's a good dog, I see. Loyal and obedient." Then he removed his hat and began to scratch around his head fretfully.

"So many of the animals are dead. The caves are full of their spirits and bones. Oh yes, where am I from? Southern Utah. You?"

"Originally, back east. I got caught up in this and..."

"An easterner, eh? And now you're trying to get back."

"Not exactly. At the moment, I'm worried about my truck. What the hell was that out there?"

"Sandstorm. A haboob, they like to call it. But now it's filled with ash. A poison cloud delivering death and woe. The dust storm itself is bad enough."

"I have some food and water."

"That will help."

"How long have you been out in this mess?"

"I came over from Texas, visiting my daughter's family. I hitchhiked, and then I started walking. I figured I'd get another ride, most of the way into Utah. I'm a Ute, you know, almost all Native American, with some Spanish.

"We know how to live off the desert. That comes

from centuries of experience. But few of us do that anymore. People try to romanticize me, as some kind of noble savage."

He laughed, in a way that ridiculed the notion. "I wear these clothes because they're comfortable and I think I look good in them. Sure, I talk about the holy spirits, the evil and good spirits out there, but the old ways are mostly gone. I've worked in garden centers and food factories; I've fought in the white man's wars. I was an Army Ranger, in 2004. That desert was ugly, not like Utah."

"So you've been overseas."

"For a short time. I hated it. I hated what I saw over there. I'm not a violent man."

"Then why did you enlist?"

"I needed to go to college. I have no money."

"Oh, well, that's a good enough reason." They were silent for a minute, as Garner reached inside his backpack for some water. Tanya curled up by his side.

"Have you heard anything from Utah?" he asked.

"No. No communications, if you mean by phone. I usually don't carry a cellphone. Have no use for them things."

"So it seems we're going in the same direction."

The man nodded to outside the cave. "Maybe we can get that truck of yours started. Keep going north."

"If so, you're welcome to join us."

"I'll give you gas money when we get to Utah."

"Don't worry about it."

Zeke looked around the cave impatiently.

"We're stuck in here, possibly for tonight. You got any hooch in that pack?"

"Hooch?"

"Booze. Liquor. Maybe some whiskey? Even wine will do."

"I, uh, I don't." He'd made a point of not taking any.

"You look at me like, 'Here's another injun can't hold his liquor.' Well yeah, I drank some in the Rangers, beer and whiskey with the white dudes. They couldn't hold it; go out into the desert and puke. Then I made corporal, because they were rewarding my leadership abilities. I was cool under fire and the boys trusted me. Then…"

He made a point of extending an index finger at Garner.

"I drank with the brass. Good Scotch whiskey and gin-and-tonics at 4-star hotels in Kuwait City. I shocked them, how well I could hold my liquor and carry on with the gents." He laughed, proudly.

Garner wondered whether the man was telling the truth at all, or weaving a tale to bide away the time.

"Wow, the women there, in Kuwait, they made me feel like a sheik." He laughed good naturedly at the memory, and himself.

"No one treated me badly, as a Native American in Iraq and Kuwait. As long as I kept blowing up and shooting enemy soldiers. Which I did. And I could party, and tell stories, and do flaming shots with the best of them. Afterwards, I prayed to the Ancient Ones: don't punish me for my sins. My war-making against men who weren't my natural enemies."

He looked at Garner with a knowing smile. "You probably thought I was some kind of cigar-store indian at first. Grave, stoic, and wise. First impressions and biases." He laughed quietly then said:

"My mouth is dry and my belly is empty, from all that walking and hitchhiking."

Garner hurriedly pulled out his water, then sandwiches, which he'd wrapped in tin foil.

"We'll have a picnic, here in the cave."

They didn't hear the wind as loudly as before; the storm seemed to have passed. The dark ash and dust piled up at the mouth of the cave like cinders flaking down from a chimney.

He handed Zeke a sandwich–they had roast beef and turkey–and they quietly ate.

"Delicious," Zeke said. "Wow, best sandwich I ever had. You know how that is when you're really hungry?"

"I do."

"We're like the old Indian cultures now," Garner added, picking up Zeke's comments where they left off. "The Anasazi, eating in caves and on cliff faces."

"The Ancient Ones, yeah, thriving here maybe two thousand years ago. Where did you come from again?"

"Las Cruces. I never told you. It was just a stopover for me."

"Do you have a woman there?"

"What?"

"Female companionship."

"You mean, like a lady in every port?"

"Yeah. That's right."

Garner peeled off a slice of roast beef and gave it to Tanya. The dog inhaled the first slice with a few chomps, then Garner threw her another one.

"I had a woman friend named Julie. She died in an accident."

"I'm sorry to hear that. Real sorry. And your wife, you are looking for her? I'm looking for my own, up north. When she finds me, she'll probably slap and nag me."

"My wife was up north not far from the eruption. I think she perished."

Zeke only quietly and meaningfully shook his head.

"I'm actually responding to a signal. Some people, or a person, who's alive up there, and calling for help."

Zeke raised an eyebrow. "So then you're helping a stranger, out of the good of your heart. That's commendable."

"Do you have any kids?"

"A son."

"Where's he?"

"He joined the Navy, wanted to be a Seal. But he washed out in training. Now he's a sailor, in San Diego working on a submarine. Don't know where he is now. One time I got a letter on blue stationary, from Australia. He's seeing the world. That's good. I saw a lot of the Middle East, more than I wanted to, and a little of Europe. The mountains, the Alps. I like the mountains here better, more space around them. Easier for a man to feel free."

"Right now, anywhere's better than here in Ash Land." Garner took a big chug of his liter water, then handed it to Zeke.

Zeke focused on his sandwich, like he was really savoring it, then he looked up again.

"Up north of here is Navajo Territory. That's where we'd be heading. I don't know how the reservations fared under the ash, but I guess we'll find out. They don't like us Utes. Ute bands used to raid the Navajos. We were the rascals." He laughed proudly, then when Garner didn't react fast enough, he said:

"You probably expected a typical white's version of an Indian, not a renegade Ute."

Garner shrugged. "I didn't expect an Indian with a name like Zeke Sanchez. What's the derivation of that?"

"I had a Spanish granddaddy. Cortez and the Indians, like this…" He linked his hands together and smiled widely, showing gaps in his teeth.

"Indians live on that rich Buffalo meat and liver, no longer. My teeth, this is what happens when you swap sugar for good meat. This beef, this is good…"

Garner looked around the small cave space disagreeably.

"I don't want to sleep here tonight. I guess I will if I have to. I'd rather check out the car."

"Hey, this cave is good enough for the lions." Garner

thought Zeke's laugh was beginning to sound more like a cackle.

When the wind had died down, they kicked away the heavy dust piled at the cave entrance, then emerged tentatively from the darkness.

CHAPTER 14

The landscape was covered with waves of drifted dirt and ash. They could see remnants of the dark storm cloud marching south, toward the southern part of the state and Mexico. They covered their faces with scarves and made their way toward the truck, the dust sometimes reaching their shins. The ash nearly buried the flanks of the Bronco and made it look inoperable.

They furiously wiped down the hood and the sides of the vehicle. Garner unlocked the doors. Ash fell down the sides of the vehicle when he did that, in small pancaked layers.

Tanya was partly choked by the dust–she shook her head and sneezed, over and over. Garner let her into the backseat for relief.

They saw the mostly buried and toppled-over motorcycle in the middle of the highway nearby. An awkward, scuffed trail led from it, ending in a six-foot heap lying under the dust, face down with only the lower part of

To The North

trousers and a pair of black boots completely exposed.

Garner and Zeke looked at each other as the former slid into the Bronco's driver seat.

"He was caught out and we don't know what his intentions were," Zeke said.

Garner fumbled for the keys and when he put them into the ignition and tried the engine, it mercifully started up. The ash hadn't yet migrated into the hood to contaminate the hoses and circuits, he thought. He let the engine sputter and run. He got out of the vehicle and dusted the rest of it off the hood, the best he could.

Zeke wandered over to the body, lying still, as if drunk and passed out. He knelt down and checked the vitals, then looked up and shook his head. Garner looked down the road, which didn't contain, as far as he could see, any of the other riders. The Bronco continued to roughly idle. He stood next to the rim and the shredded tire, looking down on it.

"Do you have a spare?" Zeke called out.

"I think so."

He went to the back of the vehicle and emptied the cargo area and lifted its covering, displaying a compartment that contained one spare and an old jack and lug.

"What I need is a forklift jack, rather than this old rusty piece of shit," he said, as much to himself as to Zeke. "This will have to do." He yanked the jack out of its greasy resting place, then set it on the ground.

Zeke came over to help, and they both got to work changing the shredded tire. It took them forty minutes. After the craziness of the chase and the storm, the task was oddly settling.

The spare was small and low on air. Garner stood up, looking north where the road led, with his hands on his hips.

He nodded toward the spare. "You know, maybe this isn't half bad. The road's covered with this sand-like gunk. It might help to let some air out of all of the tires, like you have to when you drive a camper over a beach."

Zeke nodded in agreement. "Let's do it." When they finished with that task, Garner said,

"We should keep going on this route north. Just go as long as we can. Maybe we'll make Utah."

Zeke got in the passenger seat beside Garner, just as he put the vehicle into drive and they rolled slowly north on New Mexico State Road 36, or what was left of it.

Sure enough, Garner felt like he was four-wheeling in the desert. He was glad they'd let some air out of the tires.

Because of the storm debris, it was difficult to pick up the road's path. The only way they could stay on the route proper and not veer off the highway was by following the tracks of vehicles that had attempted to flee, as well as by navigating alongside the abandoned cars, the skeletal hulks of which lay along the highway. The first one they came upon was an old Volkswagen that lay on its side. One tire sadly rotated, yet it contained no passengers. They stopped for a minute, inspecting from inside their vehicle, then continued on.

Heading into the Zuni reservation land, they had only a few hours left till darkness. The desert sky was clear, as if purified by the storm. Garner hoped to pick up 602 north to Gallup, and then Interstate 40 West into Arizona.

They were still about 250 miles southeast of Utah.

To The North

CHAPTER 15

They made their way slowly through Techado, no one home; then Fence Lake. These were tiny roadside towns that were now dead, windblown, and dust covered. They used to be full of tourists and bland, friendly residents; busy but humble motels. Cheap eats.

The hood of the Bronco felt like the prow of a boat navigating a sea of oatmeal.

In Fence lake, they passed a deserted diner that was very much in the character of the Raw Frontier. Its broken neon sign–"Bar & Restaurant"–crackled and flickered weakly.

So there must be working electricity here, Garner thought. He was tired and hungry. He figured the others were too. They stopped and pulled over next to it. A pale light glowed from within the diner. He looked through the window, but he didn't see anybody sitting at the counter.

He thought of Julie; her calm beauty, working deliberately around the diner as if nothing special had happened outside, where the dust had piled up. Her pouring coffee and promising him the leftovers.

Tanya sat quietly on the backseat, looking out the window. Garner carried her through the drifted storm debris and set her down in front of a pathetically dusted and coated tree, where she tentatively lifted her leg. He didn't want her sniffing up the junk on the ground. Then he brought her back to the car.

The sun dropped behind a butte on the horizon, casting a dying, brilliant violet light. He stood and watched it, meditatively. Despite the blissful view, Garner knew there was nothing out in that desert for him. Nothing to sustain them; yet Zeke could probably hack it better than he. The way he had wandered out of the desert, more like a spirit than a man of flesh and blood.

Darkness fell over the street, and he heard the crackling neon. The wind felt like clouds of rice.

He wanted to fill the tank somewhere, get to Arizona by the following day. Maybe they could camp out in the diner for the night, but that might mean the end of his truck.

He was afraid to shut the Bronco down for the night, even ten minutes. He feared that the dust was gradually ruining the engine. He left the vehicle running, for now. The headlights illuminated the deserted street, all dust and oil stains and shattered glass.

In the distance, about fifty yards away, a transit bus was parked diagonally and haphazardly across the road. Garner and Zeke noticed it at the same time.

Bits of ash sailed like shredded newspaper through the Bronco's headlights. They began walking through the shadows toward the bus.

"Do you know where we are?" Garner said.

The wind blew a loose shutter nearby, banging it violently against broken clapboards.

"We're in Fence Lake, close to the Zuni Salt lake," Zeke said. "That's a sacred place to Indians. There are ruins of shelters that we could stay in. It's only about five miles from here."

"Sounds like only salt to me."

"No, there are ruins. Good spirits linger there. It's good luck to pay it a visit."

"Which way?"

"That way." Zeke pointed south, down a road that intersected New Mexico State Road 36.

"We can't go too far out of our way. We have to maintain a straight path north. We need every mile; we can't stray. You know how the Bronco might be on its last legs." His voice rose an octave; he didn't want to fight with Zeke, who faintly shook his head in disagreement.

"We could stay there, get comfortable. Find more food."

"Food? From the Salt Lake?"

"The desert is full of food, if you know how to hunt for it."

Garner waved him off. "We should look inside that diner to see if there's any food."

"I suppose."

They reached the bus. The door was open. At the bottom of the steps lay a corpse, as if the driver had tumbled down the steps and died. An old bearded man with dust piled neatly in a triangle up one side of a cheek. Alarmed eyes stared toward the night sky. His arms were outstretched and rigor mortised; the fingers clutching at nothing, like claws.

"Jesus," Garner said. He knelt down and felt for a pulse at the carotid artery. Finding nothing, he shut both eyes, levering them down like trap doors.

They saw a few other bodies over across the dark road, toppled over on the sand-covered tar. They were like pictures he'd seen from WW II's Pacific War, of dead soldiers on a beach, partially buried in wet sand.

"In the diner…trying to get back to the bus," Zeke

said. "Old people didn't make it."

"Who would do that? Leave old people out here like this, with that storm coming? They had to know they wouldn't make it."

"Who knows," Zeke said. The day had been marked by peril and death, but it seemed they didn't have the energy to react strongly to it.

Zeke went over to a second body, knelt down, dusted it off, wiped his hands; brushed more of the sand off the stiffened face. He searched the man's trousers and came up with a wallet. He stood up.

"I think we should send word back south about what happened here. Notify the relatives."

Do you know that millions more are likely dead, north of here? Garner thought. But he didn't want want to besmirch Zeke's common decency.

"Wallet's empty," Zeke said. "Like someone scavenged it." He glared around the dark town, then grimaced, disgusted. "If we ever find the rat bastard who did this…"

"Maybe going north isn't such a good idea," he added. "Not that it ever was. These are all lands of death and sorrow. Funeral lands. Everything from here and northern Arizona on. The tribes never stayed at a place where nothing grows but the bones of people and critters. You need grasses, healthy rivers, and good dirt. Maybe it's best that we…"

"I can't turn around now," Garner said.

"Because you think there's nothing south of here for you."

"I've made the commitment north. I'm not turning back. You said yourself, you have family up there. What's your wife's name?"

"Amitola. It means Rainbow. She left me, you know, because I got drunk and lusted for another woman. I got caught this time, so she goes to her sister's in Colorado. The

Uncompaghre Plateau; the original place for the Utes. I didn't tell you that part, because I was still a little sick about it. When the volcano went off, I ate peyote and walked in the desert. The visions told me to go find Amitola, the mother of my son. So that's when we found each other, me and you."

"You found me. What about your visions, if you turned around? What about my vision?"

"Do you believe in visions?"

"Damn straight I do." *Honestly, it was grief and misery and loss that drove me to do this*, he thought to himself.

"Amitola, she's strong. Independent. She's probably trying to come south. Be with her son; get back to her home. She's probably still mad at me. But I could wait for her. That's the feeling I have in my gut now. Then the three of us, including you, could go back south, maybe into northern Mexico. There's lots of good land there still. We could raise horses, grow food. Make a new life. I could teach you."

"Teach me what?"

"Land skills. Farming. Hunting. Desert living."

"I appreciate the offer and the sentiment, but I'm moving ahead north. You can come with me, or not. Are you coming with me?"

It was quiet for a long moment, a weighty silence.

Suddenly the headlights flicked off, like the blowing out of a match or a candle. They stood in the street in thick darkness.

"You wouldn't survive alone. Going north. You won't make it," Zeke said.

"Thanks for the vote of confidence."

The engine in the Bronco had shut down of its own accord. The cracked neon sign sizzled like distant lightning.

"That shouldn't be your concern," Garner added. "I'm a grown-up. I can take care of myself."

"Bravery without wisdom will get you only so far."

"You didn't know anything about war, killing other

soldiers, but you were a warrior. You survived Iraq."

"I had a lot of buddies. Watching my back. It could have gone another way. In some ways, it should have. I died a few times. Many times. I came back to life, to think of it. I'm a walking ghost."

"So you're saying you've come back from the dead, and I need you to watch my back."

"You have to go north, I see, because you want to find your wife. What's her name again?"

"Kiatsu."

"You want to bury your wife, and say prayers for her soul."

"Her soul isn't at rest," Garner said. "And that makes me a restless soul. I'd just go down into Mexico to brood, and drink myself to death."

"Hmmm," Zeke said, pondering, scratching his chin. "Kiatsu. That's a real pretty name. I'd like to meet her, in person or in the afterlife." Zeke had an affable, approachable spirituality that drew Garner to him.

At that moment, they heard another loud engine, but this time, overhead. They both looked up, startled and shocked. A streak of red blinking lights shot past in the sky, heading for the northern mountains. The bright agitated bundle flew by at perhaps 3,000 feet up.

"That's no helicopter," Zeke yelled, as the sound already began to recede.

Garner had only its afterimage in his mind, a silver cylinder, lit up like a Christmas tree. They watched it disappear into the horizon behind a thin contrail, a hollow echo from its engine fading into the mountains.

"I saw something like that, over by the Very Large Array," Garner said with a new wonder in his voice. "I thought I'd dreamt it."

"The desert is full of unidentified objects. UFOs. Visions. I think we just saw one." Zeke had attained a new excitement.

"Yeah, but we haven't eaten any peyote."

"You haven't," Zeke said portentously.

"Are you telling me you've been eating mushrooms out here?"

"No, peyote comes from cactus, Mister. How do you think I made it so far, through the New Mexico barrens without much food?"

"But that was for real, what just went overhead. Wasn't it?" He was beginning to think Zeke was messing with his head, or had added peyote, or magic mushrooms, to the sandwiches.

"Sure was. For real."

"And that was no conventional aircraft."

"It wasn't."

"So what was it?"

"Your guess is as good as mine. But it came from the same direction as the Zuni Salt Lake."

Garner anxiously began walking toward the Bronco, wondering whether it had died, or just had run out of gas. He was going to let Tanya out.

"Well at least we have the diner," he said. Almost on cue, the *Restaurant* element of the sign crackled and failed, leaving only *Bar &*.

Zeke had almost talked him out of his motivation for venturing into Utah. Now he wanted to follow the phantom aircraft, as if it was pointing the way or leading him inexorably to his elusive and fateful goal.

In the back of his mind, festering, he wanted to know who left these old bus passengers to die in the Fence Lake sandstorm. Who'd emptied their pockets. It could have been the motorcycle gang, of course, or the road held even more unwelcome surprises for him.

To the flickering of the neon lights, they forced open the door and all went inside the diner together.

CHAPTER 16

A pale light glowed in the back of the Fence Lake, New Mexico diner. A man sat at the counter, hunched over, eyeing Zeke and Garner warily. He was scrawny, with only stray wisps of gray hair and an open plaid shirt. He looked down and tapped the butt of a cigarette on a full ash tray.

"You own this place?" Zeke said.

"No. Who are you?"

"Nomads, heading north."

The man scoffed, and the gesture turned into a brief smoker's cough.

"If I was you, I'd turn around and head in the other direction."

"You the driver for that bus out there?" Garner asked. He looked around at the diner's tables, which were covered with dirty dishes and cups. But some shelves above the tables contained cardboard containers and cans of food.

"Not a chance."

"Where'd he go?"

"Who knows. But I do have the keys." The man stood up, stubbed out the cigarette, and moved unsteadily to put an old corduroy coat back on. "That was some hellish storm out there."

Garner watched him skeptically. "How'd you get the keys to the bus?"

"The guy left them, in his coat in that booth over there."

"So you rifled the man's coat when he wasn't looking?"

Zeke moved and sat down at the counter, folding his hands placidly then stroking Tanya's head as the dog settled down next to him. He appeared quietly interested in how this would play out.

"Naturally, when the man left and didn't come back, I wondered whether he'd left his keys. Come on now, I told them not to go out with the dust storm coming down on us. They didn't listen. They thought they'd be stuck here indefinitely if they didn't get the bus started and go."

There was a pause, then Garner felt waves of fatigue and hunger pass through him. He made his way to the shelves.

"My name's Ken Webster, by the way."

"Brad, and this here is Zeke."

"Okay gentlemen. I was just going to go out and start up the bus. If we get it started, you can come with me."

"We have a vehicle," Garner said. "Currently, stalled."

Zeke slid an unfinished plate from where it sat three feet away to in front of him. After eyeing it with distrust, he began to pick at the leftover food, a burger and a limp pile of french fries.

"Waste not want not…" he mumbled.

Garner wandered over to the high shelves and began to take the cans down and line them up on the counter.

"We're going north, as I said. In the direction of Salt

Lake."

"That's where I came from," Webster interjected. "Salt Lake's in bad shape. They've lost control. I could truly use some companions going south. Some bad types came through the diner before; zonked out of their minds. Pretended to be customers, for a minute. They were harassing everyone in the diner."

"What did they look like?" Zeke said, in between bites.

"Like a renegade motorcycle gang. Burly, black leather, scraggly, greasy hair. Especially their lead instigator."

"What about the people who were working here?" Brad asked.

"They snuck out the back, through the kitchen, with me," Webster said. "I think they took off in a pickup truck. That's when a group of elderly people in the diner stood up and shuffled outside, toward the bus."

"That's a shame. Have you seen anybody else in this town?"

"I wouldn't know about that. Say, you have a lot of questions for a couple of strangers. Do you work for the government?"

"No."

"The feds are the only ones going into the disaster zones now. And you, apparently."

"When did you see *them*? The feds? We haven't run into anybody on the road. Well, hardly…"

"I saw some helicopters," Webster said, slipping on a thick-framed set of eyeglasses. "And a troop truck, outside of Salt Lake."

"What did you do in Salt Lake?" Zeke said, talking around a cheek full of burger and bun. He nodded toward the plate in front of him. "This ain't bad, really, for leftovers."

"I'm a professor at the university." Then seemingly embarrassed at the incongruence, Webster added, "I only have a smoke when I'm stressed, like now. I've tried to quit about fifty times."

Garner went back into the kitchen, searching for utensils and a can opener. Zeke's eating was making him hungrier.

It was black outside the diner window, with looming shadows of bent-over trees like toppled over statues. The neon Bar sign had failed; he could still hear the banging shutter, but nothing else.

He couldn't find a can opener, so he used a Swiss army knife to laboriously work the top off a can of beef stew. He came out of the back with two bowls, filled one up from the can, and dug into the thick gravy, beef chunks, and old stewed carrots with a big spoon. He filled both bowls with the can's contents.

"Aren't you gonna heat that up?" Webster asked.

"No." He knelt down and set one bowl in front of Tanya, who ravenously thrust her jaws and tongue into it, gulping it down in moments. Garner straddled a chair at the counter and began to eat from the bowl.

"What kind of a professor are you?"

"Astrophysics. I do some A.I. research. Artificial intelligence."

"Artificial intelligence…impressive," Zeke quipped, pushing the empty plate away from himself, as a way of punctuating his meal.

"So," Garner said, "with your academic acumen and knowledge, how long do you think it will take for Salt Lake, and other big cities, to get back on their feet?"

"I'm not a climate scientist. Or a volcanologist. But I can make an intelligent guess. It will take decades for the effected cities and regions to return to normal. If they ever can. This is a cataclysmic event, but I'd rather take an optimistic approach and say that man is more adaptable than we give him credit for."

"That said," he went on, "it is clear that Salt Lake is undergoing a disaster of epic proportions. People desperate to leave. Overwhelmed emergency services." His chin quivered faintly. "No one else would want to go north. That's why I wondered whether you were federal officials, although you don't look like them."

"We have loved ones up there," Zeke said.

"I see. Well, you're very brave." Ken fumbled with the set of keys, the thick-framed glasses magnifying his eyes. "I'm very myopic. I mean literally, not in the sense of my perspective. I don't drive well. That's why I've made my offer. And I have issues that make coping a bit more difficult."

"Issues?"

"An autism spectrum disorder."

"Oh."

Garner aggressively moved the knife utensil around the edge of another can. He wanted more.

"We eat and sleep first," he said. Then he thought of the "bad types" that Webster had mentioned.

"Where did those men go, who barged into here?"

"They had what looked like a converted ambulance. And a pickup truck with a camper on top of it. I think they went south on 36."

"I think we should try to start the Bronco," Zeke said. Then he looked at Ken calmly. "We're committed to head north to Route 40 West. You're welcome to come. Maybe you can find a ride south in Arizona."

"I suppose I'll have to."

Garner finished a second can of stew, then they bagged up the rest of the food he'd found and went outside.

CHAPTER 17

The Bronco wouldn't start, so they had to declare it dead. That bothered him, more than he thought it should. He felt sadness, as he imagined its dust-covered carcass abandoned by the side of the road, for the scavengers who would inevitably sweep through the town. He thought of listening to Emmy Lou under the waning starlight with Julie, then living in the Bronco with Tanya as they began this lonely journey, as if in Julie's and Kiatsu's honor.

He'd always had a weakness for his old cars, as though they embodied his memories and meaningful moments.

Zeke took the keys from Webster and started up the engine, which coughed to life in a plume of noxious diesel exhaust. They let it run for a few minutes; a fuel gauge with a broken glass facing indicated more than half a tank. Then they transferred the food, bottles of water, and other gear from the Bronco to the bus.

Garner pondered what to do with the corpses that lay

like lumpy debris beside the roadside. He thought these people should have a proper burial. He imagined himself or Zeke flung aside in the gutters, slowly buried by ash as the wind blew along the unused streets. He wouldn't want to end up in this blighted town no one knew existed anymore. They didn't have the means or tools to bury them, so they carried the bodies to the sidewalk and covered them as best they could with coats.

They'd leave in the morning. They shut the bus down and went back into the diner to get some sleep.

#   #   #

By 7 a.m. they were on the road north to Gallup, New Mexico. They watched the fiery sun come up over the eastern mountains, with ash clouds drifting across it like frayed, ugly masks.

This part of New Mexico wasn't the cold type of place, but Garner knew that as they drove further north they would hit winter conditions, made worse by the eruption.

They were on their way to Route 491 north of Gallup, which would take them into southern Colorado. They'd decided to go straight through, and not veer west on Route 40.

The bus rumbled along, past another sleepy crossroads near Black Rock, New Mexico. The desert was empty, sterile and flat, punctuated by ornate, rust-red stone formations, which Garner remembered seeing once outside of Las Vegas. The views lifted his spirits; he liked the fact that the unrestrained impulses to litter the West with new development, now quashed by a super eruption, had been resisted by this desert. It sat placidly in the sunlight, preserved in a kind of blessed, eternal state.

Or course, it had been violated by mining ventures and nuclear tests, but you wouldn't know it from the desert vistas, he thought.

"You said you spent some time up around the

Uncompaghre Plateau," he said to Zeke, who seemed to be nodding off in a nearby seat. "We going near Telluride and Silverton and Durango."

"That's where my people are from," Zeke said, wistfully as if recalling old family members. "We're Uncompaghre Utes."

"Are you going to get off there? I mean, the bus?"

Garner was reminded of an old 1960s meme, of being "on or off the bus." Meaning, were you hip, willing to experiment and challenge the old bourgeois ways? Maybe this bus trip was some kind of psychic, spiritual journey as well.

Zeke looked at him silently, then back out to the road.

"I don't know if I'll go. Maybe if my wife contacts me; if I find her. Then I'll have to stop. We're going through the Ute Reservation. I have no business there otherwise."

"Ever been to Durango?"

"Never."

"I went there with Kiatsu once, on vacation. Look at that!"

Out of the corner of his eye he'd spotted a pack of animals in the desert. They looked like wild dogs. As the bus drove past, the canines all looked up with their ears rigidly set.

"Coyotes. Probably eating a deer carcass, or an antelope," Zeke said.

"Yeah." Maybe navigating the desert on foot, if it came to that, he thought, wasn't a good idea after all.

Where the hell were they going to end up, anyways? He felt his morale palpably slip, become shaky and weak. They were still hundreds of miles from Idaho, with only the known and unknown hazards of a ruined landscape between here and there.

What the fuck am I doing in this diesel burning jalopy, with soup cans rattling around in the back, and three guys, a dog, and a pathetic water supply that I'm waiting to run out?

Then he thought again of the digital signal from Idaho, as if willfully trying to boost his own morale. Someone, alive but desperate, depended on him, and on him alone. He'd forgotten why he'd left in the first place, after Julie's death. He'd never had a choice.

He remembered what he read somewhere, advice for achieving serenity. The thoughts that plague you are a waterfall. You're standing behind the waterfall, watching them flow past.

"Yeah, we spent a week in Durango," he went on, feeling the old highway, with its crusty layer of ash and gravel, jolt along under the bus' tires.

"It was springtime. Beautiful place. We hiked, just like that first trip when I met Kiatsu in Indonesia. We loved it. We brought food in a backpack, got up to about 10,000 feet, took pictures. I still have those pictures."

He choked up a bit, like something stuck in his throat; a memory of lost passion and love.

"We rented a little cabin, made a fire, drank bottles of red wine, slept in a big bed with the window open. They had awesome blankets there, and this kind of deerskin that lay at the foot of the bed. Everything smelled like wood and pine, I recall the rustle of wind through the window. It used to drive Kiatsu crazy, me having to keep a window open. She liked to sleep, without clothes on. She was fastidious, like the Japanese are. Pale skin, long black hair, long legs, stretched out under the blankets. Like a painting."

Zeke stared at him kindly, as if enjoying the story and understanding its core meaning. "She sounds beautiful."

"She was."

"We can go to Durango."

"We don't have to."

"Maybe they have something there; gas and food."

"I don't know if I could go back there."

They'd reached Gallup. They were met by unlit traffic lights swaying like giant ornaments in the wind. A frontal system made up of dust particles swept over the sun, casting the afternoon into darkness. They spotted a few headlights meandering around the streets of the town. Garner kept an eye out for gas and diesel, but it didn't seem like anything was open.

They rolled slowly through the town, where they could go from New Mexico State Road 602 to US 491, which was going to take them close to the four corners that connected the western states.

The town was a forest of empty, faded, low-rent enticements; pawn shops and fast food emporiums and faux Spanish motels and Route 66 "attractions." They came upon a sign for a roadside Chinese Buffet that got Zeke's attention ("Closed"); then passed another unlit one for the El Rancho Motel and a *World Famous Indian Store—40% Off Jewelry*!

None of the streetlights were on; ash piled by the side of the road like silt leftover after a flood.

Beyond the crossroads and its sprawl and small-business gimcrack, was nearly featureless desert; gray tufts of grass, brittle, solitary buttes, and a darkening sky.

They slowed down through Gallup, but its dispirited abandonment made him press the accelerator, and the bus clattered over the littered, beaten up road onto 491 north. They were 480 miles from Salt Lake; about a hundred from the Colorado border.

Idaho, near the epicenter of the super volcano, was still 700-plus miles, so far away it seemed to him like going back in time.

That's what it was like, for the suffocated Gallup seemed frozen in 1959.

CHAPTER 18

Garner handed the reins over to Zeke. He felt the obsessive need to know exactly where all his possessions were, so he piled his backpack, jackets, Swiss Army knife, pistol, water containers, and food boxes onto one seat of the bus. He stared out a window to the desert flats, where he watched a string of dust that was either a dust devil or kicked up by an off-road vehicle. It went along for miles, spiraling along the sandy barrens like a dancing mirage. In front of it was a tiny vehicle that looked like an insect. Then he fell asleep.

When he woke up, which seemed only ten minutes later, he saw Zeke staring bleakly through the windshield as the gray road swept under the bus. Running his hand through his hair, too greasy and long for his taste, Garner tried to figure out where they were. Then Zeke, as if reading his mind, turned and looked back at him.

"Indian country," he said, unable to stifle a pride. "Not my people though; Navajos, Zunis, Arapahoes. We're

To The North

not in Ute country yet." When Garner didn't answer, he added, "Coming on to Shiprock, New Mexico. We're on the old Route 666, you know, the Devil's Highway. Then at Shiprock, there's a crossroads at Route 64, where people go to Four Corners and the Grand Canyon. But we're just going straight through to Colorado."

"What's Shiprock?"

"That." Zeke pointed to a rust-red, triangular formation in the western desert.

"The Navajos see it as a great bird. That's powerful medicine. It's an important rock in their story. Maybe the king of the eagles."

"Yeah, interesting," Garner said, betraying that he was too fatigued to take a genuine interest in Zeke's mythology knowledge. "How are we doing for fuel?"

"We have to get more diesel soon. At least, we're almost in Ute country; about 40 miles from Cortez, Colorado."

The sky looked cold, the early stages of dusk stained purple along sharp mountain ridges.

"We have to pull over soon," Garner said. "To make a visit to Mother Nature. Then I can take over the wheel." He looked to the back of the bus, and he could see a pair of boots balanced on back of one of the seats. Webster was crashed out back there.

Zeke found a place to pull over within two miles; an empty filling station with a Sunoco sign. He maneuvered the bus awkwardly into place next to crushed rubble that used to be a curb.

Tufts of desert grass grew out of the sandy cracks in the pavement. The deepening ash resembled the spillings from a load of concrete, before the water's added.

Pulling a sweatshirt hoodie over his head, Garner wandered behind the building to the edge of the desert. In the distance, a flock of crows flew overhead and settled down onto the ground.

They began picking at something, strutting about on their skinny legs, another anonymous carcass in the desert. Garner gazed upon Shiprock; at another time, he would have driven out there and scrambled up it.

The changing light altered the color of the rock to another shade of red; ochre. Julia and Kiatsu would have liked it.

He heard a car door slam. He quickly turned, and saw a converted ambulance parked behind the filling station, next to a dumpster. Two men swaggered out of the vehicle and slammed shut the doors. They were a tall one and a short, broad-shouldered man in a black fake-leather coat, laughing as if at the end of a raunchy story.

The bean pole finished drinking a beer, then let the bottle drop and shatter on to the broken tar. The broad-shouldered one, with long black hair and a wide-brimmed cowboy hat, hitched up his pants and gave Garner a leering grin.

"Hey, great view huh?" he called out. "Shitrock. Anyways, that's what we call it. Not sure if the locals do."

Garner started to walk back to the bus. He never did well with aggressors. Bullies. He tended to shirk confrontation. But the two strangers walked diagonally to cut him off. The other man was so skinny his scruffy cheeks were concave, and a pair of jeans slackly fell past his hips, barely covering long pretzel legs.

"I've got a question for you," the short man in the scuffed black coat said. "We've been driving so long through Nowheresville."

"I've got to go."

"No you don't."

"What's your question?"

"We're a little lost. I thought you might have a map in your car."

To The North

"We're on 491 north, just south of the Colorado border." Garner's mouth had gone dry; looking across the broken pavement, he couldn't see the bus past the blank stucco wall of the abandoned station. He thought of running.

"That where you're going? Colorado?"

"Maybe."

"Aren't you sure?"

"Listen, I don't have time for this…"

The man moved the lapel of his coat to the side and revealed a handgun tucked into his pants. Then when he noticed Garner had seen his gun, he laughed knowingly.

"Yeah, the way things are with the volcano and everything, what's happened and the cities and some such, you have to pack some protection. Dangers abound…" Then he gazed about the desert, as though he was about to say something profound, but which was only going to drip with sarcasm.

"But don't worry, about your safety. I'm not worried. You don't seem too dangerous." He smirked. The other guy had an approving, empty-headed look.

"Some cops were coming up behind us," Garner said, ineffectively, he couldn't help but think.

"I really doubt that," the man said. "We came all the up from Mexico, and it's been easy pickings the whole way. We only saw two cops."

"And they ain't too happy now," his partner boasted with an oafish grin. He had shitty teeth, Garner thought. He silently pondered the old decision not to go south with the crowds into Texas; he second-guessed himself, because it wasn't looking like a good one now.

He was in the Badlands of New Mexico now. On the Devil's Highway. No escape.

Order was breaking down, as if he just now figured that out. Survival of the fittest.

"Don't worry," the man with the black hat said again,

as if he had a natural tendency for sympathy. "What's your name?"

"Brad."

"I'm Bobby. Hey, we're both bees! This here's Trig, my comrade in arms."

"Always a pleasure."

Bobby shifted his feet, as a way of getting back to his business.

"Okay Brad, you can start by giving me your wallet and credit cards, then we'll go back to that bus of yours and see what kind of goodies you can share." Bobby stared at him quietly, then he grunted, "Hand it over!"

Garner reached into his pocket and handed the guy his wallet. He felt an emptiness, like defeat. The man took his wallet and opened it. He pulled out the dollars and precisely folded them and stuffed the wad into his front pocket.

"Somebody must take cash around here," he quipped. Then he removed a picture from the wallet; it was Kiatsu and his son Jake.

"Who's this?"

"None of your business."

"She's hot. I'd like to meet this one. Maybe you could introduce me. I'd like to make her my business. Get all naked together," he cackled.

Something moved and was triggered inside Garner; he felt the heat rise to his face.

"Give me that picture."

"Its mine now."

Garner lunged at Bobby and grabbed him by the neck and the wrist and as they grappled, Bobby shoved him away and briefly broke free. But Garner had the photo back, if creased and crumpled. Trig reached into his own belt and pulled out a blade, which snapped from its enclosure with a metallic report. He held it up proudly in the sunlight, as if it marked him as an expert. Bobby drew his pistol.

Then a shot rang out, the a metallic sound ricocheting over the hardpan desert. The knife flew out of Trig's hand, accompanied by a red spray and a scream. The blade clattered to the ground.

CHAPTER 19

Trig gripped his bloody hand, missing parts of two fingers, bent over, and howled. Over his shoulder, Garner could see Zeke, standing near the stucco wall with the pistol raised.

"Drop the gun cowboy," Zeke said. "Put it on the ground. Step away from it."

"Your friend Tonto," Bobby said. "He's not a bad shot." He bent over and placed the handgun on the ground.

"Move away!" Zeke yelled, walking towards them. Trig kneeled on the ground holding his bloody hand and whimpering.

"Tell your friend to calm down," Bobby said, as though his was the voice of reason in this confrontation.

"Shut the fuck up," Garner said. He picked the gun up off the ground, gave it a quick look, then tucked it into his own belt. "You looted those people who were on that bus. You drove them into the storm."

"We didn't do that."

"Give me my wallet and cash back."

"I need to go to a hospital!" Trig cried.

Bobby handed Garner his wallet; the wad from his pocket.

"Yeah. We're not going to kill you here," Zeke said, still covering Bobby with his handgun, and walking slowly in their direction. "That would be vigilante justice. That's what makes us different than you."

"Well maybe you had a better childhood than we did," Bobby said sarcastically.

"I was a child and you were a hood, that's probably the difference," Zeke said. In the near distance, Garner could see Webster watching them with his hands in his pockets. A cool wind blew dust around Garner's feet, a mixture of desert dirt and gray ash.

"There's probably a clinic around somewhere, but you're walking anyways," Zeke said. "Give me his gun." Garner handed it to him.

"Don't get hasty now friend," Bobby muttered.

Zeke went over and shot out the tires of the ambulance with Bobby's handgun. Four distinct reports that carried and sounded like a construction hammer. Only that sound, a childish whimpering, and the wind.

"Where's that pickup with the camp topper on it?" Garner asked him.

"What pickup?"

Garner went over and opened the back door of the ambulance. He pulled various bags of stuff out and dropped them on the parking lot, until he found a canvas bag full of dollars and credit cards.

"Where are the IDs, the licenses from those stolen wallets?" Garner asked.

"We didn't find any such things," Bobby mumbled.

"Give me a ride to a doctor and I'll show you where we chucked them into the desert," Trig cried. He was completely bent over forward in pain, as if in Islamic prayer.

"Keep your mouth shut or I'll kick it in," Bobby snapped.

"Let's get out of here," Zeke said. "I suggest you start walkin'. South. The prospects are better down there. This is good-bye."

"Ya teh hay," Bobby said, with more dripping malignancy.

"What did you say?" Zeke said, stepping forward, the pistol hanging at his side.

"It's no mystery. Just a goodbye in Indian," Bobby said.

"You're a disrespectful sonofabitch," Zeke said. "You know what we used to do with those animals in Iraq? The rapists?"

"Take it easy," Garner said.

"We took their weapons, buried them up to their wastes in the desert, and then we gave knives to the Iraqi women they raped. Then we walked away."

"Is that right Cochise?"

Zeke smashed Bobby on the jaw with the butt of the gun, and Bobby fell heavily into the dust.

"The funny thing is," Zeke said. "That was Navajo, what you said. I'm a Ute. But I'm also Spanish, and that makes me hot-blooded."

"Let's go," Garner said.

#   #   #

"I'm not a violent man," Zeke said, staring out the sooty windshield as they crossed the Colorado border. They'd left both men, standing sheepishly on the sun-baked concrete. Garner still had that image in his head, from the rear-view mirror.

"I never thought you were."

"The stuff in the war, it changed me. It does that to everybody."

"You're a good man Zeke. That's all. End of story. You've saved me twice. There's no rational reason I'm going north, but you're still sticking with me and Tanya."

Zeke, in the passenger seat, looked back at the dog in the seat behind them and chuckled. The bus wheezed and coughed diesel smoke, just outside of the small town of Delores, Colorado.

Garner looked over at Zeke. He'd neatly parted his black hair and tucked it beneath the cap and rearranged that necklace of shells and bones. The ruddy skin seemed tight and smooth on his cheeks. His eyes were calm, almost mystical. He was right; violence didn't come naturally to him. He defended the good.

They planned to stop in Delores, a small river town which they weren't sure had anything to offer them, as in diesel fuel. But the sun was going down and stopping at the town was better than running out of gas on an empty road.

They were less than 350 miles from Salt Lake—they would head east into Utah soon.

It was no longer desert terrain. Delores was set in beautiful high country, canyon lands and forest with the snowy San Juan mountains nearby. The Delores River ran through the town.

They saw open fires burning in the hills, and only a few lights in town. This town tended to be quiet during the best of times, so Garner could imagine how dead it was under up to four inches of ash. They were right on the edge of the region that had received more than 100 mm (four inches), and Salt Lake had been buried in one to three feet. This time, it wasn't champagne snow powder, it was blasted magma from a super volcano.

They pulled over on a dirt siding above the river. They figured they'd sleep in the bus.

The ash wasn't too deep there, as if it had been blown clear by mountain winds. But you could tell it was around, floating freely in the cooler, high altitude mountain air. They would eat and sleep in the bus, but Garner wanted to make a fire that they could chill next to. He still had jagged nerves from the scrape with Bobby and Trig. In a cold pragmatic way, he wished they were both dead, so he didn't have to think about them anymore.

"This is a little north of my country," Zeke said, stepping out of the bus and stretching out his arms. Along with floating flakes of ash, the air hinted of winter; the wind blew through your clothes to the skin. The breeze carried subtle scents of pine and ponderosa.

The river flowed darkly below them down a slope; Garner could hear it running over rocks.

Garner and Zeke gathered some birch bark and dried wood, making a pile. Garner placed a lit match near the edges of the birch to get it going, and soon it made sounds of snapping and rushing wind, with flames climbing high into the air and embers sailing into the black night.

They sat around the fire and Zeke pulled out an old dirt-encrusted red wine bottle he'd found in Fence Lake. Garner opened it with the Swiss Army Knife, and vouchsafing glasses, they passed it around for slugs.

"Webster," Garner said, handing the bottle to Zeke. "You mentioned you were a professor of astrophysics."

"With a minor specialty in computer science, yup."

"Okay," Garner said, raising his eyebrows impressively. "We saw a UAP the other night. I'd like to pick your brain about that."

"UAP?"

CHAPTER 20

"Unidentified aerial phenomenon."

"You mean visits from extraterrestrials."

"Do you believe in them?"

"It's not an issue of belief. Where did you see it?"

"In daylight. Out in the desert. Northern New Mexico."

"I think there's enough verifiable evidence, in the archives of military videotapes, that these are craft and not atmospheric disturbances."

Webster had shifted into lecture mode.

"That they exhibit qualities of flight not found in any of our advanced aircraft: USA's, Russia's, or China's. Sure, I'd like to look at the specific evidence myself. Break down the official secrecy on this matter. What did yours look like?"

"It looked like a silver cylinder with red lights."

"Did it hover, dart in different directions?"

"No, it just flew overhead."

"Well, you know a lot goes on in Area 51."

"We were nowhere near Area 51," Garner said. "That's in Nevada, northwest of Las Vegas."

"But we're developing a lot of advanced technology there, and they fly back and forth across the American desert. Some of these sitings might be our own. Maybe it was one of our cruise missiles, being tested." Webster took the bottle from Zeke, looked at the label myopically, as if checking the vintage, shrugged, then awkwardly tipped the bottle up and took a sip.

He swallowed and gagged, as if it was a shot of bourbon. Then he passed the bottle to Garner.

"Here," he said hoarsely. Zeke laughed.

"A little on the strong side, eh?"

"The first sip tastes like vinegar to me…sometimes…" Webster croaked.

"It didn't look anything like some cruise missile," Garner said. "It was more like a drone. Or a pod. Maybe one that could take a passenger."

"Drones are so common," Webster said. "How long did you watch it?"

"It went by fast. Five seconds I'd say. Or thereabouts."

Webster swallowed and cleared his throat. "The eyes can be very deceiving."

"I saw it too," Zeke said eagerly. "It was like a big drone, but no wings. That was no mirage."

"The last 70 years or so," Garner said. "The pilots have been tailing and chasing these objects, which have advanced flight capabilities and show up on radar. I've seen the tapes myself, on the Web."

"It's undeniable now," Webster agreed. "But NSA and Pentagon officials keep denying it, anyways."

Zeke tossed more wood onto the fire, flinging into the air sparks which flashed and mingled with the floating ash.

Garner pulled out odds and ends of food; tuna cans and garbanzo beans and the last of the sandwiches. They were running low. They had to head into town in the morning for provisions, he thought.

"We're heading into the worst ash deposition zones," Webster said, somewhat mordantly.

Garner said, "We heard from these guys back in Los Cruces that the government is sending drones into the eruption zone. Robots. Does that sound credible?"

"Very," Webster said. "The robotics can do everything a human can, but more. They can move through the ash on a purposeful mission. They don't have to breathe. They can send a constant video and data feed over a network. Verbal descriptions; air and ash samples."

"Verbal?"

"Sure. They can analyze the data on the spot. Tell us what they're seeing. Are there any survivors? Are the lights still on? Are the buildings standing? How is the ash distributed? They can be very…lifelike."

"What do they look like?" Garner asked. "Mars Explorers? Industrial robots? I mean, these ones that would be sent into Idaho?"

"They look like whatever you want them to. You've seen mannequins in store windows. You're walking by them on the street and you do a double-take, because the faces and bodies look real. Same with some of these A.I. robots."

"Sounds like science fiction," Zeke said, tipping back his hat and staring into the starless sky. "Like the movies."

"You've seen something like that?" Garner asked. "One of these androids that walks and talks and chews gum?"

"I've not only seen them but I've worked on them. I've grown fond of them. You can't help but."

"Not me," Zeke said, tossing a piece of wood onto the fire. "That's the end of humans, as far as I'm concerned. These plastic machines with computer brains will take over everything. Then they'll decide that we're obsolete."

"They come in handy," Webster said, chuckling. "During tough times."

Garner took another slug from the wine bottle, then he felt like he was hogging it, slipping further into an unhealthy alcohol craving. He handed it back to Zeke, who offered it to Webster, who shook his head.

"Hey Webster," Zeke said.

"You can call me Ken."

"That's better. Ken. How did you end up on that bus? Didn't you have a car? What else did you leave in Salt Lake, other than that professor job? Got a wife?"

"I don't…don't have a spouse." Webster seemed pretty looped on the wine. "I live alone. Actually, I'm an entrepreneur. I'm owner…part owner…of an A.I. company. I have a few partners. I own patents. The company is based in Salt Lake and naturally, when the eruption started, I didn't want to see it go up in smoke. I'd invested a considerable amount of time and money in it."

"What's it called?" Garner asked.

"RIW, Real Intelligence West. We work on robotics applications. You know, you can't retire on a professor's income. It was chaos in Salt Lake; the ash raining down. Day became night; sirens going off. Frightened clusters of people running aimlessly down the streets. Plenty of police presence, but traffic and panic like you've never seen. I didn't see a future there for my company. I transferred the assets to a Florida bank. One of my partners got angry; threatened me. I won't lie to you…"

The booze was like a truth serum.

The flickering firelight made his face seem more gaunt and pale. He went on.

"He charged me with stealing. I had no intention whatsoever of taking everything; simply preserving it. So I paid an exorbitant sum to take a helicopter to Provo, and when I was planning to rent a car, I saw this bus leaving."

"So you left all your stuff and possessions, too?" Zeke said. "What about the robots?"

"They're still in Salt Lake, regrettably. But all the patents and specifications are in digital form."

"They went to Florida?" Garner asked.

"No, it's gigabytes of data. I didn't have time to send it over a network. I have it with me, on a hard drive. So now you know; you're traveling with some very valuable data. We've done some work with the government…the military…"

"What kind of work?" Zeke asked. "Killer robots? Jesus it's cold!" He pulled a dowdy old blanket closer around his shoulders.

The sun went down and it seemed to drop 20 degrees.

"We worked on machine learning; what was happening between the ears. The ability to take orders and reason. They don't want soldiers on the ground anymore. Only robots. They believe that's the future."

"Who's they?"

"War makers," Zeke said. "What did I tell you? We soldiers are obsolete. It's time for me to go into the bus," he added. "I need to get warm!"

They shoveled dirt and ash onto the flames and stamped out the remaining embers, then moved into the bus. The aired smelled fondly of smoked wood. The mountains and canyon walls were black shapes above the tops of the trees. The moon cast a spectral light onto the river.

If you stared at the moon long enough, something that looked like a torn sweater would drift across it. Garner could only hear the water flow and the rustle of wind through branches.

CHAPTER 21

They woke early, just before sunset. Hungry and thirsty for a real cup of coffee, and cooked food, they wandered down a dirt road to the center of town, wondering what they'd find. Their instincts told them that something was open. Zeke had an old horse blanket, the one he had slept in, over his shoulders, and a wool hat.

The feeling reminded Garner of walking down the road to the Raw Frontier. And once again, Julie.

"I don't like the cold," Zeke said. "It makes me want to crawl inside myself."

"I'm not keen on it either," Garner said. He felt a shiver go through him. Webster stayed in the bus and requested a coffee if they found any. Zeke and Garner found that amusing and presumptuous.

"But I'll take cold over extreme heat," Garner mused. "I can't get comfortable in the heat. If it's cold, I just put on more layers. I sleep better. Of course, if it's…"

"A dry heat…yeah yeah I've heard that one before."

To The North

Zeke pulled the blanket tighter around his shoulders. You couldn't tell whether the flakes floating through the air were snow or ash.

"One time I was driving down a dirt road in my pickup," Zeke said, looking straight ahead at the road. "Really cold out, and snowing. It was a hilly road that people had trouble with in the icy conditions. I came upon a car that was flipped on its side after smashing into a tree. I pulled over and got out and ran over. Inside I could see a lady, face half covered with blood.

"I could smell gasoline, could see broken glass on the inside of the car. Her mouth was moving, but no sound was coming out. I looked into the backseat, the window was all clouded by cold. There was a baby in the backseat. I ran back to my truck in the dark and grabbed a crowbar, came back and had at the back seat window, until I'd smashed it in. The baby was strapped into one of those car seats; it took me a while to get it loose. Seemed like forever. Damn, I said to myself, that gasoline smell is strong, I got to get our asses out of here."

He kept looking straight ahead as he talked.

"It was intense cold, frigid. My hands were killing me. I finally get the baby out of the damned seat; I was half-in, half-out of the car. I wriggle out of the window, still holding on to the kid like it was a fragile piece of glass. She has one of these tiny-baby knitted caps on, and a little baby coat, but not enough. I put the baby inside of my coat, zip it up, and the car blows up!

"So now I'm on my knees on the side of this steep road with the baby's head poking out of the top of my coat, and I'm thinking about that lady burning to death in the car.

"But I can't do a thing. Not a thing. I take the baby inside my truck, blast the heat, and wait for the ambulance to come.

"They come, put the baby inside the ambulance and

leave for the hospital. They get the ID for the lady from the license plate. It turns out it wasn't even the lady's baby; it was a friend's, she was just baby-sitting. Doing her a favor."

"Shit."

"Life ain't fair, is it?"

"Not much of it."

Nothing was open in town but a very small fire station. Yet a tiny convenience store was open; they could see the pale light through a window. It was kitty corner to the fire station. They talked to a firefighter who said the store had hot food, and they shouldn't go in the direction of Salt Lake, but they had some diesel fuel and they'd be able to fill half the bus's tank with it.

Then they walked over to the store and bought some food and more provisions. Garner felt lucky, fortunate they'd found it. The coffee wasn't half bad; in fact, it made Garner feel like a different person. He knew couldn't start the day without coffee; he called it "liquid confidence." It was more like, to him, "elixir of life."

They sat down on a couple of stools in front of a short counter, and ate the food that was available: egg sandwiches, beef jerky, and crullers. It had been a long time since Garner had a cruller or even remembered that name for an elongated donut. For a few moments eating made him forget about his quixotic tour through a stricken, ash-covered landscape.

Zeke looked up at him, with sincerity in his eyes, as if he had to reveal something.

"I have to go look for my wife. I'm going back to the Uncompaghre Plateau. I can't go through this region without looking for Amitola. She's out there somewhere. I have to follow my vision. I talked to her in a dream, just last night. We were standing by the water. It must have been a lake in Colorado."

"You mean you're leaving?" He was expecting that

Zeke would stay in Colorado, but denying it at the same time.

"Yeah. I hate to do it to you, but I have to connect to my wife."

"I'll give you a ride there."

"Don't bother, you can take me to one of the crossroads. You have your own vision to follow. I'll see you on the return leg. We'll see each other again."

Damn, he's going to leave me with Webster, that dork, Garner thought to himself.

Just when they were about to leave, two backpackers came into the store. They hardy spoke to anyone, and bought only a few liters of water. There was a man and a woman, both sturdy and looked to be in their twenties.

"Where're you two headed?" Zeke asked them.

"Salt Lake," the man answered, after a pause. "Or thereabouts." He had a glazed look, Garner thought, like eyes on speed.

"Where are you going?" the man asked them.

"I'm going in that direction," Garner answered. "Eventually, Idaho."

"Nobody can go there," the stranger bluntly replied.

"Who do you work for?" Zeke asked.

The two people had dark-green, bland uniforms.

"U.S. Fish and Wildlife," the man said.

"Fish and Wildlife," Zeke repeated, hinting at skepticism. "Do you have wheels?"

"If you mean a vehicle, yes, a Jeep," the man answered, then paid for their bottles at the cashier's.

"Have a nice day," he said, somewhat flatly. They left out the screen door. The woman gave them a friendly, half-smile.

"First government officials I've seen on this trip. Which is strange," Garner said. "You'd think we'd see troops, and rescue personnel, instead of just these two people."

"Seemed phony types to me," Zeke said, shrugging.

They left and went back to the bus, where they gave Webster some cold coffee. Then they started up the bus and returned to quiet downtown Delores to partly fill the tank with diesel. They paid for the fuel with cash, and went on. They felt refreshed, and Garner thought, on a more solid footing.

Delores seemed like a nice mountain town, far from smothered with ash, even though it was at least half shutdown. Garner wouldn't have minded staying there. But both he and Zeke had other places to go; as Zeke would put it, their visions to follow.

# # #

They headed north on Route 491 to the junction of 191 in Monticello, Utah. Moab, Utah was more than 100 miles away; Garner thought they should skirt Salt Lake, with all the problems there. He could figure out a way to do that.

He was losing Zeke; that seemed inevitable. He was sure he would drop off Jack Webster somewhere south of Salt Lake. Then he and Tanya would be alone again, and he would have to get used to that all over again.

Zeke was quiet for a while as they rumbled along to the Utah border. The ash deepened on the sides of the road, like grungy snowbanks, and scattered like powdered cement across the roadside. Garner began to sink into a black mood; he knew what they were driving into.

Then he thought of the distressed messages from Idaho, which he'd copied and read. Re-reading them at the roadside when they stopped for a break helped bolster his spirits.

Then Zeke announced that he would stop and get off in about 30 miles, and from there go east to Colorado on a route that went through La Sal, Utah.

CHAPTER 22

"We won't forget you, will we Tanya?"

They were in La Sal, the bus pulled over near a rough trough by the side of the highway. Nothing was left in this tiny town but a couple of bland brick buildings, one a post office, and a row of Old-West style wooden homes with narrow porch decks drifted with ash. No one was home.

They all stood out by the roadside with Zeke, who only carried the small rucksack that Garner had met him with.

The dog stood next to Zeke, who stroked her fur. "I'll see you guys on the rebound," Zeke said. "You'll take care of yourselves, right?"

"You're just going to start walking here?"

"That's right. My spirit will show me the way. I have a feeling Amitola is in Naturita. That isn't far; maybe 30 mile." They were standing at the intersection of 191 and Utah route 46, which went east into Colorado toward Naturita and Telluride.

"We'll take you there."

"You don't have the fuel. You need to save it to get to Idaho. Besides, look at the view that I have! I'm blessed!"

Above the gray, powdery scrub land and red buttes they could see the snow-covered La Sal mountain peaks. At least the sky, at the moment, was semi-arid and blue. It was warm in the sun. It was enough to make you forget about the super eruption.

Garner felt the impending loss of Zeke's talent and companionship, but he stayed quiet about it. Zeke was a wandering soul, and there wasn't anything Garner could do about that.

"I hope you find your wife Zeke. Did you take enough food?"

"I have all the food I need, from the desert. Here, take this." Zeke stepped forward and handed him a pipe and a small plastic bag.

"No." Garner held up his hand.

"This is a gift from me; it would be an insult not to accept a gift of peyote from a Ute. It's bad medicine to do so. Smoke it in the desert, if you need to heal, or if you're lost. It will open up your spirit and show a different path."

"Oh, alright." Garner slipped the pipe and bag into a front pocket of his shirt. They gave each other a broh hug.

Zeke turned to leave up the road, then he pivoted around again.

"Keep your head high and your eyes on the road, Brad," he called out, smiling. "I hope you find your people in Idaho. I'll catch you on the southern trip; maybe in Delores again, sleeping by the camp fire under the stars, right?"

"Listen dude," Garner said. "I gave you my cell phone number. When everything gets recharged and the networks are back up, call it and tell me where you ended up. Take care of yourself."

He and Tanya watched Zeke walk up the empty road, a purposeful saunter in his step, with his round black hat and the blanket draped shawl-like around his shoulders. They watched until he was a tiny figure, then they turned back to the parked bus, which seemed a whole lot emptier now.

CHAPTER 23

Garner kept heading north, driven by a restless, agitated spirit, made more so by Zeke's departure. The engine of the bus rattled in a way that concerned him, and the road carried the swirling, often blinding aftermath of ash and dust storms. At times they had to slow down, grinding through thick piles that crept across Route 191 like sand drifting across a beach road.

They passed Moab, slowing only to look for fuel, but the town, a tourist's and recreational Mecca, had been abandoned. Webster had wanted to get off at Moab and head into Colorado and south on a bus, but there were no transportation options there. Utterly lacking in Zeke's open-road skills, the professor could only sit quietly behind Garner and morosely stare out the window.

It wasn't a pretty picture. They entered a windy part of the Utah canyon lands, which kicked the ash up in the air and made the daylight seem like gritty dusk. They drove through a kind of fog. Garner turned on his windshield

To The North

wipers and headlights. The scene through the window was like driving a subway car through a grimy tunnel.

At least a foot of ash had fallen in this region since the Yellowstone eruption. Salt Lake City was on the border of the worst zone, which had an estimated 40 inches or more of ash piled up on every square meter of the ground there. That was the state of affairs in Idaho and elsewhere.

"You said there no was communications at all in Salt Lake?" Garner asked, partly making conversation to break the monotonous silence inside the rattling bus.

"Partial communication," Webster muttered. "Localized."

"What do you mean by localized?"

"People still have satellite communications that function. So there may be a few nodes where you can make a Web connection, perhaps with working networks like the military's. Some of those Google server farms may still be up."

Garner stole a glance at the fuel gauge; they only had a third of a tank. Things seemed suddenly desperate. They were entering a blasted No Man's Land. They didn't have much food, water (a couple of day's worth), or fuel. *Maybe we should turn back and get on 46 in Zeke's direction,* he thought.

But that would be giving up. The windshield wipers thumped mockingly; he turned them off for a moment. *Soon I'm going the reach the point of no return.* I won't have the gas to turn back.

Thinking only of his family's last route by car, and the faint signals from Idaho, he bore along as if the prow of the bus headed upstream, a river of dissenting thoughts pushing at him from the benighted north.

# # #

They'd gone a hundred miles past Moab. He stopped once, at a filling station in Wellington, Utah, parking the bus beneath an old, dying hardwood tree.

The roadside stop looked from a short distance like it might be open, but he found it empty and looted. He parked and wandered inside. Smoking, burnt-out wires hung from the ceiling. The inside of the station was scorched by fire and filled with the worthless debris from rifled drawers and a refrigerator that contained sour milk and rotten sandwich meats.

On the wall, someone had spray-painted an eye inside a triangle. Beneath it was "Novus Ordo Seclorum." Webster stood behind him as Garner hastily sifted through the boxes flung on the floor for anything that could be of use. Tanya was just outside the door, drinking water from a bowl.

"New order of the ages," Webster mumbled.

"What?"

"That crude graffiti. Look at the dollar bill, and you'll see that all-seeing eye inside the triangle and novus…" He reached into his pocket and pulled out his wallet, withdrawing a dollar.

"Novus ordo seclorum. That's Latin for a new order."

"I'll say it's a new age," Garner said bitterly. "Let's go. There's nothing for us here. Whoever was here last was interested only in mindless destruction. They might have gas in Provo."

"I doubt it. I think it's going to be worse," Webster complained. "Nothing but lawlessness, from here on out." Ash and sand had reclaimed the parking lot, laying about in lazy piles, as if produced by men who were digging holes then gave up. Garner pulled the buff back up over his face, bent down, and picked up Tanya's leash.

His voice was muffled and tired. "I'll let you off in Provo. You'll be able to get a ride south, chances are. For me, it's Idaho or bust."

"I knew I should never have gotten on that bus in the first place," Webster droned. "I've almost made a complete circle."

"Another way to look at it is that except for Zeke, you'd probably be dead." I'll be brain dead if I have to spend another day with you, Garner thought to himself. What was it about tech-heads that made them so self-pitying? Maybe they were spoiled or deluded by the ease with which they settled into those high-paying positions.

When they got outside a pickup truck approached on 191 south at speed with its headlights on, fish-tailing through the soot that obscured the road. Webster began waving his arms, but the truck never stopped. They'd only seen a few vehicles on the road that day. At any rate, Garner thought it was evidence that there was fuel somewhere.

As they walked back to the bus, Garner looked out at the desert, which the wind had sculpted into shapely waves. They looked like small sand dunes. He spotted a half dozen men on horses, making their way north a mile or more off the highway. They rode slowly on black and copper-colored breeds.

He thought of Taipei, and his lonely grave out in the desert near Julie's place and Las Cruces.

"I wonder where they're going?" he said. One of the horsemen seemed to have his hands bound behind his back, and his horse was being led by another man on horseback.

They got back on the bus, and as they started it up and drove back out onto the highway, Garner slowed the vehicle and kept watching the horsemen. The men came to an old wooden house at the end of a dirt rode. Three of the men dismounted, including the one leading the bound man's horse. They approached an old thorny tree that made a black silhouette against the desert horizon.

One of the men threw a rope over a tree branch.

"This is Mormon territory," Webster said. "They make the laws; they look after things. You have to go by the rules of the tribe, once you come into this desert."

"Maybe 200 years ago," Garner muttered. He braked

and the bus rolled to a stop.

Webster looked at him with a quiet smirk. Perhaps Garner had to admit that segments of society had devolved the farther north they went, and the closer they got to the eruption epicenter.

The horsemen positioned the man with his hands tied behind him under the tree branch; a man came forward and fitted a noose around his neck. It didn't look like the man who sat on the horse was protesting; with his head bowed down, he seemed like a statue depicting resignation. Garner rubbed his weary eyes with the bottoms of his hands; he temporarily turned off the ignition, to watch in silence.

One of the riders came forward and slapped the rump of the horse, which galloped off abruptly and left the man twitching and hanging by the rope. The desert wind came up; the ash flew up and obscured the silhouettes of the posse.

"Jesus Christ. No," Garner said, almost only to himself. A wave of loneliness overtook him. He had entered badlands, not homelands.

"Novus ordo seclorum," Webster declared darkly.

CHAPTER 24

They never found diesel. The gauge hovered on empty by the time they'd cleared downtown Provo, Utah. The town hadn't fared well, buried by more than three feet of ash. Like snow in the high mountains, it was piled higher in certain places, sometimes toppling the walls of buildings. A route for cars plowed down the middle of Main Street, but the wind and depth of ash had made the effort look inadequate and half hearted.

Provo was where they ran into the vast pilgrimage on Interstate 15, heading south. Everything had been remote and depopulated up till then; the change was shocking, as if a crack in the earth had opened up, pouring forth forlorn masses of underground people.

A somber migration of refugees, as if driven by war out of cities, trooped in rows down the road, carrying or pushing their possessions in carts. Their facial expressions were flat and exhausted; the children had more energy but looked fretful and confused.

There were thousands of them; Garner had never seen anything like it. *Take a big stadium rock concert and multiple it by 20*, he thought.

A truck or sedan here and there rolled down the breakdown lane. More of them were abandoned by the side of the road; some with busted windows and adorned with graffiti. *God is dead* and *To Hell with it* and *Super Vol Rules*.

The surrounding desert had the Sahara look that they'd seen in the canyon lands; the ash sculpted into successive waves that were almost picturesque, if you didn't know what they were made of.

Members of the Latter Day Saints church were famous disaster preparers, but few of them could have properly prepared for the blizzard of toxic soot that had settled over their region.

Garner rolled slowly along the north side of Interstate 15, waiting for the bus to run out of diesel. The refugees filed in an orderly silence down the highway south, some of them dusted head to toe with ash, looking like a lost tribe of white mud people.

At one point, a fleet of vehicles, the size of troop trucks, came down the highway south. The crowds parted. The cargo areas of both trucks were jammed full of body bags.

The bus stopped for good on the outskirts of Salt Lake. The scene was gray and despondent; the wide empty north lanes of concrete highway and drifts of ash and a sad sea of humanity flowing down the opposite lanes.

Garner could see the dark Salt Lake skyline across the highway and trees.

He stood up from the driver's seat and swayed, exhausted. He quietly walked to the back of the bus and lay down on one of the backseats and pulled a coat over his head. They still had more than 300 miles to go, if they ever could get to Idaho, he thought. He fell asleep to the sound of boots and shoes scraping and murmuring voices, including the shouts of children, carrying across the windy open spaces.

#　　#　　#

It seemed like he'd slept for 12 hours. The procession outside was oddly comforting, and he'd locked the door of the bus, since a small crowd of people had gathered there, assuming the bus might deliver them to salvation. Or at least to Mexico.

For a while he watched the crowd, hunting for the faces of Kiatsu, Jake, or Abby.

He sat down in the driver's seat, stared out the windshield, and pulled his hands down his face.

"I had a dream that me and Kiatsu were back in New Zealand together," he said absently. His mouth was pasty; he picked up one of their plastic bottles and guzzled it.

"Before we were married. Do you ever get the impression that your memories were only dreams, that they never really took place? I thought of that when we went through Wellington, Utah." He noticed the crowd across the highway lanes hadn't ceased; its numbers had only thinned somewhat.

"You see, Wellington is my middle name. Like the Duke, but, you know, I doubt I have a drop of royal blood. Brad Wellington Garner; my parent's must have added this ostentation on a whim. An egotism. So I always wanted to go to Wellington, New Zealand, since I was a little boy. That's the capital of New Zealand, you know."

Webster was only half listening. He seemed mesmerized by the crowd flowing by, which was like a silent protest march.

"Kiatsu and I flew to Wellington from San Francisco. We took a cab into the city. The sun was shining; we passed a beautiful urban beach called Oriental Bay. We got to the hotel, checked in, and went outside to walk along the Bay and discover the city.

"We sat in a cafe by the water. I remember the sun on the water, the sailboats in their moorings and the different colored sails, the way the sun reflected off the skyscraper glass. The color of the harbor was purple and teal. I thought, I'm finally in Wellington. This is what I was thinking when we drove through Wellington, Utah.

"Wellington has a well-earned reputation for wind. We walked around a building to the end of a pier, I could see out across the Cook Straits to some green mountain slopes, and the wind ripped Kiatsu's hat off. This nice straw hat with a yellow ribbon. I rescued it before it went into the water. The wind was like that on a mountaintop; we just started laughing uncontrollably."

Garner chuckled to himself, reminiscing.

"I still have the pictures with me from that trip; Kiatsu with different dresses and hats, with Wellington Harbor behind her. Everything in the sunshine. All we did in Wellington was walk, all over the city, drink coffee, drink wine, sit in cafes, and make love in our hotel."

He swallowed hard. He looked over and he noticed Webster was watching him and listening.

"That was the first real trip I took with Kiatsu, after we met in Indonesia."

"You must have really loved her," Webster said, uncharacteristically thoughtful.

"Yes, I did."

After a moment, Garner looked over at the seat containing the folder of Idaho messages.

"Do you know where we might find a web connection? I mean, in Salt Lake?"

Webster looked at him incredulously. "No, I don't. Everything's ruined here. The utilities are inoperable. Even the generators have probably run out of fuel. I don't know why you're asking me this, as you must already know the answer."

"There's always a working connection somewhere." Garner began pulling his things together into the backpack. "You were an A.I. guy, a techie; I figured you knew where to look for one. They're underground, and they're probably run by Homeland Security, or the like."

Webster shrugged. "What are you going to do now?"

"Start moving, north."

"How?"

"By flapping my wings. How do you think. I will have to start by walking." He still had Kiatsu, and the dream, firmly in his mind. She pulled him north, a mysterious form of magnetism.

"Just walking north, aimlessly. It's not survivable."

"Maybe not. But maybe it is."

Then after a minute of silence as he finished packing, "We can't stay forever in this bus. Or I should say, you can. I can't. I think at least I can try to contact a network. I want to see if I have any messages from my family…or otherwise from that Idaho signal."

"Are you going to take the dog?"

"Of course I am. I'm responsible for her."

Webster looked vacantly out the window. "There were about three million people in Idaho, Montana, and Wyoming. What happened to them? They stayed put and tried to survive." He was thinking out loud now. "They tried to go south. They went to Canada. They died."

"Some of them might have made it west to California." Like my family, he thought.

Then Garner looked up and out the window. "Hey wait. Weren't they those two people we saw in Delores?"

About fifty meters up the road was a Jeep, with a man and a woman standing next to it. They had dark green uniforms and wore small expedition backpacks. Garner watched the man assertively shoo people away from the front door of the Jeep as he opened it. Both of them got inside the vehicle as Garner hopped down the bus steps.

CHAPTER 25

Garner walked along the breakdown lane until he was next to the Jeep's passenger door. He circled around to the front. That door was closed, but he knocked on the window. The woman was in the driver's seat; she rolled the window down and smiled at him pleasantly.

"Do you remember me, from Delores, Colorado? The convenience store?"

"Of course I do," she said without hesitation.

"My name is Brad Garner. I'm searching for my family members."

"Well, as you can see yourself, there are thousands of displaced people on the road. Have you looked for them there?"

"Yes. But they're farther north, in Idaho." The man next to her shrugged noncommittally.

"We're leaving now," he said.

The woman, still showing a half smile, said, "I wish you luck in finding your family members. These are difficult times. But there's always hope." She began to roll up her window.

"Wait wait," Garner said urgently. "Which way are you going?"

"North," the man said, then added impatiently, "we can't take anyone. If we agreed to take one person, it would be unfair to the others."

The man had a monotone and slightly too rational way of talking, Garner thought.

"What are you doing up north?"

"That's...classified," the lady said.

"Listen, wait a minute," Garner said, desperately buying time. "There's a network signal up there; I'm following it. Near Ketchum, Idaho."

The window was open halfway; she rolled it down a little farther.

"What kind of network signal?" the man said, mildly interested.

"Forum messages over the internet. Cries for help; recent ones. Not far from the epicenter of the volcano."

"Do you have the messages?" the man asked.

"Yes. If you can give me a ride, I'll share them with you. I'll do some of the driving—whatever you need. I have some cash left; a few provisions."

"We don't need this," the man said, sharply. The woman averted her eyes and the window went up. The two people then had a rapid discussion, which to Garner was only muffled. He got the impression the woman had advocated for him. Then the lady rolled down the window.

"We'll take you as far as the Idaho border. We're going in that direction."

"Thanks so much. I can give you the GPS coordinates for those messages."

"Get in back...with the dog," the man said, with a clipped delivery.

"What about me?" Webster said. He stood right behind Garner, next to Tanya, who sat on the ground.

"We didn't say we could take any more," the woman said coldly.

"I'm only going as far as Salt Lake, where I'll look for another ride south. I'm a computer professor from the University of Utah. I don't want to stay around these parts; we saw a lynch party back there."

"Where?" the man said.

"On horseback, out in the desert," Garner said, getting in the back. "We have room for him to slip in. He's not going 50 miles."

"Alright but make it quick," the man said. "This isn't a sight-seeing ride."

They all got in and the Jeep accelerated in the gravel of the breakdown lane, leaving a cluster of disconsolate refugees in their wake.

"What do you have there?" Webster asked the man, who typed into a laptop. It was connected to a larger console beneath the dashboard.

"It's just a computer for storing data. Observations."

"Data on what?"

The man looked back at Webster from the passenger seat, irritated.

"On the conditions, after the volcanic eruption."

"Who're you reporting to?"

"Fish and Wildlife, and other agencies, of course," the woman said.

"Uh huh," Webster said.

"So you have a connection?" Garner asked. "To other computer servers?"

"You might say that," the man said. "We can't say anything more."

They seemed awfully tight-lipped for government types sent to deal with a disaster, Garner thought. He caught

Webster looking at the back of their heads intently.

"You didn't tell us your names," Garner said.

"Laura," said the woman, absently.

"Lance," her partner said, not missing a beat.

"Okay Laura and Lance," Garner said eagerly. "Do you have a way of charging up a cell phone?"

Lance looked at him silently.

"Do you have a charger?" he said, finally. "A cord?"

"Yes, I sure do."

"Okay, maybe later we charge up your phone." He returned to his laptop screen and resumed entering data.

They kept driving towards the outskirts of Salt Lake. Garner was surprised to find a lot of woods, so accustomed he'd become to the desert and its hardpan sameness, bordered by dun colored mountains.

They kept climbing until they had an overview of the muted city. They could see the mountains in the distance, carrying a deep cloak of gray, ash-mingled snow.

Horizontal columns of pollution-colored fog sailed between the skyscrapers, like blurry, airborne billboards.

The sun, low on the horizon, cast angled sunlight across the mess of ash piles that went on for hundreds of square miles. It didn't look like beautiful hiking and ski country anymore. It looked like the surface of a dead planet.

"That's shocking…awful," Garner murmured, almost to himself.

"What is?" Lance asked, distractedly.

"The ash in this region—the view really makes it hit home."

"At least 80 centimeters," Lance stated coldly, as if talking about snow depth or a piece of custom built furniture. "A Salt Lake-Ogden-Provo Metropolitan area of 1.21 million people, and 80 cm fell on them."

"Not 1.205?" Webster said sarcastically. "And these millions are flesh and blood people? So called meat space?"

Lance grimaced back at him. "We should discuss where you should be dropped off," he said.

"Well certainly not on the open road," Webster insisted. Garner looked at him quizzically, wondering what he was getting at.

They kept climbing on the rural road that went northeast, before, Garner assumed, they rejoined the highway in the direction of Idaho. Even the suburbs, which had sprawled across the dry land for many miles, were blanketed by ash, making the region look depopulated and bombed out.

Now Garner remembered what it reminded him specifically of—the view from the plane when he took it on business from Chicago to the Pacific Northwest. They'd fly over the northern border terrain of Minnesota, North Dakota, and Canada. Having lived exclusively in suburban and urban areas, he gazed upon this landscape in awe; how did humans fail to fill its emptiness? Vast stretches of plains of snow, punctuated by vertebral mountains, dark squiggly lines or wider arteries for the frozen rivers; and the glaring absence of any settlements. The scene reflected a bleak, harsh beauty.

He used to stare out the window and think, how long would he last trying to trek across it? Not even the isolated river or road snaking across the steppes showed any human signs. What happened if the plane skidded down on it? The land's unconquered space made him and everyone else seem puny and insignificant.

But there was no beauty or even harshness to the view of Salt Lake he had from above; lazy columns of black smoke trailing beside unlit, seemingly empty skyscrapers. No signs of life. The gray steppes beyond the urban center sat under an empty blue sky, with even the mountains tarnished and off-color.

They stopped once and both Lance and Laura, without saying anything, stepped outside with air-sampling devices and worked for a while, taking samples and connecting the devices to ports in their laptops.

As they wandered outside of the Jeep—they'd removed the ignition keys—Webster turned to Garner and said, "very efficient worker bees, aren't they?"

"They're a little aloof, but I need the ride. I also need to take Tanya outside." Garner opened the door and attached a leash to the dog, and they walked over to the edge of a field where Lance and Laura were.

The two "Fish & Wildlife" agents paid them no heed, until Laura looked up and said, "we're only staying eight more minutes."

"How's the air quality?"

"It's unhealthy. High particulate levels. It would be unacceptable under normal circumstances."

"Where are you from?" Garner asked.

She looked at him and her face relaxed somewhat. She blinked strenuously, as if urging herself to recall something. "Ithaca, New York. I went to Cornell University...biology and chemical engineering...You?"

"Vermont."

She acted as though smalltalk was a struggle.

"Pretty," she said offhandedly. "Skiing and sleighs and maple syrup. Green mountains."

She really wasn't engaging for someone so pretty, Garner thought. She was shapely and slim, almost as tall as Garner, with medium-length brunette hair. Beneath the uniform, he detected the sign of muscles, like she hit the gym and practiced martial arts.

Surely, many men had been attracted and come on to her, but she appeared to have no ability for the typical nuances of flirtation. She had a hard-headed confidence, but little feminine flair. She had an unaffected, almost autistic side to her personality.

"How far are you really going?" Garner asked. "What

are your plans?"

She paused. "Well, I suppose you can know. There's no harm in it. We're going straight to the epicenter of the volcano."

"You don't say? We saw all those folks on the road…those must be the survivors of Salt Lake."

Laura looked to the horizon again, at the sad skyline, but only briefly because she couldn't have her task interrupted. "There may be some left in town–perhaps as many as ten thousand. Possibly less. The urban zones are not our mission, however."

Then she bent forward, removed a spade, and dug into the earth, placing some of the soil and ash mixture into a ziplocked plastic bag. She stood up again.

"What are you measuring in that dirt?"

"Toxicity. Heavy metals."

"What's Lance's gig?" Garner wanted to probe this enigmatic couple's background.

"What do you mean?"

"What's he doing with you?"

"Lance is also a scientist."

"Are you two an item?"

"Item?"

"Do you go out together? Are you lovers?"

She scoffed. He laughed, which felt good, for once.

"We are merely colleagues, who have been sent as a team to investigate the eruption."

"Do you have a boyfriend?"

"Why are you so interested in my…my romantic involvements?" He was making her uncomfortable, which manifested as irritation and greater shyness.

"Because it's a surprise to me that someone who is so attractive wouldn't be involved with someone…man or woman."

"I think it is none of your business."

"You're probably right. What do you like to do on a date?" He pressed on, because it felt good and light-hearted to once again playfully chat with a lady, like Julie. Even get on her nerves. "Do you like movies, dinner, red wine?"

"I like my work," she said bluntly.

He looked again at the Salt Lake skyline, which brought to mind lower Manhattan on 9/11. He paused as she walked back to the car then, "All those survivors, likely clinging to life. How come the Army hasn't arrived, or Coast Guard rescue helicopters? You must be privy to that kind of information, working for the federal government."

"The environment is dangerous, even for rescue workers. The eruption has only ceased recently. They'll be coming soon…the military agencies, FEMA…"

"I hope so."

CHAPTER 26

They continued on the road that connected with Interstate 15 north, at around Ogden, Utah. They had bypassed Salt Lake City proper, which left Webster the odd man out. He moped in the backseat. The Jeep rolled along through a fog of ash kicked up by a mountain wind.

"Make sure windows stay closed," Lance said with a martial air. "The air outside is toxic."

It was difficult to see, then suddenly a human form appeared in the dimness. He carried a sign and stood off to the side of the road. They slowed down as they approached him. The sign said "Slow" and he wore one of those yellow reflector vests.

As they moved closer he turned the sign around to "Stop." They stopped alongside him.

Lance looked at Laura, but didn't say anything as he rolled the window down.

"Is there any problem ahead?" Lance asked.

The man's mouth moved but nothing came out. He

wore glasses and was partially covered with dust.

"Sir?"

"You're supposed to stop here," he finally said.

"What for?" Lance said. You could hardly see anything, the visibility being perhaps 100 feet. "There can't possibly be a construction project ahead. These agencies aren't functioning."

The man gaped at Lance with a blank, confused expression.

"In a few minutes, when the sign says slow, you can move on," the man said, in a hollow voice, as the dust swirled around in the gathering darkness. "But at a safe speed…"

"What's your name, buddy?" Garner asked from the back seat.

"Frank."

"Where do you work, Frank?"

"I work for the City of Ogden in the Highway Department."

"And is the Highway Department functioning now?" Lance snapped. "That isn't possible, and if you continue to stand out there, without protection, you will die of ash inhalation."

"He's right, Frank," Garner said, but in a softer tone. He leaned forward over the front seatback. "Do you have a place to go Frank? To get inside? Do you live near here?"

"I live at 1205 Riverside Lane, in our house…"

"Well, you better get back there," Garner said. "Got some food and water? Just hang tight, until the emergency personnel start arriving. It's not safe outside."

"He's right," Laura called over from the driver's seat. "No one should be outside now."

"We don't have time for this!" Lance hissed at her.

Frank looked at Laura and slowly nodded. "When my shift is over," he mumbled. He turned his sign around to Slow. "You can move on now."

"Hey Frank, do you need a ride to your house?" Garner asked.

"We don't have room!" Lance barked. They nearly didn't, with Tanya, Webster, and Garner in the backseat. Frank was covered nearly head to toe with white dust. It had caked on the top of his shoulders.

"We can take him that far," Garner said. "It probably isn't a long way." Lance only shook his head curtly.

Then Frank called out "no!", and began to back away. "You have to obey the sign! It's the law! I'm just doing my job!"

"We have to go," Lance said, and rolled up his window. "Crazy man. A lunatic. We don't need it."

"Traumatized," Webster said. "It's not his fault."

"No, it's not," Laura said. "Human frailty; a trauma syndrome. Perhaps he'll realize he really is in danger and must go in soon."

"I hope so," Garner said. But he had the impression the man was committing slow suicide, because of what he had seen, and what had happened to his loved ones. He could relate to that. They all could; he thought, again, of Kiatsu. A lump formed in his throat. He rolled the nearest window down and stuck his head out.

"Hey Frank, get your ass out of there! It isn't safe! Just go home!" Frank turned to look at the departing car, as though he wanted to take the advice, but something imponderable prevented him from doing so. He put the sign up toward the road in the opposite direction, then was lost in the murk.

Garner was suddenly starved. He wished he could go back to the Raw Frontier Diner. Or that at least, a similar place, with blazing red neon and a warm light softly bathing a dining area seen through a plate-glass window, would appear around the next corner.

In reality, nothing appeared within miles but a gray

blizzard of ash, with more malignant soot piled up by the side of the road.

# # #

They continued on. The ash on the route deepened. Garner got out a map and studied it.

"Where do you want to spend the night?" he asked. He figured they had about 290 miles to go before they reached his Idaho destination. That would be, as soon as tomorrow, but not if the roads were blocked, which looked increasingly probable.

Lance looked back at him from the front seat, but didn't say anything. It seemed he was having a little spat with Laura.

They had been unerringly straightforward up till that moment, showing little emotion.

Garner had heard Laura say in a measured tone, "we should have done more for him."

Lance replied calmly, "when an insane person decides to commit suicide, it is tragic, but if we have access to no medical personnel, experts, and resources, then we can do little to prevent it."

"Ultimately, we are here to save civilians. He was, obviously, a civilian in need."

Lance didn't say anything for a minute, then stated in a low, vaguely testy tone, "Let me drive now." She pulled over to the side of the road.

Dusk fell and made it difficult to see either side of the road. Flakes of ash clogged the darkness and danced in front of the headlights. Lance got out and walked over and took the wheel of the Jeep, then pulled back out onto the road. They kept traveling at a moderate speed, through a suburban neighborhood where the ash drifted as high as the mailboxes, then uninhabited woodlands.

Finally, they reached the intersection with Interstate 84, which they took north, on the outskirts of Ogden, Utah.

They weren't far from the Wyoming or Idaho borders, and only about 250 miles, as a crow flies, from the Yellowstone epicenter.

They passed Ogden and entered Interstate 15, but the ash deepened and drifted across the deserted concrete lanes, slowing their progress to a crawl.

Garner wondered how much gas they had left. He got out some of their remaining food, a peanut butter sandwich he'd pasted together with about half a dozen others from an old scavenged jar. Strangely, he hadn't seen Laura or Lance eat yet.

"You guys hungry?" he asked from the back seat.

"Not yet," Lance replied, opaquely.

"Do you mind if I check for those messages I talked about? The ones online?"

"No I don't mind. But I think it would be better to check these messages when we stop at the next refuge."

"What do you mean by refuge?"

"Any kind of enclosure that we can find, like an abandoned house or commercial building."

They approached one near Tremonton, Utah. The big parking lot had only two vehicles hastily parked and suffocated with ash drifts. The single-story building was unlit, but Garner could still make out the blue Motel 6 sign, the "6" in bright but pealing red.

The Jeep, with its thick treads plowing through the soot like dried mud, came to a quiet halt in front of the motel. The rooms were all dark. They all got out of the Jeep, removed their luggage and bags, and hurried over to one of the doors. Lance quickly jimmied the lock with a metal tool, impressing Garner with this street-smart skill, and they all entered the pitch-black room. Garner pierced it with a columnar beam from a small black flashlight, the last working one he had.

CHAPTER 27

Open luggage spilled clothes over a queen-sized bed. There was a tired, drink-stained bedside table, and the wallpaper had a cheesy western scene with wagon trains and Indians on horseback standing watch on buttes. That made Garner think of Zeke, and he got out his cell phone.

"I have to charge this up, too."

"Okay, but just this once," Lance said. Garner had trouble thinking of him as a federal official; he didn't know what Lance was. But he certainly carried an arsenal of fancy gear. The portable battery he used for charging devices had multiple plugin nodes. He felt lucky.

As Garner's phone charged, Webster slumped on a spongy couch in the corner, and soon could be heard snoring.

Predictably, none of the wall outlets worked. It was cold inside the small motel room, and now Garner had a full appreciation of what it was like when the electricity grid went down. Night was night; food was short or nonexistent, gasoline was rare. He idly thought, it was cold enough to snow, which was hardly distinguishable from the airborne ash.

They'd moved into what was possibly a semi-permanent winter in North America.

"How are we doing on gas, Lance?"

Typing furiously into his laptop, Lance looked up.

"We have enough for the Yellowstone region."

Garner filled in the blanks.

"But not the return trip…" He sat on the edge of the bed. "Who are you messaging there?"

"Headquarters," Lance replied, without looking up. "It's all about Salt Lake City. Bad air quality, power down, massive refugee problem on the road; unknown number of casualties…well, you know. You were there."

Laura had a headlamp on; she wandered over to the bathroom. When she tried the bathroom tap, it worked, miraculously, emitting a weak stream.

"My goodness, there's water here. I'm going to…wash up…" She partially closed the door, and Garner could see her, through a crack near the door hinge, removing a zipped vest and a pullover shirt, revealing a tank top and bare, muscular arms.

As she splashed water on her face, shapely, prominent breasts were visible, then she turned and pulled the tank-top over her head.

He could see the small of her back and the bra strap. She bent over and splashed water on the nape of her neck, still failing, as if on purpose, to fully shut the door. She smoothed her hair back, arching her back.

Garner glanced at Lance who, transfixed by the laptop screen, couldn't have been less interested.

He saw Laura pulling on her layers and shaking out her hair; it was a new, womanly side to her he hadn't noticed before. She opened the door and their eyes met; hers were wide open and wet. Self aware. He could tell she knew he'd been watching her.

She looked down, mimicking being busy by wiping her hands and arms with a towel. Garner also got the impression she'd wanted him to watch her pour water over the tops of her breasts. Maybe she was tired of Lance's all-business, cerebral exterior.

"Little more than a trickle," she commented. "But there seems to be plenty left." Deep inside, Garner felt a twinge of guilt and imagined the time he and Kiatsu lay on a beach together on the North Island of New Zealand, an empty Champagne bottle lying in the sand; arms and legs entwined.

Then the image made him sad.

He wondered, again, what Laura's gig was, romantically. At the same time, he was aware it had become an obsession of his.

"How old are you Laura?"

"Twenty-seven."

"Did you have any boyfriends at Ithaca? Or I should say, how many boyfriends do you have?"

She hesitated, and her silence revealed her intransigence, as well as deepened the mystery.

"Yes, you're interested in that, aren't you? We talked about that before."

"Well?"

"Boyfriends? None that I could say. Coffee sometimes, after class. A movie. I'm just too busy."

"I can see that, at the moment. But the rest of it surprises me. Men are men, and you seem to have great qualities. Did you just spurn them?"

"Spurn? What's spurn?"

"Rebuff them; constantly say no when they express an interest." He wanted to be respectful; not tease her too hard.

"Something like that."

Garner laughed softly, shaking his head, as though in sympathy with the frustrations of the college men who must have gathered eagerly around Laura.

Webster had woken up and was watching them both intently.

"Don't you have physical urges?" he asked Laura.

"Dude," Garner said to him, remonstratively.

"Of course, I have physical urges," she said nervously. Lance looked up from the laptop disapprovingly.

"Maybe you should make yourselves useful," he said, to Webster and Garner. "Look around the motel for food and bottled water. Take the dog for a walk…"

Tanya stood by the closed door, slowly wagging her tail. Garner thought of standing on the wet kitchen floor of the Raw Frontier diner with the door half open, almost having left her with the old cook.

"What kind of urges?" Webster asked, placing glasses over his myopically expressive eyes. "Hunger. Sleep. Sex?"

"Cleanliness," Laura said, zipping up her jacket, watching Webster with a seething look.

"What's Pi, then, to the 26th decimal point?"

Without hesitation, she said, fixing the jacket around her narrow hips, "3.14159265358979323846264338."

Webster fixed Garner with a knowing, insolent expression.

"Good at math," Garner said, then "I'm going to have a look around this place. With Tanya." He headed for the door, as Laura sat down next to Lance and studied the laptop screen.

Webster stood up, stretched stiffly, and followed Garner out the door.

"What's your problem?" Garner said, when they'd shut the door behind them. He pulled the buff up over his mouth. He wanted to see the sun again. The wind was bitter and caustic.

"She's an artificial," Webster said. "They both are."

"An artificial?"

"A synthetic, an android, whatever you want to call it."

"Nonsense."

"I'm not kidding you," Webster said, talking excitedly. "I should know. Haven't you suspected it? The flat reactions, the machine-like efficiency, the bodily, plastic perfection…"

"That's impossible. You're dreaming." Webster couldn't convince him of that, despite his A.I. cred. As Zeke had called it, science fiction.

Webster went on, pressing the point. "It's eminently possible, with existing technology. Cutting-edge, for sure. I'd like to take them apart, see what's on the inside."

"I'll bet you would."

"Did you see how quickly she answered the math problem? The inability to talk, maturely, about feelings and desires?"

Garner thought about her movements around the bathroom sink. "The unwillingness around men like you, maybe," he said, pushing back on Webster's annoying assurance.

"So this is how it works," Webster went on. "The feds, maybe the CIA, send in the most advanced technology, to the worst ash-deposition zones. It's a win-win; it's safer than putting real humans at risk, and they get to test the technology. Maybe these are advanced prototypes."

"That's…unbelievable," Garner said, though he found Webster's confidence off-putting. "Lance is just…one of these careerists; an arrogant asshole. He sees this catastrophe as his moment, a way to further his career, impress people."

"Have you noticed they haven't eaten anything, the entire time."

"I've seen them drink water."

"Perhaps their moving parts require hydration, but they contain no flesh and blood. No organs. They have no need for metabolism."

Garner didn't want to grace Webster's claims with the credibility his own speculation would give them. He walked Tanya in silence, but only as far as the Jeep. He changed the subject.

"They must have a kitchen at this place. We should search it." The leftover peanut-butter sandwiches weren't cutting it; he was starved, and cold. He needed meat.

True, he hadn't seen Laura or Lance eat yet; perhaps they were just discrete about it, and were munching meals-ready-to-eat in the background.

The night was as black as a cold cell, a fog hovering over the empty, unlit highway. They went back to the room; Garner wanted to check the Idaho messages again, see if there were any new ones.

He wanted to look at his recharged cell phone. They were located at the intersection of I-15, which went north to Pocatello, Idaho, and I-84 northwest to Ketchum. They were about 20 miles from the Idaho border. No one was migrating south on the highways, as if few if any were alive to make the trip.

He heard the wind whistling in the darkness.

When Lance let him check a working network with his laptop, Garner found new messages from the same forum as before. *Someone* was alive up there.

CHAPTER 28: DECEMBER 1, 2025

This time he could post a reply to the forum. Dated December 1, 2025, the new one read:

This might be the last message!! things have gotten desperate...I've run out of food...all are gone...mostly dead!! please answer!! please pass it along!! we can't survive much longer...a few more days, maybe...where are our rescuers? me and Gavin...we can't move!! its poison outside and full of them...it's so dark out the window I'm scared!! I have faith but not much longer!!

John 1:5

Jenny Lane, Saint Luke's Hospital, Ketchum

This time she gave a name–Jenny, and a specific location, a hospital in Ketchum. He typed the address for Google Maps, but the app was down. He would look at his own western maps. Now he knew where he was going.

He typed in,

We're coming to get you Jenny, hang tight. Hopefully we'll be there within 72 hours at most.

But Garner didn't want to get her hopes up. He went

back and changed the message to: *We're going to get there as soon as possible within the week. Don't move, unless you're already in the hands of emergency responders! Sincerely, Brad Garner (at the Idaho border).*

Then he sent the message.

Without making false promises, he figured that was enough to give Jenny some hope. Who was she? He guessed: a mom, who was injured, or burdened by young children so she couldn't move, or both. He handed the laptop back to Lance.

"St. Luke's Hospital in Ketchum, Idaho. A person still alive. Barely, it sounds."

"So I assume that's where you want to go."

"Correct."

"Ketchum, Idaho..." Lance ruminated. "That's where Ernest Hemingway lived, at the end of his life."

"A great American writer," Laura stated, somewhat sophomorically.

Garner got up and reached into his bags for his maps, unfolding one on the bed.

"We're here..." he traced with his finger, to Tremonton, Utah. "And I have to go here." He measured the miles roughy with index finger and thumb. "Two hundred twenty miles, if we stick to I-84 and go through Twin Falls, and catch Route 93 north."

Aptly, the first town they'd hit approaching the Idaho border was Snowville. Might as well call it Ashville.

They would be officially entering the zone that received greater than a meter, or 40 inches of ash. Maybe some places received twice that or more, a height of debris taller than him. Spread everywhere. He wondered if the roads would be passable at all.

He shut off his flashlight and picked up the cell phone where it had been plugged into Lance's charger. He switched it on; it came to life, casting a pool of light onto the bed covers. He left it on the covers, went into the bathroom, and stuck his face into the sink, greedily lapping up a trickle of cool water.

We can't even melt snow because it's contaminated by the ash, he thought.

He came out of the bathroom, grabbed the phone, opened the door, and went outside. He let the various logos–Verizon and Samsung–silently load and fade from the screen. Icons appeared at the top, and a fraction of a bar.

*So a phone network exists…*he thought. Miraculously.

No message replies appeared, no responses to all the texts he'd sent Kiatsu. *C'mon baby,* he said to himself; *send me a signal. Give me some hope. Load up.* He gave it another minute; two, three, four. Nothing. He felt his spirits sink; his mind swam in images of his family again, a sea of grief, regret, and guilt. He cleared his throat, and dialed Zeke's number, the one he'd given him outside of Delores in Colorado.

He fully expected not to connect, but he did. Another miracle; a voice message from Zeke. It felt good to hear his voice.

I'm not here compadres, but leave me a message. A short one; I don't need to listen to your drunken ramblings. Your favorite hombre, Zeke.

He talked quickly, "Hey Zeke! It's Brad! Did you make it, to Naturita? Did you find your woman? Hey listen man, I've got a working cell phone for now and the number is…" He quickly read it out.

"I'm close to the Idaho border and I'm going to Ketchum, be there in…" But click, the message recorder shut down on him. Alright, Zeke had his number now. Maybe he could connect with him on the trip back south. If he didn't go west to California. Maybe not; even San Fran and L.A. were coated with an inch and a half of this crap…

Still no messages from Kiatsu…

The phone dropped to his side; he shivered in the

wind. He opened the door and went back into the hotel room.

Laura and Lance were sitting on the bed looking at him blankly.

Lance cut right to the chase, as was his wont.

"We're not going to Ketchum. I'm sorry, but we said in the beginning we'd take you to the Idaho border."

"Where are you going?"

"We're going to the epicenter. Take more readings. This is our mission; we need the data."

"But you saw that message. There's someone, people, Jenny and Gavin, alive up there. We have the means to rescue them."

Lance exhaled impatiently. "There are probably more people alive near Yellowstone. This is of critical importance. We have to report to headquarters exactly what conditions are at the epicenter. We have to take seismic readings; take debris samples. We have to measure the gases in the air. Surely you understand the importance of reporting directly from there."

"You'll be killed yourself," Garner said, his voice rising. "…By toxic spew from Yellowstone, or more explosions. There's nothing to sustain you, in terms of supplies; it's all blasted to hell."

"Ketchum would be the same."

"But someone's alive there. We know that. Yellowstone's been blasted to Kingdom Come, and all you're going to find there is ash, rubble, and fissures dribbling molten rock. The air is poison. You know that; it's full of sulfuric acid, like a poison planet."

"We knew our mission was dangerous," Laura said. "It was part of the agreement."

"Part of the programming," Webster quipped from the other side of the room. "Risk-taking, self sacrifice; no tendency to hesitate. Power through with the mission, no matter what. It's all written in; coded."

Garner shook his head with fatigue and frustration. "How come you don't eat, anyways? Me and Tanya are starving, and we've eaten much more than you two."

Laura removed from her pack what looked like a protein bar; she unwrapped it, took a nibble and idly chewed it. "See...we eat."

How did I end up with these two, at the Idaho border in the middle of nowhere in a blasted landscape? He realized again the irrationality and madness of his journey; its mindless faithfulness.

How come I wasn't with Kiatsu, Jake, and Abby, when they needed me most?

I've run out of food...all are gone...mostly dead!! the message repeated in his head.

He wasn't finished with Lance and Laura.

"You didn't drive that Jeep all the way from Washington, D.C., or wherever you originated."

"Edwards Air Force Base," Laura repeated blankly. Lance shot a sour, disapproving glance at her.

"We came in an aerial vehicle," she said.

CHAPTER 29

"He deserves to know," she pointed out to Lance.

"This information is classified. It can't be shared."

"He's a partner of ours." Then she looked at Garner again, with what he took to be a longing.

"We flew in an AAV–an advanced aerial vehicle–to Northern New Mexico, where the Jeep was waiting for us. And all the gear and supplies."

Maybe they were "artificials," and Webster was right, Garner thought. He still couldn't get himself close enough to believe that; she was too real. He'd seen her body; it was sculpted to perfection, but real enough to him. The training and indoctrination just gave them these robotic personas.

"How far will you take me into Idaho?"

Lance exhaled, as though Garner represented a great burden. He picked up the map, which lay unfolded on the bed.

"We'll take you 50 miles into Idaho, where I-84 intersects with I-86. Then we have to take I-86 north to

Yellowstone. I-86 goes to I-15 north in Pocatello."

"We should take him to Ketchum, as long as we're going that close to it." Laura looked at him, and Garner smiled in a strained and hopeful way.

"It's another 125 miles from the intersection where we must go north. That's too far out of our way!"

"What…are we just going to leave him by the side of the road with his dog, in a pile of dust?"

Garner was impressed by her passion; the empathy. That wasn't artificial.

"Maybe another search-and-rescue operation will be going towards Ketchum; he can hitch a ride with them."

Garner thought of this advanced aerial vehicle, and what he and Zeke saw over the New Mexican desert. The UAP.

"What does your AAV look like?"

"That's classified," Lance muttered, folding up the map.

"How come you didn't take it farther north?"

"We needed to be on the ground," Laura said.

Garner laid back on the bed.

"What does this AAV run on?"

"Rocket fuel, of course," Lance said too quickly.

Laura took a deep breath and exhaled, as if torn by something.

"If you really have to know, are interested…" Laura said. "A salt solution. It's advanced, we told you that."

"Lt. Laura Gaines," Lance said firmly, like a father at his wit's end with a recalcitrant child.

He hadn't seen the Jeep get any gas, either. "And the Jeep?"

"It's an experimental engine…salt…" Laura said, eyeing Lance rebelliously.

"And what do you run on?" Webster blurted out from the shadows.

"Piss and vinegar," Lance said, staring at Laura.

Garner thought of the Zuni Salt Lake way down in New Mexico, not far from where Trinity went off. The UAP flying overhead from the Lake's direction.

Just then, from the other side of the motel door, from the ash fog of night, they heard a screech like the whinnying of a horse.

CHAPTER 30

Garner stood up and went to the door of the Motel 6 room, carrying his pistol. He'd heard the muffled whinnying and stamping. He opened the door partway. Flakes of ash drifted in from the cold darkness. He whisked them away like a spider web one stumbles into.

"It was my impression Tremonton was an empty town," he whispered back to the others. Through the crack, he saw the thick, boney legs of a white horse, shifting over the ground like a synchronized dance step. The rest was lost in the dark swirl of dust, like moths against the night sky.

"It seems we might have guests," Lance said. "But you don't have to carry that gun around. This is not a diplomatic way to greet a stranger."

Garner thought about Lance's cold tone with the scared sign carrier back on the road. And he didn't want to be lectured anyway.

"You never know what their motivations are," he said. He peered through the crack again. "You just never can know."

He could see flashlight beams stab the darkness. He heard a few gruff voices. He thought of the posse. "Especially this far north." He gripped the pistol harder.

Laura stood at the front window and parted the shade.

"They seem to be leaving. They look like shadows; three, four people on horseback. No, they're going across the parking lot. Perhaps around back…"

Garner had cut the room lights; Lance clicked them back on.

"Clearly…" Lance said with an uppity assurance. "They're looking for shelter and food, just like everyone else. We can ignore them. For now." He walked over and shut the door.

"I hope you're right," Garner said, feeling a tingling of dread, that black spirit he'd had trouble dispelling on the road. Webster stared at him from across the room.

"It's that posse we saw hang the man," Jack recited in a monotone. "The men who tried to rob us at the gas station. They're not likely to forget. I'd lock the door and keep it locked. I'd keep the handgun loaded."

"Now don't start jumping to conclusions," Garner answered. But he latched the lock, as he would've in any motel.

Still standing at the shade, Laura turned back to the others. "They're gone. So strange, riding horses in these conditions. They're going to kill the poor animals. They can't breathe. How would they water them?"

"The vehicles must be breaking down. Three, four feet of ash, and it's simple for tiny amounts to ruin the engine. The region is reverting back to the Old West," Garner said.

"The Old West," Webster quipped acidly. "Lawlessness, anarchy, and corruption. Vigilantes, hangings…"

"I'm going to get some sleep," *and leave the pistol by my pillow*, Garner thought. Webster's bitter ramblings exhausted him. "We should go at sunrise."

"Agreed," Lance said, going back to his laptop. "We should waste no time to get to the epicenter."

"I don't know where I'm going to go," Webster mumbled pitifully. "Anywhere, but to go commit suicide at the epicenter, with a couple of…cellular ambiguities."

"You can take the next wagon train south," Lance shot back, eyes not leaving the laptop screen. Garner laughed.

"Well, we only have two beds; I'm taking this side, Tanya's over here…hey Laura, I'll make a lot of room, and you can take the rest of the bed." Anyone sleeping next to me but Webster, Garner thought. He had to admit he craved Laura's companionship. The warmth. The feminine vibe. She was real enough to him.

He heard Lance's tapping, then the lights went out again. The mattress depressed gently as Laura lay down next to him. He searched the darkness for sounds of the men outside, but heard nothing but wind against the walls.

He wondered if Lance was jealous; he could feel it in the air…an inhibited anger and envy.

Laura lay down on top of the blankets; he was already beneath them. The air was cold; the motel had no heating. After a minute, he sensed her shift around. He rolled around in Laura's direction; she'd pulled part of the blanket over her. He loosened his own grip on the blanket, and tossed another section of it over the exposed part of her torso.

He watched her shoulders go up and down with the breathing. He reached over and felt for his pistol on the side table. He felt warm, purposeful; he was protecting someone again.

He pulled the blanket up to his chin and fell deeply asleep, imagining the road north. He'd examined his maps before laying down. He had just 200 miles left to Ketchum, Idaho, and he'd made it almost 1,000 miles already from Las Cruces.

From the land of the centimeter ash, to the land of ash as high as a cornfield in August.

# # #

The evening was quiet, except for a mysterious knock coming from elsewhere in the dead motel. He figured it was possibly the pipes: freezing, thawing, and popping.

He thought he heard someone laugh, followed by more laughter, heartier and vaguely crazy, but then it went silent as he lay in bed listening.

Lance was up before sunrise. Garner looked over and Laura was still asleep. She'd slept silently. *Is sleeping something they can do?* he could hear Webster say. But the whole claim they were synthetic was something he'd tried to set aside days ago. Survival and reaching his goal is what mattered the most.

Lance stood looking out the window, then seemed to go back to his laptop in the dark. Garner had found the cheap-o Mr. Coffee the day before, but it was useless without electricity. His stomach growled too. He found one of the beef stew cans he'd harvested from the diner back in Fence Lake. They still had matches and a couple of crusty, stainless steel pots and pans.

He went outside. He made a crude little fire, out in the parking lot as the sun was coming up, then heated up the stew and water. It kept him busy and occupied with a low-level goal: food. He thought of being in Ketchum at the end of the day. In maybe two.

He shared the food with Webster, who followed Garner around like a whipped dog. He seemed frightened; dreading some form of abandonment. Garner made cheap coffee by dissolving it in boiling water, sifting the grounds from left-over envelopes in the motel room.

Laura rolled off the bed and gathered her things into

the backpack, yet once again, neither she nor her partner wanted any food, Garner noticed.

The Jeep started up fine, and they sat idling in the parking lot. Lance glanced back at Webster, expecting him to make a decision.

"Are you staying, or coming?" he finally asked.

Ken opened his eyes wide, in a near panic. "Do I have a choice? I don't see a bus stop around here. In fact, I don't see anyone else here, except for those ghostly renegade horsemen from last night, and believe me, their presence doesn't inspire confidence in a southern journey. Me, alone? No, I'll choose companionship, for now," he said, looking out the window at the empty highway entrance ramp.

"Don't get me wrong…I appreciate the ride," he added meekly. "And the company." He looked at Garner and Tanya, sitting with him in the backseat.

"Then we'll get moving," Lance said decisively. He peeled out in the sand and ash of the parking lot and headed up the ramp to Interstate 84 north.

The highway was empty, except for a few tire tracks that wended their way through the dust blindly towards the surrounding scrub, with no signs of a vehicle, as if it had blown away with the tumbleweeds and shredded mesquite.

The wind sculpted the ash across the road in waves. Lance put the Jeep into low gear and they began the slow grind north. Thirty-five miles to Idaho.

CHAPTER 31

The landscape was stained black and red in places, from the smoke of recent forest fires. Still at the wheel, Lance glanced back at the others absently.

"The volcanic ash was so hot it lit wildfires," he said. "We have to be careful." Dirty brown rags of ash plumes sailed across the sun, which had only just risen. Ugly black plumes rose in the distance from still smoldering fires.

Garner wondered how anyone in these parts survived the eruption. They'd run away, or were lying around dead in the woods somewhere. They drove the empty road into the crumbled remnants of a town called Blue Creek, Utah.

The long abandoned settlement had wooden homes that had collapsed onto their foundations, as much by neglect as the cataclysm just north of them.

It used to be a railroad stop; tourist guides even referred to it as a ghost town.

It had taken them an hour to go less than 20 miles, the Jeep bogged down at times in ash that rose to the bumpers. They swerved a snake's path through the dust, with Lance slamming the vehicle into four-wheel drive. Garner could hear the high whine of the gears as the vehicle fought and bumped past no more than a handful of broken homes and barns.

He watched Laura stare through the windshield at the empty, featureless expanse buried with what looked like shifting sands. It used to be desert with some hills and sagebrush. Now it was almost uniformly covered in a sad blanket the color of dead skin. The landscape could have been a corpse itself. But Laura seemed oddly at peace, contemplative, considering where they were going.

"Great engine in this rig," Garner said, breaking the awkward silence. "However much I miss it, I'm not sure the old Bronco could have made it a mile through any of this crap."

"As an engine that runs so well on a salt solution, hypothetically, I'd like to see the specs for the design," Webster said.

Lance grimaced and grunted, "That would not be possible."

"Why?"

"It's a technical document that I would not be permitted to show to you."

"I'm an A.I. researcher myself, so naturally I have an interest," Webster said, in a friendlier vein. "I've worked on artificial brains, the neural equivalents of humans, for the intelligence agencies. That's why I'm interested in where you and Laura came from."

"I don't see how we have anything to do with that."

"Where were you born?" Webster asked, seemingly testing again.

A long impatient silence from Lance, then "Gaithersburg, Maryland."

"What did your parents do?"

"They were a professor in art history and a civil engineer who designed bridges. What is this, a job interview?"

"I'm just the inquisitive type. Don't take it the wrong way. I'm from New Jersey myself; my father was a mathematician. My mother, well, I guess you'd call her a homemaker. I think she could have done anything she wanted to do professionally, with her smarts, if she had the opportunity."

"Lack of equal rights and opportunities for females in the workplace," Laura said, as if by rote. "Breaking through the glass ceiling, is necessary, for a more optimal society."

"You seem to have led an interesting professional life, yourself, Laura."

"I'm…satisfied."

They passed barren fields with a few lonely shells of wooden structures. Everything was in ruins, belying the casual chat they had.

"Lance, did you have a happy childhood there in Maryland?" Webster wasn't letting go.

"Of course," Lance said, as if everyone did.

"How many brothers and sisters?"

Lance was quiet for a minute, then responded, as if reaching his irritation limits, "you can stop your annoying questions now."

"I have something you might be interested in," Webster said, digging around in his luggage bag. He produced a red plastic disk with a black connector cord. "The collected works of Kenneth Webster. These are the specs for the working brain of an advanced form of artificial intelligence; a man's…or woman's…brain. But better. It's all there." He placed it on the plastic shelf next to Lance that held the emergency brake lever.

"Plug that into your laptop and take a look. I have a feeling you'd be able to comprehend it. It's a neuromorphic chip, but of the most advanced form. I own the patent for it.

It can understand several languages, create natural speech, control arms, legs, and torso, compute math, of course, do everything, at speeds that leave us mere mortals in the dust…so to speak. I'd be interested in what you think."

Lance looked down disdainfully at the hard disc.

"I don't think so," he said.

"Digital machines perform better than human minds, in almost every respect," Webster added proudly.

"Almost?"

Garner glanced out the window at the buried roadside and fields, temporarily bathed in a jaundiced sunlight. It looked like a giant beach, without the sea. He thought of being alone, perhaps tomorrow.

"They haven't been live tested yet." Then Webster nodded knowingly at Lance and Laura.

Lance maneuvered to the side of the highway, in a huff, ash bunching to the hood of the Jeep. He stopped the vehicle, abruptly, then glared back at Webster.

"Just what are you getting at, with this line of questioning?"

"Nothing, really. Just thought you'd be interested in my work."

"Do you think I'm synthetic, some kind of machine? A prototype? Is that what you think?"

"Well, I wouldn't know. You have an amazing ability, how else can I say it, to go without food."

"I'm sick of your idiotic questions. You lunatic scientists. You're ruining everything, with your doomsday inventions. Maybe this will settle it for you."

He pulled a hunting knife out of his gear pack.

"Lance, put that away," Laura said.

He addressed her, defensively. "You know, he thinks the both of us are machines. Like blood, human blood, doesn't flow in our veins. Here…"

He rolled up one of his sleeves.

"Don't do this," Laura said.

Lance looked at his bare arm, as if fascinated by it for the first time. He placed the tip of the knife on the underside of his forearm and drew it across, making a red line. Carmine blood began to seep out of it, like a tiny tide flowing out. He looked up at the others, faintly pleased.

"You see…that should settle things, that I'm human."

Webster looked at him eyes agape, chin slightly quivering. A large spot of blood pooled on Lance's forearm, as he clenched a fist. He appeared triumphant.

Laura furiously rifled through her own gear bag and produced a roll of gauze, which she quickly applied by wrapping up Lance's forearm and taping it over.

"That was a rash, illogical thing you did," she scolded. "We don't have time for it. This could cause problems for us later, for our mission. Self injury; I can't comprehend it. Don't do it again."

"Some people don't listen to reason," Lance muttered, clenching and unclenching his fist, still proudly watching the dark blood stain on the bandage.

"I have a lot of blood," he claimed dreamily, still staring at his forearm. "I have more than I need."

"We are wasting our time now," Garner said, aggravated at the direction things had taken. "Here by the side of the road in the desert. You said you'd take me another one hundred fifty miles north. I thought we could make that by sundown."

Then, from the backseat, Tanya began to bark at something outside the windshield. They all looked up. A large truck, heading south in the other lane, rolled slowly towards them, headlights on. Then another behind it, and another. It was a convoy, and appeared military.

"This is a good development," Lance said. He started the engine and pressed a button on the dash, which operated a blinking red light on the roof of the Jeep. Then he got out of the Jeep. He closed the door and stood next to the road waving his arms. Tanya kept barking.

Garner got out too, and closed the passenger door. Laura got out and followed him. The first truck slowed down. It was the first vehicle they'd seen, except for a few sedan and pickup carcasses at the side of the highway, since Salt Lake.

They saw a man, in a green khaki uniform with a HazMat mask on, in the driver's seat. The man rolled down his window; lifted the mask.

"You stuck here?" he yelled out.

"No," Lance said. "Who are you?"

"Western National Guard. I'd turn around and go south if I were you. There's nothing up there. There's nothing to survive on. It's very dangerous."

"Where are you going?"

"Salt Lake…they're opening up a hospital. We have casualties."

"Do you have room for one more?"

"Are they hurt, or ambulatory?"

"They're not hurt or sick. They just need a ride."

"Well, then I think so." The man looked back at the other trucks idling behind him, impatient to get going.

Lance opened the passenger door on the roadside.

"C'mon Webster, get out. This is your ride home."

Webster looked down sheepishly, then began to gather his things. He stuffed the hard disc back in his luggage, and got out of the car. Tanya stuck her head out, sniffing the vaguely contaminated air.

Garner looked down at the ground, coughed, looked at Tanya, then said, "Can you take one more, too, a dog?"

"Sure," the driver said. "But we have to leave now. We have to make the city by daylight."

Garner looked over at Tanya, then walked over and began to pet and stroke the fur on her head and back. Tanya still stood on the backseat of the car with her tail slowly wagging.

CHAPTER 32

"Listen kid," Garner whispered. "This is as far as you're going. I'm not going to bring you up into that mess, but I have to go. This is my thing. I don't want you to die up there, just because you were with me. That's the last thing I want. You've been a wonderful companion. I couldn't have gotten this far without you. Thanks for being there for me."

He thought of the early days, which seemed oddly about a year ago. Driving north from Las Cruces on a dark, lonely highway with only Tanya in the backseat. He had a lump in his throat.

He knew he was doing the right thing.

He reached over and lifted the dog out of the car and carried her in his arms. They walked over to the back of the truck. He could feel Tanya quivering. Dogs knew.

He walked over to the man's open window. "I can give you some food…she's eaten lately…she's had water."

"That's okay. We have plenty of food for her," the driver said. He seemed nice and like he'd had a dog before.

"You can just bring her to the back of the truck. They'll take care of her in there."

"Is she going to be okay in Salt Lake?"

"Sure thing. We need more dogs at the base."

"Which one is it?"

"The headquarters over in Sandy."

"Is Salt Lake survivable though?"

"It's getting better. They're bringing in supplies."

"Okay."

He brought her to the back of the truck, which was open with a stiff canopy fastened over the top, as a roof. The space was full of cots with prone people covered in blankets. Some lay under I.V. devices. A guardsman pushed a tarp aside and Garner handed Tanya to him. The dog was still trembling.

"Bye Tanya!" Garner said, lingering. "Be a good girl now. These people will take good care of you." He swallowed hard. "That's a good girl. I'll see you in Salt Lake. I swear I will." Tanya kept looking at the man who received her in the truck. He kept petting her and smiling. Then Tanya looked back at Garner, panting and then whimpering in a way that was barely audible. Garner turned and slowly walked back to the car.

"No worries, Tanya."

Then he said to himself, "No worries, Garner."

"You should wear a HazMat mask outside," the driver called down to him when he walked by. "Do you have one?"

"Yes," he said.

# # #

Webster carried his things to the back of the truck. He appeared glad to be going south, but also uncertain about leaving, having been tossed out of the Jeep by Lance. Garner offered then shook his hand.

"Good luck to you," Webster said. Then he seemed

to shift away from farewells. "Why don't you just get on the truck, with me and the dog? It's suicide, going any farther. You heard the man; there's nothing alive up there."

"That would be giving up. Anyways, he's wrong about there being nothing alive up there. I have to go. I have to finish what I started."

"I can see that." Webster turned and threw his stuff in the back of the truck. Then he lurched back to Garner. "Don't trust those two. I'm telling you, they're synthetics. I know one when I see one. They're not selfish, they're worse than that. They're programmed for a mission, and only that. You're not part of the mission; so you don't fit into their plans."

"They've gotten me this far."

"I'm telling you, don't trust them with your life."

"I get your point…"

"…Because when push comes to shove, they're not going to choose you, they will aim only for the outcome they are coded for."

"I get it."

Garner turned aside and walked back to the Jeep, getting in the back, now feeling alone. Lance started up the vehicle, and they pulled off into the slough of the road ash. They continued in the northbound lane, which as far as they could see had no other vehicles.

Garner watched the convoy of half a dozen trucks disappear in the distance. They couldn't have contained 200 casualties, he thought, with six trucks. There must be millions more. There must be a lot of people still alive, if his own signal is still transmitting.

He felt like he knew this person Jenny, without knowing a thing about her life, and only reading about four cryptic messages from her.

She lived at the center of his days, like two strangers who are flung together because the ship sinks and they share a boat.

They were on a lifeboat together—he, Jenny, and who was it? Gavin. And Tanya and Zeke. He was going to fetch the two who'd signaled for help, then reunite with Zeke and Tanya in Salt Lake. It seemed like a plan, if only that. This thought lifted his spirits.

"Can I drive?" he said to Lance.

Lance sniffed, then glanced in the rearview mirror.

"Do you know the stick, the clutch, and the four-wheel drive?"

"Yes."

"Then okay...in twenty minutes."

It seemed weird without Tanya, like when Zeke left, but different. He felt he couldn't hack the separation psychically. It made him feel more lonely and less certain of his path.

Soon, he switched seats with Lance, took the wheel, and the change moved his mind off who wasn't there anymore.

# # #

The wind swept across the desert scrubland and shaped waves of bone-white ash and dust across the highway lanes. The Jeep plowed through it, making at times only 15 miles per hour. The engine ground to well over 3,000 r.p.m., he noticed from the gauge, but never appeared to falter.

They were a few miles outside of Snowville, Utah, which was not five miles from the Utah border with Idaho.

Salt, he thought. The accelerator felt like a familiar gasoline-powered one, the motor revving lustily when he pressed it, but he knew the tank contained no diesel or gas.

"How are we going to get more fuel?" he asked Laura, next to him in the front seat.

"We don't get more fuel."

"The energy is infinite?"

"No, but we have plenty in the tank, you might say, to

reach the Yellowstone epicenter."

"How are you going to get home?"

"How are you going to get home?" she answered enigmatically.

"It depends."

"On what?"

"On what happens in Ketchum."

"Well, as for us, a helicopter will come. We'll come look for you."

"That would be nice."

"And we have enough fuel, and that's why we will take you most of the way to Ketchum."

"What about?" Garner nodded his head back to Lance.

"You don't worry about him," she said, with a brisk confidence he'd only noticed once before, when she displayed no modesty in front of the sink and mirror at the motel. "He'll do what I say, eventually."

She'd pulled her auburn, soft hair back and zipped a black sweater up to her chin.

"Are you wearing make-up?"

She looked away shyly then smiled, as if against her will.

"Yes, a little lipstick…and something else. This air is destroying my skin…"

"You look pretty."

"Thank you."

Outside the windows, the flat, sandy barrens oppressed his eyes with its sameness and the knowledge that it was mostly ash and withered plants, no longer tufts of grass and living cacti. On the northern horizon, the mountains were scorched black.

CHAPTER 33

They decided to stop in Snowville, just short of the border.

The air tasted caustic. They put their HazMat masks on and stepped outside into the empty crossroads.

In the distance he saw a ranch that had collapsed under the weight of debris. A lonely tractor sat in a field, and another fenced-in lot was littered with the partially buried corpses of what he thought were cows.

The airborne soot was abrasive, like sand on a windy beach.

"We have to get inside," Garner said. The only place around was a small roadside building that must have been something in its heyday–Molly's Cafe read the battered sign.

Focused on one task, Lance silently took air-quality samples and captured G.P.S. coordinates with his devices. Garner and Laura walked over to the diner. A screen door opened and smacked closed in the wind. Nothing else at the roadside was open; they tried the front door and it too was broken.

They entered, leaving Lance outside in a dismal dusk that had arrived too early, cloaked by pollutants and the clouds of distant fires.

Molly's was an old-fashioned rectangular cafe with a long formica counter and cheerful but tattered red vinyl-covered booths.

"Anyone here!" Garner yelled out. Nothing but another wooden crash from the screen door.

"Boy, I wish the cook was still here," he quipped, collapsing into one of the booths. "But this will be fine for tonight."

"A roadside diner," Laura said with an impressed dreaminess. "Americana at its best."

"You said it honey. Corned beef and hash, with biscuits and great coffee. Blueberry pie with a scoop of vanilla that melts over the top. No, maybe apple pie with a slice of cheddar cheese."

"Cheese with pie?" she asked wondrously.

"Of course." But this conversation was making him starve. He got up to check the kitchen, with confidence, given what he'd found before.

Lance still wandered around in what increasingly seemed like an alien atmosphere. Another planet's.

"What's he doing?"

A weak, angled sunlight leaked through lopsided shades; Laura stepped forward to look out the window.

"Taking more data…observations."

"When is enough enough?"

"You can never have too much data, in these situations. We only have one super volcano. Humanity must survive it. We must move on, and for that we need to study."

So you are a part of *humanity*, Garner thought, as if he was still debating Webster.

"I miss Tanya," he said, changing the subject. "But I

made the right choice. Now I don't have to find food and water for her, and she's heading south. She's in good hands."

Lance came through the door roughly, stamping the dust off his feet. He thrust the mask off his face, which resembled a coal miner's. Garner went back into the kitchen, where he found used pots and pans on the floor and a rancid smell of old cooled pan grease.

Fly paper hung from the ceiling with black crunchy dots stuck to it. There were cracked framed photos of farmers and pilots and softball teams, giving the kitchen a personal touch and once again driving him back in time.

Right away, he found dry goods on the shelves: oatmeal, baking soda, salt, rice, a plundered box of Ritz Crackers, which he seized. He took a handful of the stale wafers and crammed them into his mouth. They made a salty mush. He kept looking, until he found the big chrome institutional refrigerator.

The handle had been tied shut with a bungee cord; he found that odd, but then he considered all the broken doors he'd found already.

He heard Laura and Lance talking in the main restaurant, a heated exchange, to the degree they ever became hot tempered with each other. He thought they were talking about him, and the plans to drive him farther north.

He took out his knife and cut the bungee cord, then the door released. Jarringly, a thawing, frozen corpse, curled in the fetal position, rolled out and thumped on the floor. He jumped out of the way and yelled; in a squeamishly slow-motion manner the body uncurled itself on the floor.

The corpse was male with white hair and beard; it reminded Garner of the Raw Frontier cook, same attire, but much skinnier. The body, the skin, also became bluer, as if he was watching him ripen. The man was clearly dead, so Garner pushed the heavy body aside, so he could gain access to the fridge.

There was still the matter of the freezer and its other contents.

He looked up and saw Lance standing in the kitchen entrance.

"What do you have there?" Lance asked, grimacing with white teeth through a soiled face.

Garner made sure by touching both the wrist, and the neck area where the carotid artery was located.

"It's a dead man."

"Did you find him on the floor?"

"In the refrigerator."

Garner stood up and went over to eye what was inside.

"Why was he in the refrigerator?"

"Beats me. Well, I can guess. Somebody put him there."

"He was killed, or died, and someone put him in the fridge…"

"And tied up the door."

"…Because the door was malfunctioning."

"No, I think it was because they trapped him in there. He was a captive, poor soul."

"Why the refrigerator? Why bother? Unless you wanted to save…the flesh. That's cannibalism; that's animalistic and depraved. An action that is a grave violation of human rights, and the basic precepts of civilized human behavior…"

"No, I just think whoever did this decided at the last second to shove him in there. Spontaneously, a cold-hearted gesture. Maybe he was giving them a fight."

It was like Lance had to think everything into its logical conclusion, based on preconceived notions. It was how he worked.

"This is more than just a volcanic eruption zone," Lance said, portentously, then he walked out.

Garner searched the inside of the freezer. The interior walls had several inches of frost build-up; he scraped it off into a bowl. He wanted to let it melt for water.

He removed a full ice tray and set it on the counter. He probed around the rest of the space but found it empty.

In the rest of the fridge he found half a stick of hardened butter and a partially eaten turkey leg stuffed in an old bread bag, which together, he considered a feast. He set them both on a plate, then he went back into the restaurant.

There might have been a few other scraps of food in the kitchen, but it was getting too dark to bang around in there.

He sat down at the counter with the plate and looked at the food, admiring it. These days, it took less food on a plate to impress him. He looked up; Laura sat in a booth, Lance stood at the window, snapping pictures.

"You want some of this?"

"No," Lance said, but Laura seemed interested.

"What is it?"

"Ritz Crackers, butter, and a turkey leg."

"I probably can eat the crackers and butter; then again, no. I'm a vegan."

"Since when?"

"I always have been."

"Okay." He pushed the box of crackers down the counter towards her. "Then at least have a cracker. They're salty. In this case, that's good. You guys seem to really like salt."

Lance seemed disinterested in everything going on inside the cafe, and put his mask on and went outside. All of a sudden, Garner heard a guttural motor start up, and the lights came on.

CHAPTER 34

"I'll be damned!"

Garner saw Lance pass in front of the window, then he came partway in.

"I found a generator, in the back. I don't know how much fuel is left."

"What a treat." The motor kept running in the back of the building.

Garner scanned the now illuminated wall and his eye fell upon a partially empty amber bottle with an old faded label. Behind it was a western mural of southern Utah, including some red-rock formations and Apaches or Utes on horseback standing on a butte. He got up and fetched the bottle.

Lance had the door halfway open. It was dark out; a pool of light fell upon the paved entrance to the diner, which was covered in drifted ash. Bits of the dust danced about like moths. You couldn't see the highway.

"Given that a corpse is lying in the kitchen," Lance

said. "I don't like the idea of spending the night in here. I'll sleep in the Jeep. I have to work late anyways. I have to backup and transmit my data."

"I'd like to stay inside the diner," Laura said, calmly asserting herself.

Lance nodded noncommittally and said, "We leave at sun-up." Then he left again and shut the door.

Garner took two juice glasses from behind the counter and set them down on the Formica surface. He opened the bottle, which was a Knobb Creek whiskey. He poured the liquor in one glass.

"You want a drink?"

"Three fingers on two ice cubes," she said, after thinking for a moment. He smiled, sensing a faint restoration of tradition.

He cracked the ice tray and put ice cubes in both glasses. He noticed a juke box on the other side of the diner, glowing red neon. He poured the amber bourbon in both glasses, handed one to Laura, who stood up from the booth, almost ceremoniously.

"Cheers," he said. He sipped half of it; smooth as silk with a bite in the back of the throat.

Laura brought the glass to her mouth and ever so slightly tipped it up so that her lips were moistened. Then she made a glad-sounding "hmm," lifted the glass up a bit more, and took a genuine sip.

She swallowed hard then said hoarsely, "My gosh!" He laughed. She laughed. *That was genuine*, he thought. You can't fake that, or simulate it with "artificial intelligence."

"Let's see what they have for music." He walked over, put both palms of his hands down so he leaned on the juke box, and searched inside the old, brightly lit machine.

"Johnny Cash, Bobby Darin, Frank Sinatra–got any favorites?"

She blinked, paused, then answered, "I like them all."

"Consider it done." He put on Mack The Knife and Walk The Line and Summer Wind.

He turned around and found her swaying to the music, drink in hand. She put the drink down on the counter.

"The music is swingin'…it's rad…it makes me want to boogie woogie," she murmured, still moving her hips to the beat. She said that more like a shy girl who was ready to take the wraps off, than a robot, he thought.

She was cool, and he had to admit, naturally sexy. He finished the drink, then came over and started to dance next to her. The mere pleasurable movement allowed him to escape their dismal surroundings, if only for a few minutes. By Summer Wind, he had a hand around her waist and another held aloft, and they waltzed across the narrow diner linoleum together.

"You dance divinely," he said.

"As do you, kind sir."

He thought of the inhospitable desert and this pool of light they occupied; what a sight they'd make, two people dancing in the ricky ticky diner with the juke box playing, if somebody came upon them by surprise.

Laura's hand was warm, slightly moist. Her lower back, through the jersey, felt like a real skin texture to his hand. Her expression was demure. Then she rested her chin on his shoulder.

"We don't need all these lights on…" he whispered into her ear. He turned off all but one, the red glowing juke box. She willingly put both arms around his neck.

He looked out the window to see if Lance was watching, but saw nothing.

He felt like he had guzzled a powerful tonic, but it was only the dancing and Knobb Hill, and Laura.

"Does Lance dance?"

"Are you kidding?"

"No. I was kind of wondering if he would mind us

doing this?" *Does he feel jealousy?* Does she? he thought.

She only smiled and glanced away, rendering that notion ridiculous.

"We're merely colleagues, as I mentioned before. Besides, it is important to…take a break, de-stress, sometimes. You'll run down your systems."

"My systems are kind of revved up right now."

She looked at him quizzically. They kept dancing to Ole Blue Eyes, then she glanced at him with a questioning look.

"Am I…a good dancer?"

"Exceptional. You have smooth moves."

Smooth moves, she whispered, as if learning a new complement.

He thought of the slow dance with Julie near the cliffs in Las Cruces. This was the same. This was something they both needed.

In a way, he wished Webster was here. Webster could see her drinking whiskey, dancing, and behaving in every way like a real woman.

He thought he detected cologne around her neck.

"You smell nice, too."

"Oh…" she murmured, embarrassed but pleased.

"You're full of complements tonight," she said, frankly. He could sense her enjoying herself.

"I give credit where credit is due. By the way, I know I can't possibly smell nice, after everything we've been through. And minimal baths. But I appreciate that you don't mention it."

"I want another drink," she declared.

"By all means." He filled hers up with Knobb Hill, and she picked the glass up with a sly smile.

"Bottoms up," she said, knocking it back. Then she grinned widely, bright-eyed. No longer the shy girl.

"Turn off all the lights."

"You mean the juke box?" he asked.

"Yeah." He did as she said.

"Now we go over to the booth with the blanket," she said, assertively taking his hand. He had no resistance in him. It was the whiskey, and desire and fatigue and her willfulness. And beauty. He was jelly in her hands.

They burrowed into the booth together. Quickly, her shirt was off. She was on top. Other layers began to go. She was only a dim, shapely female figure in the darkness, hair dropped down, breasts–firm, pliable, wet with sweat–eyes glinting in the night. She moved against him; she had him in her grip.

Yes, she was real.

CHAPTER 35: DECEMBER 3, 2025

When daylight broke, he woke up with his shirt off under a blanket. At some point, she'd shifted away from him so they could both sleep. If she'd slept very much. He'd also tugged back on his pants, but didn't remember doing that. He still wasn't sure about her, their, animal comforts, but he was convinced of her humanity. And her sexual skills.

The first complete emotion he felt upon awakening was guilt. He hadn't formally found, or buried, Kiatsu. That feeling lingered.

Laura was up and putting her things together in her gear bag. The lights were bright and harsh inside the diner. She seemed reticent.

He stood up reluctantly and put on the rest of his clothes. His first thought was, we are within 180 or so miles of Ketchum. We'll be there today or tomorrow, if I'm lucky. He thought gloomily that if they didn't make it soon, it will be because of some disaster that befalls them. The road ahead was full of such calamities, no doubt, most of which were impossible to predict.

Garner found scraps to eat from the day before on the counter. Laura looked fresh as a daisy, unlike him, he was sure. She came over and sat down next to him.

"What do we do the day after?" she said, with curiosity, as if she was doing a study. Absent the whiskey, music, and darkness, a romantic naivete had substituted for desire.

"Well, we start by being nice to each other," he said, chewing around the mold on an old pie crust. Then he stood up, opened his arms, and hugged her.

She still gave him the impression of having lived in a bubble. Everything was brand new. She was asking him for instructions, on how to conduct a love affair.

Just then Lance came in.

"Everything is ready," he said, brusque and authoritative. "We have to go."

Laura looked at Lance with a straight face. "Fine." Then back to Garner with a half smile, enjoying their rebellious secret. He wasn't so sure that Lance didn't know. The guy was some kind of genius. A mind reader.

"You two, I assume, got a good rest in here? We have a long day. An important day."

"Yes, I slept well," Garner said guardedly.

"I'll bet you did."

"Was the Jeep okay?"

"Good enough, for me. I worked on the data input…then rested. Let's go. Let's get out of here."

"Did you notice anybody coming down the highway last night?" Garner asked as he went through the loose screen door to the cold desert air, pulling on a jacket.

"No, nobody. You'll sit next to me in front, alright?"

"Okay." Garner pushed his backpack into the backseat of the Jeep and shut the door. The HazMat mask dangled around his neck; he'd need it if he did any walking.

He'd shoved some more food scraps from the diner into the backpack: a partly moldy package of white hamburger rolls, the rest of the Ritz Crackers, the stale pie crust that had no filling, and the prize…a hardened chunk of old Canadian bacon that hadn't gone quite bad.

The rest of his breakfast was going to be the bacon and the pie crust with gummy, dehydrated peanut butter smeared onto it. He'd scavenged that jar way back in Fence Lake, New Mexico. Now it was almost gone.

He thought of the dead body moldering back in the kitchen, not only tragic but senseless. Why would someone do that, under the present disastrous conditions in Idaho? What was the point in assaulting someone, where survivors were barely scraping by, and where the volcano itself has left hundreds of thousands dead?

He settled into the seat beside Lance, with Laura in the back, and they drove slowly back out onto I-84. He watched Molly's Cafe recede in the cloud of dust the swerving Jeep left behind.

Nothing about I-84 resembled a highway anymore. What used to be four lanes was obscured by the soot and blown-over desert sands. There was no boundary anymore between concrete and land; everything looked like "side of the road" and desert scrub. The Jeep jerked off the road more than once, as Lance, impatient, pressed the accelerator. It was off-road driving.

Soon, they passed a toppled over Welcome To Idaho sign. The view was buried scrublands with distant rolling mountains, the slopes striped with wildfire-scorch marks.

Garner could hear the "wooo" of the wind striking the sides of the Jeep. He'd pulled on all the layers that he had, along with the shell of a coat. It was suddenly winter. The sky was gun-metal gray.

He got out his map, unfolding it in his lap. They were headed for the intersection of I-86, which went north toward

Yellowstone, and I-84, which traveled northwest.

Garner leaned forward from the backseat.

"Are you taking me to Ketchum?" A heavy silence; only the wind buffeting the Jeep. He had to know for sure. He could feel the grinding of the thick tires through the bottom of his seat.

Lance took a deep, aggravated breath.

Laura declared, "Yes."

"Are you mad?" Lance said, his anger rising. "Do you see the slow progress we are making here? I can't go more than 30 kilometers per hour through this junk! Ketchum will take us three hundred kilometers out of our way! We'll be lucky not to lose two whole days!"

"What about the helicopter?" Laura seemed to be reaching.

"What about it?"

"Perhaps we can summon it to Ketchum."

"The helicopter is only for extraction from Yellowstone, when needed." Lance was on the edge of exasperation. "It's not a taxi cab!"

"Okay then," Laura said defiantly. "If you leave him at the intersection, I will go with him."

"That would be insubordinate," Lance snapped. Yet he seemed defeated, and unused to that position. "You have a mission," he said. "We cannot complete it by separating."

"I won't condone leaving Brad on the side of this wasteland, alone, with no transportation."

Wow, she called me Brad, he thought. It was a new outward sign of intimacy.

Lance stared through the windshield at the desolate land, where now a light snow mixed with the ash. The view was lunar.

"He came here of his own volition," Lance argued. "He had a plan. We agreed to bring him to the border. We've already changed that once. He's not a victim. He's a man going north, illogically. I can't jeopardize the mission, because he won't listen to reason."

Lance glanced over at Laura for a reaction, but received none. His shoulders came down. He sighed.

"Alright, we take him to Ketchum. Only to be dropped off at the outskirts. Agreed?"

"Agreed," Garner said, sitting back in the seat.

Garner watched a large bird, a golden eagle, settle on the top branch of a sad lone tree that sat in a field. The eagle impassively watched the Jeep plow past the field, then it lifted off the branch again and arched south, propelling itself with only a few swipes of its wings.

"Did you see that?" he cried out, hopefully.

So a heartbeat still exists up here, Garner thought.

They drove slowly past a tiny windswept, buried town called Juniper, which had not much but a large farm that looked like it had been hit by a tornado. In another hour they cruised silently past the turn-off for I-86, which went northeast to Pocatello and Yellowstone.

It had a burned-down fueling station and convenience store, only a charred shell and piles of black and white ash. Black ash was largely local; white ash was deposited by the volcano. He was becoming an expert on ash.

Kiatsu, Abby, and Jake were just about here, Garner thought, when he received the last message from them. He'd read it like dreaming a nightmare, red-eyed driving through somewhere like Arkansas, with them far out of his reach.

He half expected to see their sedan, a rented Nissan Versa, buried by the side of the highway. *Bye my love*, she'd written, in a concluding text. *We'll be okay. Don't worry. Take care of yourself. We all love you.*

She'd never really told him where exactly they were, but it could have been here. He knew she was on I-86. He thought of a car with Jake and Abby in the backseat.

He continued staring out the window at the ruins of

southern Idaho.

To The North

CHAPTER 36: DECEMBER 5, 2025

They could go no farther. The road into Ketchum was completely impassable. This is where they would leave Garner. He was on the laptop looking for a message, for the final time. Now he would go in there on foot.

He'd completed about 1,200 miles of an odyssey into the worst super volcanic eruption in human history. But not quite.

Someone had to be alive in there.

Garner began putting his things together; he'd moved into the backseat for that purpose. He had winter gear on, a knitted hat, gloves, the HazMat mask, and his expedition-style backpack. He had only a little food and water. The hospital was a few miles.

He was glad he didn't have Tanya.

Using Lance and Laura's satellite connection, he'd intercepted one final message. It read like a response to his last message.

Received. So appreciative. We don't have time. Food and water

are gone. Please please please help! You're so kind!!
Jenny and Gavin.
St. Lukes Hospital, Ketchum, ID

Jenny and Gavin, I'm coming, Garner whispered to himself.

"So you're going to swing back and get us, right?" he asked Lance, who stood by the car in a HazMat mask. His voice sounded hollow behind it.

"Us?"

"Me, Jenny, and Gavin."

He looked aside as though pondering the notion, then said, "This is where we use the drone. We might be able to save you some time. And us."

"I didn't know you had a drone. You mean, one of those bumblebee-sized ones?"

"No, moderate-sized with advanced camera. Range of 20 miles. It's in the cargo area."

He went to the back of the Jeep, which was pushed up against what was nearly a wall of ash.

Laura stood outside the vehicle wearing protective gear. She approached Brad, and once out of whispering earshot of Lance, she said, "We will wait for you, here. It doesn't make sense for us to leave, when your destination is only a few miles away. Do you want me to come with you?"

"No. you should stay with the car and Lance, as long as you're sure you can convince him to stay. Surely, that will help."

Lance came out with a hard case containing the drone, and set it on the ground. As he opened it, he looked up. "We'll be able to efficiently inspect the hospital grounds from this distance."

He took the drone out of its box, placed it on the ground, and picked up the handheld controls. Soon the machine whirred and was aloft. It made one circle about 100 feet above, then it disappeared over the swaying tree-tops.

Lance opened the vehicle then sat in the front seat with a screen opened to what the drone could view. It took less than a minute for the local neighborhood, including the hospital, to appear. It was the five hundred foot view: a river, a forest, the nearby highway, and a cluster of buildings. The hospital campus.

No movement could be seen, cars or people. Parts of the hospital buildings had caved in, and piles of ash were all around.

Lance steered the drone closer in. They could hear the buzzing of its motor. At one hundred feet they saw cars in the parking lot, a few upended or burned; an empty bus stop, buildings and parked cars across the street. No other signs of life.

A large brown truck sat in the St. Luke's parking lot.

The grounds appeared as if a flood had gone through, leaving piles of silt.

"I see nothing," Lance announced, after the drone had made several passes. "No signs of life. It's possible we have wasted…"

"I'm going in," Garner interrupted him. "A little more than two miles. They're probably in the building." He snuck a look at his watch, still ticking. "That will take me forty five minutes. Maybe more."

"We keep the drone above you," Laura said firmly. Lance only glared at her.

Hoisting his backpack, Garner began trudging up the state road where the hospital was. He wore the HazMat mask over his face. He could tell he was at altitude; his chest quickly tightened. He was undernourished, generally exhausted, maybe a bit hungover from the Knobb Hill.

This was the final leg.

The ash was deep, at times like wading through snow.

So I get there and I find Jenny, and I'm thinking, a young boy.

I get them outside, Laura and Lance see us, from the drone, then they come help. We could put them in the back of the Jeep.

That last message, though, was a little off; impersonal. Almost strange like, saying expected things. "Received." She's probably on her last legs, Jenny.

He thought of sitting at the counter at the Raw Frontier with the sheriff and seeing those messages for the first time, almost a month ago. It felt like a year or more. He felt like an empty vessel then, especially after Julie died. That was the last straw. This gave him a reason to go on. He supposed he was badly depressed then, and drinking. But he had a purpose now. He'd come to the end of the road.

He thought he heard the drone overhead; he looked up and saw dully through the mask, a glint against the gray sky. The wind blew through the trees around him. The breeze carried odd flakes, more like chips.

The mountains were high–up to 9000 feet–and still majestic. He was cold; it was gloves weather. But he was warm yet almost suffocated behind the HazMat mask and knit hat. The air was shitty, he thought; it carried the ash, snow, or both, like loose insulation from a decrepit attic.

Not fit for man nor beast, he thought, of the general atmosphere.

He'd covered about a mile at a plodding pace. Minutes went past, slowly, thoughtfully. He was almost there, at the end of the long journey.

He was passing homes, big ones, McMansions even, and businesses, all vacant, in ruin. No movement, except for the tree branches in the wind, and the drone perhaps above him. He could hear his labored breathing through the mask; the wind as the rushing of forced air around behind his head gear.

He thought absently that these buildings could be scavenged later, for supplies.

He'd never been to this part of the West; Ketchum

actually was considered a famous resort and ski place, when those kinds of places existed just moments before the eruption of Yellowstone. In the minutes after the eruption, every form of luxury lifestyle was rendered obsolete. How circumstances can change, in a second.

He laughed to himself, then he remembered that there were two starving, suffering people at the hospital coming up.

He passed Cold Springs Drive; the highway was wider now, more navigable, and was surrounded by undeveloped lots. They probably wanted this to be a golf course, he mused. He saw the hospital buildings in the distance, maybe a quarter mile.

At one point, he stopped, rested, lifted his mask, and drank water from a half-filled liter bottle. His mouth was too pasty to be satisfied. He paused every few seconds to catch his breath. Between the poor air quality and altitude, he never could be completed satisfied.

He used the opportunity to stare up into the sky; he saw and heard nothing. No whirring, no glint, no eagle. The sky was the off-white color of stale pudding. He put the mask back on and kept going; Hospital Drive.

He turned in there. He saw the brown truck. It was the same one, like a UPS delivery van. It seemed to be in a different place than when he saw it from the drone, but he couldn't be sure.

He stood in the driveway and yelled, "Jenny!" He cupped his hands over his mouth. "Jenny! Are you here? Are. You. In. There!" His voice sounded hoarse and isolated. Not loud enough. No answer.

He thought he heard muttering, then startled he quickly looked to the other side of the parking lot, where the wind hurled the top of a trash can across the gritty pavement.

He yelled again, no response. A lonely echo from brick siding and plate-glass windows reflecting the slate gray sky. Then he saw a light on the third floor.

CHAPTER 37

He went to the hospital entrance. The door was locked. He removed the mask, looked straight up the door and facade of the building, and cried out for Jenny again. But he was met with silence.

The trash can minus its top sat ten yards away. He dragged it over to the entrance, picked it up, and hurled it through the door glass, which shattered violently. He smashed the rest of the way through and went in.

Old messages came to mind: *We're at the end of our rope...please help!!*

As expected, the hallways were empty, the front desk vacant, but its drawers rifled. The area existed in suspended animation; tipped over wheelchairs, papers strewn about, elevator doors open but non-functional. The hall had an astringent chemical smell. He shuffled through the halls, mask dangling around his neck, until he found an exit door and a flight of stairs. He went in, and up. He caught his breathe at the second floor. He opened the door and went into that hallway; it was in shadow and displayed the same disarray.

He called, "Jenny! Gavin!" This had to be the place…he'd seen the light on the third floor…

He went back to the stairs. *Twelve hundred miles, a super eruption, he'd never given up…*

He burst through the third floor door; dull, cluttered linoleum, wheelchairs and gurneys and abandoned I.V. units. Wires hanging limply from a ceiling, where panels had fallen out. A light on at the end of the hallway. He yelled once more then dragged himself along.

He reached the open door, entered. A broken fluorescent light flickered wanly. *There must be a generator puttering along somewhere…* He heard the distinct soft motoring of one or more computer hard drives. But no people were in the room. "Jenny!" he cried out again, with a faint lilt of desperation. "Are you here? Anybody here? Gavin?"

Empty chairs with rollers on them; two cluttered desks, that medicinal smell. Bland, off-kilter framed landscape pictures on the wall. He saw one computer at the end of the room.

The screen was on; he approached to look at it. A window was open on the screen, and a program ran by itself. In the window, he saw a message thread, similar to what he had seen when he logged in with Lance's laptop.

The program ran silently. Then, as he watched, automated typing appeared, tracking across the screen, writing a new message. *help us please…if you can…time has run out…thank you kind sir…thank you so much for your time…Jenny and Gavin.*

The cursor blinked once per second, ominously and mockingly, at the end of the sentence. He stared at it, for the longest time. Just the cursor blinking, like the final heartbeats of a terminal patient.

He formed the words with his mouth, but didn't hear

them, even as he spoke: "It's some fucking hacker, some message-writing virus left on the terminal…"

It's some ghost in the machine…an awful joke played by insidious hackers who escaped when they could…or didn't…

He turned away from the computer, picked up his backpack, and put it back down. He lifted the swivel chair, hoisted it over his head, and smashed the computer terminal with it, twice, three times, until the computer was nothing but pulverized plastic, glass, and smoking circuit boards.

He grabbed the backpack and left, back down the third- and second-floor stairs.

When he reached the parking lot, he saw the brown delivery truck parked nearby. One of the back doors creaked in the wind.

"Well lookie here, fancy meeting you again. Especially in these sorry parts."

He looked to the side and saw Bobby, from way back in Shiprock, New Mexico, the same crappy, marginal, venomous appearance. He was dust-covered, and wore goggles, cowboy boots, the same worn-out coat. He carried a sawed-off shotgun, held in one hand and partly raised.

Garner stared at him silently.

"Where's your pal Tonto?"

"Do you mean Zeke? He's long gone. In another part of the country."

"*Really*? I'd need proof of that. What does he have, a private plane? You see, my partner Trig is still looking for his fingers, or a suitable replacement." He laughed humorlessly. "That was no fun back there in the desert. The way you left us. We've been looking and looking for you. I guess persistence pays off."

Garner was surprised his mouth hadn't gone dry. Maybe it was because he didn't care anymore. It might be time to go over the edge, finally, he thought.

He didn't ask for any of this stuff, a computer virus instead of flesh and blood, Bobby and Trig on the open road; but he'd gotten it anyways.

"Wasn't that you on the horses?"

"Down there in Utah? Sure. We got tired of the saddle and got us another truck. It's been a fine time since then. You'd be surprised how easy it is to take free withdrawals from banks, casinos, whatever, after a big fucking volcano. It's like all the people scurry away, like they didn't value the cash enough in the first place."

"Or maybe in a disaster of this magnitude, only the cockroaches are left."

"Haha, very funny."

Trig walked over from behind the truck. Bobby had the shotgun leveled evenly at Garner. Trig wore a glove on the hand that was shot.

"Give me the gun," he said to Bobby.

"Revenge is sweet," Bobby said. "But its not really you I care about. I want Tonto. Something tells me you're not telling the truth about his whereabouts. Maybe you can pony up about that, before I use a different tactic, than being nice as I am. He's probably somewhere in that building, right?"

He handed the weapon to Trig, as if having a change of heart.

"Why would I ever tell you? Two vultures, looking for carcasses."

"Speaking of carcasses," Trig said. He loaded a round into the chamber of the shotgun with a loud click and snap.

"Now now," Bobby murmured, with a leering grin. Trig raised the shotgun. "These kind of shots are heard for miles around. Tonto will hear it and come running. Let's save a round for him."

Garner saw Laura creep out from behind the brown truck. She was as silent and graceful as a cat. With a remarkable whirl, her body torqued, flew through the air, and kicked Trig with such force that Garner thought he saw her foot enter his chest. She completed the move by smashing a gloved fist down on his head, forcing a spurt of blood from his mouth as his body collapsed in a heap. The shotgun clattered to the ground.

The move had the force and agility of a well-tooled machine.

Bobby ran across the parking lot and tugged a handgun from his belt at the same time. He emptied the clip at an onrushing Laura, just as Garner snatched the shotgun from the ground, aimed, and blasted Bobby off his feet.

Crackling gunshot echoes carried over the ash-strewn concrete and the empty suburb. The smell of cordite wafted over the scene; a dramatic silence. Garner dropped the gun and ran over to Laura.

CHAPTER 38

She lay on her back, staring wide-eyed at the sky.

He was on his knees next to her. Then her eyes met his. They seemed warm, kind, lost in a memory.

"I had enough time, to get both of them," she whispered. "The calculations were correct…I'm sure…this makes no sense to me…no sense."

He watched a thick dark stain spread over her chest.

"We have to stop the bleeding," he said, tensely. "You're going to be okay."

"Stop the bleeding," she whispered, more in consent than fear. "Stop the bleeding."

He had nothing but his kerchief, but made himself busy unzipping her jacket to press the cloth against the wounds. The others were sprawled and lay still in the scattered ash nearby.

When the jacket was unzipped, he found more blood, but also an odd split in her chest and rib cage. He pulled the cloth aside, to reveal what was beneath. She watched him unblinking.

"Put pressure on the wound," she whispered, instructionally. Unblinking. "Add gauze and bandages…get the patient to the Emergency Room as soon as possible…"

He pealed the torn garment away, and beneath the flesh and blood artifice he found circuitry; plastic encased wires mashed together like muscle and capillary, and cracked, tiny advanced-plastic motherboards. An acrid vapor arose from the opening in her torso and the crushed motherboards; the smell was more like overheated solder, than blood.

"Apply pressure…gauze and bandages…turn patient to the side…monitor blood pressure and alertness…" Then she blinked, her mouth moved, and one eye began to roll back, until he couldn't see the iris or pupil anymore. The light went out of her eyes and he heard a faint high-pitched whirring from somewhere inside Laura, until it stopped.

He let go of her and stood up unsteadily. The three bodies were completely still, except a flap of clothing would move in the wind. Piles of ash began to push up against the corpses, then sift over their faces.

After another minute, he went through Bobby's pockets and found the keys to the truck. He stepped up into the van's cabin and started it up. It coughed to life. Leaving the engine on, he went to the back and opened the doors wide. He then picked up Laura's body, cradled it gently, and placed it carefully in the back of the truck. He put his backpack in there.

He was cold and shaky; the tips of his fingers and nose were raw. He leaned against the truck, dropped his mask and put his hands on his face, grinding his palms into his clouded, misted eyes.

He shut the doors in the back and returned to the driver's seat. He backed up the truck and slowly exited the parking lot on to local Route 75 again, which he took south.

After a few minutes he stopped sobbing and talking

to himself. He planned to drive south until he reached warmth and desert or ran out of fuel, whichever came first. North offered nothing to him anymore.

CHAPTER 39

He drove without stopping. The truck lumbered slowly through the ash piles. Hours went by; he didn't see anybody. Time flowed unnoticed. He reached I-84 south and headed down, like an automaton, toward Utah. He drank leftover water but didn't eat anything, staring straight ahead bleakly.

A glimmer of fire shimmered from the east. The airborne ash dissipated notably. One time when he pulled over to piss, he heard a jet's roar overhead, above the clouds, headed for the epicenter. The land still had the sameness of dead gray and black ash, having cast off its distinct color tones of yellow grass and green forests and snow-capped ridges.

When he reached Utah, he breathed a sigh. He was very low on fuel; he assumed the engine took diesel. Once he pulled over to an abandoned Shell station but the pumps didn't work. He broke into the convenience store section and scrounged around for packaged crackers, Plantar's Nuts, and a few bottles of water and lukewarm Mountain Dew, which he greedily guzzled in one take.

He felt feral, feeling over his beard, bruises, and cuts; half-starved, like a scavenging animal. The eagle he'd seen was far better off than him, and deserved more than he, Garner thought.

He thought of the peyote and pipe that Zeke had given him. His cell phone was dead.

He was down into Utah, towards Salt Lake, when the fuel finally ran out. He was making decisions and moving robotically, not sure what he was going to when he reached the city, if he did.

The desert was blinding with sunshine, and warmer than Idaho was. He rolled the brown van to a stop behind a dust-covered car that was half-on, half off the highway. He saw a form in the front seat.

He stepped down from the truck and walked over and a found an older man with his head back against the head-rest of the driver's seat. Gaunt, blue, and dead. A pen rested in his hand, and in his lap, a letter.

Garner went back to the van and removed his backpack. For a while, he stood and looked at Laura's body. Surely, she was gone. Or maybe "decommissioned." He'd checked carefully for signs of life. Then he'd placed a tarp over her. He put his backpack back on, shut and locked the door, committed this location to memory as best he could, then he went back to the sedan. He reached inside the vehicle and closed each of the man's eyes.

He looked around him. The road couldn't be straighter, the land couldn't be flatter and more dry. The sky bluer than he'd seen it in a while.

He took the pipe out of his pocket, then the little packet of peyote. He spread them on the warm hood of the car. It seemed too precise an activity than he was presently equipped for; pinching the ground up plant and stuffing the tiny pipe bowl with it.

After a few minutes of this, he took a match and he lit the contents. He placed the pipe in his mouth and inhaled; the bits of plant matter glowed and pulsated. Then the pipe emitted a lazy thread of vapor.

He exhaled the smoke. Took another puff. Smiled, thought of Zeke, and laughed. Zeke would approve. He walked over to the driver's window, which was down, reached in, and removed the letter.

"Let's see," he said out loud.

Dear Gretchen,

I hope this letter finds you. I just wanted to tell you that the last 20 years have been the best years of my life.

Garner looked away and said to himself, approvingly, "agreed. It has." He went back to the letter.

I can only wish that you are doing well, and safely rescued in Austin. These have been trying times. I did my best to drive away and self rescue, but obviously it wasn't enough. Know that I didn't suffer. I hadn't food and water or sleep and my heart was giving out, so I'm taking some Aspirin and going to sleep. Simple. I gave all my heart to you and it was the best decision I ever made.

A Good Samaritan will find this letter and deliver it to you. I know the world still has them. Sleep well my love. I am.

Forever yours,
Weldon.

The Austin address was written beneath his signed name.

"Weldon," Garner said, to the desert. "You're a good man. You did your best, just like I did. That's all someone can do, give their best. I'm going to deliver this letter, just like you said. Rest easy, buddy. Things are only looking up from here."

He folded the letter carefully and put it in his backpack. Then, the pipe still lit, he began walking south into the desert.

CHAPTER 40: DECEMBER 7, 2025

He saw one tree in the desert ahead of him; a Joshua. A few saguaro cactus were about, but nothing else stood tall amid the sand and rocks. The tree had a bird sitting in it; he thought it might be a vulture. The bird emitted a rainbow halo. He's seen and stared at a similar shimmer in the east, from the vast fires lit by Yellowstone; but to him that was only an amazing light show.

When he closed on the tree, he could see the bird was the eagle. It watched him approach impassively, its head turned to the side.

"Hi eagle," he said. "Me and you, I guess we're in the same boat. Trying to make it in this desert. Don't be afraid of me."

But the eagle lifted off and arched toward the west.

"Don't leave me eagle!" Garner cried. "Don't leave me!" As if it heard and heeded him, it stopped and landed not far away on a pile of boulders. He thought he saw squiggles of phosphorescent yellow, red, and orange on the ground,

To The North

and that they were snakes coiling slowly in the sun. Fireworks still lit that had fallen to the ground.

He finished a bowlful of peyote. He sat under the boulders and caught his breath. The eagle lifted off again and morphed into an Unidentified Aerial Phenomena, slicing through the sky with unimaginable skill, speed, and a mournful grace, especially as it became smaller against the sky. He got up and walked…

"Don't leave me eagle. Don't leave me now," he spoke to the sky. "I need you to follow. Please don't go. Please stay with me eagle."

Another form appeared in the desert distance; it was an old-fashioned plane, he discovered. A group of people lined up to board a 1950s vintage aircraft, sitting in the desert. It included one of those roll-away stairways that he remembered from old clips of JFK and Jacquie arriving somewhere. He waved at the people as he approached. He walked faster.

Abby, Jake, and Kiatsu were in the line. "Kiatsu!" he cried. "Kiatsu, it's me, Brad!" She looked at him and smiled, ever so calm. She still had really long black hair, down to her waist.

He walked up and embraced her. It felt so good to hug her, to hold on to her; she stroked the back of his neck gently. When he pushed away, they were on the front lawn of their old home in the suburbs. Jake and Abby were getting in the car to go to school.

"Stay with me, Kiatsu."

"Follow the eagle," she said. "Be careful. You don't look like you're taking care of yourself. You could do better, Brad. Just follow the eagle."

"Kiatsu!"

She got into the front seat of the car, shut the door, but turned to look back at him. "We have to go now, but I care about you."

"It's not my fault?"

"You're quite right. It's not your fault."

"I wasn't always there. I was emphasizing my work over you guys. I wasn't there, when Abby and Jake were born."

"No you weren't." She looked away, not angry but thoughtful.

"But, you still love me? You still forgive me?"

"We do," she said frankly, looking back at him. "We love you. Say we love you kids!"

"We love you dad!" he heard, as the car pulled away. She was smiling the calm smile, the one he remembered so well. Then the auto became the vintage plane, as the old wheels rumbled across the desert away from him, in a cloud of white dust.

He was alone again.

CHAPTER 41

He made himself keep walking toward the sun as it dipped in a riot of lurid tones. He was weirdly indefatigable. He was almost flying.

He watched his feet walking along the parched ground, crunchy rocks and sand and less ash and wonderful cholla cactus. He stared at the spiny green yet softly outlined plants. He took an incredible concentrated interest in the sound his worn boots made in the sand.

Then he heard the eagle cry above him, a screech that held a startling command.

"Eagle, it's you!" he cried out gratefully, as the bird struck out with its wings above him. But his tongue and his cracked lips were all pasted together and the words didn't come out sounding right.

The eagle soared hugely overhead, backlit by the sun. He kept walking until it was dusk; the eagle circled in the distance. The desert was full of brilliant colors and flat outlines. Piles of red boulders appeared, like Picasso cubes, and he spent quite a while admiring them.

"Eagle, you didn't leave me. I knew you wouldn't," he said as if the eagle stood next to him. "You must have endless faith to stay with me. After all I've done, after everything that's happened. The greatest faith in the world. You're the eagle of profoundest faith..." he said, as he staggered forward, collapsing onto a hard desert floor.

Fires licked on the eastern horizon, the western line was hot pink, then he was enveloped in black.

He woke up with a splitting headache and intense thirst. He looked up from where he had been sleeping against his backpack. He saw a flat, empty road through the desert. It seemed to travel a hundred miles in a perfect straight line ending in a washed-out, shimmering blue, with flat rocky desert on either side. The eagle was standing on the road, with a limp something hanging from its mouth.

The eagle flew from the road, and dropped the floppy carcass near him. He staggered to his feet. The eagle flew away in the distance. The bird had a way of gliding along in the wind without flapping its wings.

"Thank you, eagle," he said. "I will never forget you." He didn't know how long this peyote trip had lasted and how long he'd walked. The road was still there, a paved glare, when he slowly raised his head.

He scuffed over to the carcass; a large dead jack rabbit. It was partially eaten by the bird but with much of its hind legs attached. He went over to his backpack and then recalled that he hadn't dug into the pack once during his peyote time. The inside of his mouth felt like walking on the desert sounded.

He frantically unclipped his backpack and removed a full liter water bottle and desperately uncapped it and guzzled until the water dribbled and spilled down his cheek. The finest water he'd ever tasted, along with the eagle he'd met with the profoundest faith.

He found his Swiss Army knife, pulled back the blade with some effort, and went about slicing into the jack rabbit. Then he laboriously ate as much of the fresh chewy uncooked meat as he could, in tiny, red, sawed-off pieces.

He kept drinking water, until it was gone. Sober, he got that small feeling of faith in the day ahead, and having won some success.

Down the road was a town, a tiny cluster of buildings baking in the desert sun. He thought he could make it, even though he was utterly exhausted. He figured cars or trucks would come down the highway.

He started walking.

A mile seemed like two, or three. He began to have to concentrate to put one leg in front of the other. He briefly considered dropping the backpack and leaving it by the side of the road. He stopped and scanned the sky, but it was pale blue and empty, like the inside of a bowl.

"You're going to have to make it through today without the eagle," he said, almost comically, but also as an admonishment. "The rabbit was delicious," he added.

He now had no food or water. It was much easier to tramp along, much easier to travel the desert, he thought absently, while on peyote. He felt around in his jacket and discovered the little hard pipe and a plastic packet. He put the backpack down and pulled the pipe out. He hadn't even noticed that it was carved in the likeness of a southern Indian, perhaps a Ute or Apache, with his arms crossed on his chest.

The pipe had a little ash in the bowl, and the plastic bag was empty. He put them back in his pocket and kept going.

Finally he reached the town, if you could call it that. It amounted to no more than a collection of dark buildings and utility poles toppled over in front of them, and a crumbling Welcome To… sign that he didn't bother reading, due to the smear of sweat he couldn't quite rub out of his red eyes.

It looked like a dead railroad town from the 19th century. He saw no railroad tracks. He dropped to his knees for a moment, slipping the pack off his back and onto the ground.

Both palms of his hands were on the ground, which was warm with centuries worth of ground-up rocks.

"Maybe this is where I end it," he muttered to himself, staring at the coarse ground. "Every story has an ending."

Then he raised his head and looked at the sky, fully expecting to see the eagle. "Find water and food, fool," he whispered, standing unsteadily. But he couldn't see any storefronts, franchises, or the merciful diners, only decrepit, wind-blown homes with dust and ash pushed up against every crevice and porch.

He stared down that glaring, straight-as-an-arrow road; still no vehicles. The road was wide as it went through the buildings, and he picked up his backpack and walked along the sidewalk, until he heard the muffled, faraway screams.

CHAPTER 42

The sound came from one of the homes, a short-lived, almost bird-like screech that carried in the dry wind. He put his backpack down in front of the house, which had peeling clapboards, and a warped porch with a partially collapsed porch roof.

He heard nothing, then a moan. A woman's deep moan. He pulled opened the broken front door through a stiff pile of dust. He entered the house. A boney cat sprinted away from him in the hallway. He heard "Oh," and then another drawn out moan from a room up a flight of stairs.

He smelled piss.

"Hello!" he cried, out of a parched throat, but there was no answer. He climbed the creaky stairs to the top.

He found a room with an open door, just as another cry issued forth. "Gaah!!" He entered and saw a woman laying on her back in bed.

"Oh Jesus, I thought everyone was gone!" she gasped. "Can you help me?"

"I'll try. What's happened to you?"

"Oh God, I'm having a baby, idiot!" Then she attempted to lift her head off the pillow. That's when he noticed her big abdomen distending the loose nighty.

"I'm sorry! I didn't mean that!" Then she grimaced as another spasm went through her. "My water's broke! I think the head is showing. I can't stand the pain anymore. I just can't stand it!"

"Is there any water?"

"There's nothing, no! At least, I don't think so!"

He looked around the room; clothes strewn about on the floor and on shelves. The covers on the bed, bunched up. He grabbed a couple of shirts that seemed clean; took out his Swiss knife. He sliced the shirts into random misshapen strips.

"What are you doing? Holy crap!"

"We'll need these for the blood…I mean the water…I mean for whatever it is that comes out!"

"Now that's wonderful!" she yelled to the ceiling, bitterly.

"Shit, I've never done this before," he said. "Where the fuck is everybody else?"

"They got the hell out of here when the eruption started!"

"And they left you here, pregnant?"

"Ug-g-g…Gaah! We can talk about my sorry history later okay!" Her head went back with the face contorted in a fierce grimace.

"Okay, I'll see what I can do. First, breathe right? Didn't they tell you about the breathing? Start breathing in and out! Do it!" And he started pushing air out of his pursed mouth by way of demonstration. That worked, she started to breathe rhythmically, if in gasps. Between the gasps, she cried lustily.

"Help me with my legs!"

"Okay, wait, what's your name?"

"Katie, Goddammit!"

"Shit okay, my name's Brad!"

"Gee thanks, Brad. Oh God!"

He moved forward and took one of her legs and draped it over his right shoulder. It was heavy and thick-thighed. He put the bare sole of the other foot against his other shoulder and pushed against it, like a football player blocking. Close up the view was bloody, the scent was pungent and godawful.

The sheets were in disarray and soaked, reddened.

He could see the wet round top of the head, with little sparse black hairs. The color of the scalp underneath was ochre.

Outside the window he could see a spacious empty desert with nothing moving, as if they were alone in Utah.

"Push. Okay?"

"I'm trying!" She made a sound of exertion like a weightlifter. He was watching the head.

"Harder, okay?"

"I'm trying asshole! Mmmmmmm!" Her face was all scrunched up and sweaty with the effort.

"Alright, it's coming!"

The little slimy head now appeared, big and distended. He pushed on the legs. She turned her head to the side and moaned, as though something deep down about it gave her pleasure.

"One more biggie."

"Yah right!"

"I think one more will do it. The head is out."

The shoulders got squeezed out. The infant's face seemed wet and pinched. Garner reached down and hooked two fingers each into the armpits and gently pulled, the strong legs still pushing against his shoulders.

He was ignoring the screams, which were expected

and seemed as if they came from another room in a hospital.

The infant was completely covered in slime and streaks of blood. The eyes were pressed tightly shut. The resistance began to slide away, then he stepped back and held the whole baby aloft, his hands under the armpits, little curled up legs moving in the air, the umbilical cord heavy and wet against the sheets, like something bulky, alive, and in the way.

Sunlight streamed through the window and shined against the wet skin of the child.

He began to laugh uncontrollably, a wet, effusive release. Katie was crying, a form of weeping and laughter packed together.

"Sturdy little fella," he said. He gently handed the baby down.

"Oh what's so funny…what's so funny…just what's so…" she said, her voice winding down with an immense relief drifting over her.

"There," he said, handing off the infant, which she took to her chest. The baby opened his mouth and began to whimper, kicking its miniature, but muscular legs. The eyes hadn't opened yet. She wound him up in a sheet and hugged him to her. "A boy," she said. "A boy."

"Yes," he said. "A boy." The sunlight poured across the wet bottom of the bed.

He went downstairs and stood outside on the porch to catch his breath, leaving Katie and the child alone for a while. A few clods of weeds blew silently across the highway. The town was still; almost preternatural. No other vehicles or people.

He stood in the sun for a while. He didn't hear a thing from upstairs.

He went back inside to the kitchen on the first floor. After a short search, he found a few dry goods in a pantry. He put them in a satchel he'd found along with some clean-enough but crusty hand towels and went upstairs.

Katie lay in bed breast-feeding the boy. She was palpably relaxed and happy, all but glowing.

"Thank you," she said, with a weary, grateful smile.

"How's the kid?"

"Fine. But I need help with the umbilical. I hate to ask you for help again."

"You mean...?"

"Yes, cutting it off." She looked down at the boy lovingly, then back at Garner. "I'm sorry I swore at you. Gutter mouth, me."

"No offense taken."

"I've named him Brad, at least for now."

"What's your last name?"

"Lawson."

He nodding approvingly, rubbing his bearded cheek, then changed the subject. "I found this stuff downstairs."

He set the satchel on the floor and pulled out a bag of sugar, a box of Cream Of Wheat, an ancient plastic container of Marshmallow Fluff, and a cardboard container of iodized salt.

"It's a start. Maybe you would like some of this Cream Of Wheat? I'm making some for myself."

"With salt?"

His eyes aimed dreamily out the window at the desert; looking for something, he didn't know quite what. "Salt," he said a moment later. "She ate salt for nutrition. Her stuff ran on salt."

"What?"

"Nothing. I'm going to use the salt on some old potato mix I found downstairs."

Then he heard the truck changing gears on the highway down the block.

#   #   #

Later, Katie said to him...

I saw your wife when we were all trying to escape. I think it was her, from your description. An attractive Asian lady with long black hair and two kids and an older guy in the car. A four-door. They were part of the caravan of escapees I was part of, a huge traffic jam. She was calm, that's what I remember. So few were. People were screaming at each other, there were some gun shots, and I saw people abandon their cars and start to run. The pyroclastic flows were coming, everyone realized and feared.

Katie spoke from a clear memory; the baby sleeping beside her…

We were in the car behind hers. I remember because an Asian lady got out of her car—we were all stopped then—and went to the back to get a cooler of food, I assumed. She let the two kids out too, to stretch their legs…a little boy and a little girl. She was so calm and deliberate; she even smiled at me. No, I don't remember what state's plates the car had.

She got back in the car; the traffic moved toward an intersection. You could either go south toward Utah or west toward Washington. It was six of one half a dozen of the other. We went toward Utah; I was so pregnant. I stepped out of the car to get some air at one point, and she was getting back in her car. She turned and looked at me, smiled, and mouthed the words "good luck."

I think that was your Kiatsu.

CHAPTER 43

The white tents stretched for miles across the desert. This was a part of Southern California called the Great Basin. It was an impressive sight, when he stood on a nearby hill and looked at it.

He'd reached this federal refugee camp after a long ride with some truckers from Utah, and after one day he felt the need to make himself busy. There was a lot of red tape and conformism with FEMA, but finally they let him do something useful: ladle cheap beef stew and mashed potatoes into styrofoam bowls for refugees.

He stood behind a table and spooned out food to those who filed past him, people of all ages, genders, and races, who wore their experiences in the dust on their clothes, and in their tired faces.

There were almost one million refugees of the super eruption in this camp alone. They'd driven or trooped down from Montana, Wyoming, Utah, Idaho, and other worst-hit parts.

Similar camps had been set up along the Canada border, and run by Canadian officials and military. Some of them housed up to half a million. The problem now was cold; the winter was going to be harsher worldwide because of the layer of volcanic debris that settled from Yellowstone into the upper atmosphere.

That's why some of these camps were established in the hottest deserts. They'd swapped a problem of ash-contaminated, cold air for a lack of water, but Garner wasn't complaining.

His cell phone worked sporadically but he didn't see any messages from Kiatsu. He would hold out hope for his family until he heard otherwise. At the moment, he was a bedraggled vagabond with lots of difficult miles on his body, and in his mind.

He'd left another message with Zeke. People were more upbeat than they'd been in a month; the deaths from the super volcano had been much lower than estimated and believed, more in line with the 2004 Indonesian tsunami than the horrific initial predictions.

Now if Rainier, Mt. Saint Helens, and the San Andreas fault would only stay quiet for a while, Garner mused.

Trucks were coming in and out with supplies where he was, near Thousand Palms, California, when one day he heard the familiar low-timbre roar of a Harley motorcycle's engine.

A guy with a helmet, funky goggles, and a faux leather get-up that leaned more to Elvis than motorcycle garb, pulled up to the mess tent area where Garner was doing his job.

The driver parked the motorcycle, which attracted a group of fascinated refugee children. He stepped off the bike and took his helmet off, releasing long dusty black hair.

"I'll be damned!" Garner cried out, a smile breaking across his face. "Zeke! Zeke Sanchez, you old rascal!"

"Brad!" Zeke yelled back. "Lookin' a little worse for wear, broh, but happy to see you alive!" They met in the dusty interval between tents and embraced. It felt great not to be wearing HazMat masks and running for your life.

"Where've you been?" Brad asked.

"I've been to the coast. Decided to take a ride, clear my head. I got your messages and decided to surprise you."

"It's great to see you, buddy! By the way, Happy New Year!"

"Happy New Year! Hey, where's the Champagne around here?"

"As soon as I'm through with the beef stew we'll start making mimosas. Did you ever find…what's her name again?"

"Amitola? You bet. When she saw me she slapped me and kicked me, cussed me out. That's when you know your Ute wife still loves you. Yeah…we still can't stand each other in the way of close-up living. So, she was probably glad to see me go off on my bike. What about you, any sign of…"

"Kiatsu, no. But I heard a story about her."

"The stories will lead you to her. I feel it in my heart."

"I trust your instincts Zeke. That's one thing I learned."

"Listen, what about that signal you were following? You know, the signal in Idaho?"

"It turned out to be nothing. A stupid computer bug or virus."

"Fancy that. This life is strange as fuck all, isn't it?"

"You said it Zeke. Hey listen, you hungry?"

"Sure as shit I am. What else else do you have here?"

"All kinds of food guaranteed to fill you up and give you the runs."

"I ain't picky."

"Zeke, you know, the other thing…"

"What?"

"I smoked the peyote. All of it."

"Where?"

"In the Utah desert. In fact, I can't say exactly where, I was tripping so bad."

"Did you see an animal?"

"Lots but mostly an eagle."

"You saw an eagle?!"

"It helped me, in fact, stay alive."

"Wow man, that is some powerful medicine! You discovered your spirit animal, and it was an eagle! That says a lot, you know, about your heart, and your soul. You're going to make a bonafide Indian one of these days broh. Then what happened, you walk out of the desert?"

"I came upon a town, and I helped a lady named Katie deliver her baby. She named it Brad."

"No shit! Man, I knew you had it in you. You had it all."

"What are you going to do now?" Brad asked.

"I'm going to get some food in my belly, then we're going to talk about our next trip. You can ride on the back of the Harley with me, that is…" He looked around the busy, crowded camp. "…If they don't still need you here. I guess I could hang out and help a bit. But then we'll go back to Utah; we'll look for Kiatsu some more. Commiserate with the eagles."

"It's a deal Zeke." Garner took his smock off for a minute, then they walked away into the dust and crowds and children running about, under the clear, hot sun, with their arms around each other's shoulders.

CHAPTER 44

The next day, Garner paid a visit to the white Red Cross tent, erected amidst the vast desert refugee camp. He was banged up and badly bruised from his journey, and he wasn't sure he was healing fast enough. It wasn't a question of where he was gouged; there weren't too many places on his body where he wasn't gashed.

He stood in a long line to get re-patched by a nurse. Zeke Sanchez waited for him outside the tent.

When he finally reached the nurse, he sat down in a chair and took his shirt off and rolled up his pants. You could still see his ribs, but the nature and exertion of the ordeal had left his body taut and muscular. Unlike the U.S. continent, blasted and polluted by a super volcano, he felt in better shape than he was a year ago, as long as he could get fully healed. When he looked around the tent, he noted that the same could be said for the other refugees. The population had lost weight due to the closure of so many markets and food franchises, and the forced marches so many people had undertaken.

What doesn't kill you makes you stronger, he thought, noting the truth behind the cliche.

The nurse had an accent. She was pretty, with shoulder length brown hair and a tired look. Her eyes carried a warm knowledge, and at the same time a glint of mystery.

"Tch-tch, this knee contusion needs to be drained, as it has a small infection. And stitches…just a few…" she said.

"Go ahead and do it. I really appreciate it."

"Right now? We can wait for the doctor."

"No, you can do it."

She looked at him warily, wondering if he was quite real.

"Where are you from?" he asked.

"Italy, originally."

"How did you end up here?"

"I was working for a hospital in Los Angeles. Then I came here to help."

"That was really nice of you."

"I'm going to give you one round of antibiotics."

"Thanks. Can you spare some extra bandages and tape for my kit?"

"Of course."

"What's your name?"

"Giovanna."

"I'm Brad."

"Okay Brad." She wasn't in the mood for new friends or flirting, even though that wasn't his intention. She bent over to the task. First, she made a small adjacent incision and squeezed the wound on his knee, which emitted a pussy, diluted red fluid. She wiped it off his skin with a gauze, wrinkling her nose and tossing the pad into a medical waste bin.

The wound was a bit smelly. It lay on the side of his knee, with pink flesh open to the air and looking angry. He couldn't even tell her how he'd gotten it.

It could have been grappling with the thug Bobby. It could have been falling to his knees in the desert. This stuff just happens.

"You ready?" she said, getting out her antiseptic stitching tools.

"As much as I'll ever be." It felt good to be repaired and administered to. She was low-key and capable. Giovanna inserted the needle and made the first few stitches.

She looked up. "How're you doing?"

"Just fine. Keep going. You're doing great." He only felt a slight sting with each insertion, then the tug of the black stitch thread. Either his ordeal had toughened him, or his body had gone partly numb, he thought. She ended up putting in six stitches. At least he hadn't been shot, he mused, during the exchange with Trig and Bobby back in Idaho.

She taped bandages to wounds on his ribcage and arms and back.

"What happened to you!" she said, putting the finishing touches to one of the dressings. It was meant to be a light-hearted question.

"What didn't happen to me."

"Did you fall out of a car?"

"No, I fell onto the desert. Over and over again."

"Okay, well, you should have the dressings looked at again, and the stitches out in a few days."

"Much obliged," he said. "Is there anything I can do to help here?"

"Not right now." Another man waited in line behind Garner; the man was shivering and gaunt and had a yellowish pallor. Garner stood up and stepped aside.

"I'll check back later. Thanks again, I'm grateful for your help."

"I hope you feel better," she said, already shoving a thermometer under the other man's tongue.

He walked slowly to the exit of the tent and stepped outside. It was like coming out of a quiet theater into a bustling city street. Crowds of people mingled or hurried past, raising a dry dust. Seemingly stray kids played and ran, as if being a refugee was the best thing that had happened to them lately. It probably was, Garner thought, given that their bellies were full and they didn't have to go to school. Yet.

He looked around and took in the full extent of the refugee camp; white tents in orderly, war-encampment emplacements, and everywhere on the flat desert basin, thousands of people milling about in the dust and the piercing sunlight.

The 800,000 or so people took up a big space nearby Thousand Palms, California. In the distance, he could see hundreds of wind turbines in the San Gorgonio Pass, going about their lazy rotations as if nothing had happened to the western region during the last three months.

He found Zeke loitering outside the tent, shooting the breeze with people. He was wearing a tan Stetson Garner hadn't seen before, and sunglasses.

"Where did you get that hat?"

"Bartered for it."

"What did you have to give up?"

"Some of my weed."

"Well at least it's been legal here in California for quite some time."

"I'm not sure about federal camps, though," Zeke said, clutching the hat in a stiff breeze. A door flap started striking the tent violently. Dust devils blew around the camp. They could have been on the Arabian peninsula, among Bedouins.

"When do you want to go?" Zeke asked.

"Are you bored here?"

"A little restless. That's all."

"We'll leave soon." He thought he'd get his bandages

changed one more time, and do some more shifts at the mess tent. He hoped he could have Giovanna for the nurse.

"You can help some more at the mess tent. We only have about half a million more mouths to feed."

The strong sunlight suddenly dimmed, and a dark, unnatural shadow passed over them.

CHAPTER 45

The sun had been steady up till then, and Garner had spent many an idle moment basking in it in a folding chair. But now he looked to the horizon at a black, roiling bank of clouds, approaching from the east.

"That doesn't look too promising," Zeke said, removing his sunglasses.

"I thought it never rained here." The clouds boiled and contorted, as if something giant and black grew inside them and was trying to break out.

"It rains in the desert, and when it comes down hard, it flash floods. You have to stay away from the canyons and arroyos then. It's like hitting concrete, instead of a sponge." Then he looked around warily at their flat terrain.

"They couldn't site this place on higher ground," he said almost as an afterthought. "They didn't have the space or the time."

The black weather system reminded Garner of the thunderheads of his eastern youth, but more darkly, of the

Yellowstone ash clouds. The camp was cast into shadow. Without the sun, people began to disperse and scurry around for cover. Scanning the vast, restive camp, Garner couldn't help but be reminded of an ant colony someone has stepped on.

The wind picked up. "I'm going back to the tent and get my stuff together. Do you want to come?"

Zeke shook his head. "I've got my bike parked over there. I'm gonna move it. I know where you are."

Garner walked fast toward his own tent. It looked like there had been another giant explosion in the east, given the clouds, but the western horizon was placid and blue. It offered a delusive promise.

Garner knew it was a weather system, because the Yellowstone calderas had mercifully gone dormant.

A shadowy curtain crept across the camp, then he heard thunder.

He walked faster. It wasn't that he distrusted everyone around his belongings; the refugees had been on their best behavior, as if they had a common understanding of the shared plight. But Garner couldn't afford to lose what little he had.

All he had, other than a few changes of clothes, were: a first-aid kit, the Swiss Army knife, empty water bottles and tucked away, non-perishable food like jerky and nuts; his cellphone (not charged), handgun ammo he'd taken from Bobby's body, and his own pistol which he still kept on his person. He also still had a wallet with IDs and a small amount of cash: U.S. and Canadian.

He heard the rumble from the sky again. Then shouting. He went inside the tent and seized his backpack and stepped outside. He saw curtains of hard rain traversing the desert, driven by high winds. They moved closer to the camp. Black clouds obscured the tops of the San Jacinto mountains; flashes of lightening struck the forests, followed by loud claps of thunder.

People fled inside the tents and tied the door flaps shut, then the rain struck all at once, a violent patter against the canvas walls. Some merely stood outside and rapturously let the water run down their bodies, loving rather than fearing rainstorms.

He stood under a small canvas patio roof. He noticed that fast moving rivulets of water had already formed at his feet.

Just moments before, it had been sunny, hot, and the sky as empty, blue, and calm as a distilled sea.

Objects began to float past him; sticks and cardboard trash and plastic bottles. He looked up and through the sheets of rain he could see Zeke struggling in the wind to park his motorcycle, put the kickstand down, and shelter it to the side of a tent.

Then he heard cries and saw a woman clinging to the trunk of one of the few palm trees, as knee-high water, and growing, flowed on either side of it like a rapids. A man waded through the water to help, reached out, seized her hand, and they both stumbled and fell into the fast-moving run-off. The camp was being flooded.

He cupped his hands over his mouth and yelled. "Zeke, we've got to get higher up! Fast!" The increase in water depth was instantaneous and astonishing.

People were already forming long chains by holding hands and frantically trying to scramble on top of tables and solid containers piled next to the tents, as well as onto the roofs and hoods of the few vehicles.

The rain drummed with a loud and hollow sound on the metal surfaces, muffling the shouts and screams. Hoisting his backpack, he waded through floodwaters past his knees, to the entrance of the Red Cross tent. He had in the back of his mind, not everyone can be saved. *There are more than 800,000 people in this camp. They can't all be rescued. We do what we can, with what we have.*

He opened the tent flap; the tent was filling with water, and the sick and injured were huddled in groups. He saw Giovanna trying to fight the rising waters and wade through the current and shove a box full of medical supplies to the top of a shelf. He yelled to her, "Giovanna!" She turned her head. She was already soaked up to her waist.

"We have to get to higher ground! The tents aren't going to hold!"

Maybe the floodwaters won't rise anymore. Maybe the rain is abating already, and we've seen the worst. Maybe not...

"I can't leave these people!"

"But you can't stay! It won't hold!" The tents seemed flimsy and temporary, under the hard rain's assault, which drummed violently against the canvas.

A boy stood by the door in the sloshing waters, grasping himself, his teeth chattering and chin and exposed boney legs trembling uncontrollably. Garner grabbed his arm, just as Giovanna yelled "Everyone out!" The tent swayed and its wooden support structure creaked like snapping hardwoods in a gail. Tight as a drum, the soaked canvas walls vibrated violently.

When Garner opened the flap door to the outside, it was like standing next to a fast-running, shallow river. Boxes, chairs, sticks, branches, and other debris swept past. Crowds of terrified people waded through the rising flood, clinging desperately to each other, some falling and thrashing in the water as they were carried away, then struggling to stand up again.

Tents had collapsed. They looked like the sails and masts of a crushed marina after a hurricane's storm surge. It was as dark as dusk.

Through the sheets of rain, Garner saw a Land Rover with a big Red Cross insignia slowly rolling through the floodwater, which rose to its headlights. It looked almost amphibious. At the wheel was Zeke.

CHAPTER 46

Garner pushed the skinny boy toward the vehicle, still with his gear on his back. Other people were crying for help, but at that moment, he had to ignore them.

The sagging tent redirected the floodwaters somewhat, but he knew he had to step into the current with the boy.

"What's your name!" he yelled into the storm.

"Sam!" the boy said, pronouncing carefully and straining to be heard.

"Okay Sam, one two three…and we're going to walk toward that Jeep," he screamed into the trembling boy's ear. The kid just nodded, gripping Garner's hand. He hadn't held a boy's hand since Jake when he was little. Garner formed a tighter grip on one skinny arm, which felt like the slim end of a small baseball bat.

He took one quick look behind him at Giovanna and the other frantic patients. It was regretful, but the tent was going to collapse at any moment, and it was every man for himself and whomever he can carry.

Realizing the kid wasn't going to make it in the current, he picked him up and slung him over his shoulder.

"Follow me!" he called over his shoulder to Giovanna, who'd reached the tent exit. In truth, he thought he'd might never see her again. As he entered the floodwaters he felt his stitched knee buckle with the weight and he fell in with the kid gripping him around his neck and they were instantly carried into the center of the cold stream. The tent creaked and leaned over and crashed in a loud heap behind him.

He saw arms and legs and a shock of Giovanna's hair go into the churning waters. The flood swept past like a swollen river.

It was chin deep already, which shocked him, and they were both carried swiftly along in the flotsam and jetsam of debris. Sticks and chunks of furniture and people's clothes; even an oil-and-gas slick rushed by, pungent and odorous.

The froth had a chop on the top as the water moved swiftly along, and some of it went into his mouth. The kid was ragged-dolled in the current beside him; he saw the little head go in, then break the surface again gagging and spitting. He still had the kid by the arm so desperately and he thought he had to be separating the shoulder but he wouldn't let go and he was haphazardly rolled over on his side with an awkward sidestroke, when netting flew down and slapped on the water ahead and beside him.

He'd forgotten about the Land Rover, but there it was. Idling in the waters about five meters away, and Zeke had tossed one of those ladders made of cargo-net material into the flood. Garner grabbed at one of the rungs and held tight. Zeke tried to reel them in.

The current was intense and forceful, and now Garner and the boy dangled at the end of the net, the waters rushing past their feet. He kicked furiously with his legs to get them closer to the Rover; he had a vague, sickening sensation of the bandages peeling off of his legs and the stitches pulling loose like a broken zipper.

Zeke unlatched the front passenger door. Garner grabbed onto the metal handle of the door, hung on, and laboriously hauled himself aboard, swinging the boy before him, like a wet sack. Zeke took the boy into the front seat and yelled at Garner to close the door, or they'd flood and sink the Rover.

Garner threw his backpack into the backseat, shut the front door, and climbed into the back, where there was more room.

Large pieces of the tent were now floating by. Through the clouded car window, he saw Giovanna clinging to one of them.

Garner shoved open the back door and lunged for a piece of canvas, so he could pull her to safety, but he only managed to plunge face first into the floodwaters, where he rapidly caught up to Giovanna and her own island of flotsam.

As he maneuvered up beside her, she rolled her eyeballs at him, as if the destruction of the camp was simply one more of the super volcano's inconvenient side effects.

It now appeared that they were floating through a fast-moving lake, such as one receiving run-off from a waterfall or river. The rains had passed over. The desert appeared to be covered by a mirror, but the glass was pierced by floating tents and even car rooftops. You could see the sky reflected in it, and a thousand heads, with accompanying arms, bobbing along the surface.

The rain curtains fled to the west, as ragged tears appeared in the black clouds, with sunlight streaming through the cracks.

He heard helicopters overhead, and saw a few canoes and dinghies with their occupants pulling flood victims aboard. Once again, he floated past the Rover, which plowed at about 10 m.p.h. through the soiled, murky waters.

The passenger window came down, and he saw Zeke, still gripping the steering wheel, gesture for them to swim over.

"Get on the roof!" he yelled over to them.

CHAPTER 47

Garner climbed aboard first by stepping on the back bumper and trailer hitch, which was underwater. Once he had hauled himself onto the roof, he grasped Giovanna's outstretched hand and gave her a boost. Then they both were out of the water as the Rover motored along like an old fishing boat through a bayou.

Soaked to the skin, they squatted on the roof, hugging their knees, until the sun appeared from behind a cloud. The temperature abruptly rose 20 degrees. The flood began to subside and drop in depth, spreading over the desert like water dumped on a concrete floor.

They reached a flat, straight road that went through Sky Valley. Zeke pulled over on a tiny gravelly rise on the roadside. Water dripped from everywhere, and there were ping noises from the engine, the smell of burned diesel, and stains of what looked like muddy seaweed on the sides of the vehicle.

Garner and Giovanna both gingerly climbed down

from the roof. It felt reassuring to step on solid ground. His knee was killing him, but he was almost too distracted to notice.

In the distance, a spontaneously formed river flowed through what used to be blinding white desert, which was now littered with miles of flood debris. Some of it was high and dry already; tree trunks and squashed tents and 55-gallon drums; propane containers, hulks of cars, parts of homes. Tiny black dots of people wandered through the wreckage, and trucks drove slowly through it.

The little boy got out of the car and sat on his haunches, then began to dig in the sand.

"What happened?" Giovanna murmured bleakly, gazing off to the east, where the remainder of the black storm clouds stood like mountains.

"Volcanos generate abnormal, extreme weather. My guess is that there's more of that to come."

"Oh, great."

Zeke stood by the mud-stained car. "I lost my Harley," he said absently. "Goddamned flood; I want that bike back."

"I have to go back," Giovanna said, as if gathering her wits reminded her of responsibilities. "We have to find out where this boy's parents are. And all the trapped and injured refugees…My God…"

The boy looked up from the hole he was digging and blinked. "They're gone. My mom and dad. They're dead. I'm sure they are."

"How do you know that, honey?"

"Because they stayed in our house and the volcano got it. The black clouds and the fire. They put me on the bus with the other kids and there wasn't room for adults and there was only one man driving," he said eagerly, as if he liked being the authority on what happened.

"Where was this?"

"Idaho. I came all the way here. I got sick, and I was in the hospital tent, and this flood came. Things are crazy, aren't they? Well you know. You were here!"

"His name is Sam," Zeke added.

"Well don't you worry, Sam. We'll take care of you."

Sam's abandonment seemed to take the steam out of Giovanna's plan to return to the flooded Red Cross site. She had someone to take care of now.

"We should keep driving to higher ground," Zeke said. "This road goes to 62, and we can take that up to Joshua Tree. The high desert. I came through there on my bike. Damn, I loved that bike. I lost my Harley! Shit!"

"It can't compare to losing your life," Giovanna said, with wisdom and a faint smugness.

"We'll get you another one," Garner added. He didn't want Zeke to keep setting Giovanna off. For some people, including crusading, sensitive women, Zeke took some getting used to.

The road was all but clear of water as they drove. Garner wondered if the road had ever seen any standing water, it was so typically baked and parched. The summers reached 120 degrees F. After a few miles, the Rover clattered onto Route 62, and they headed north, climbing through a small twisting pass.

Giovanna and Sam sat in the backseat.

"Where are you expecting to go from here?" Giovanna asked.

"We'll spend the night at Joshua Tree, then discuss out plans from there."

"We should probably return the vehicle then to the Red Cross." Zeke shrugged but didn't answer. Giovanna didn't ascribe to their modus operandi, Garner guessed, of seizing transportation when you needed it to save lives, and worrying about returning the wheels to the rightful owner later, because she didn't have to up till now. It was what he and Zeke had been doing since New Mexico.

"Do you have any kids?" he asked her, changing the subject.

"No, no kids," she replied almost gratefully in her Italian accent. "I've been working in medicine." She made child-rearing seem like a luxury she couldn't afford. There was a defensive note to her tone.

"Is your husband a doc too?"

"He was."

"Where does he live, California?"

"My husband was killed," she spoke to the window, and the hot, empty landscape it displayed. "A plane crash in the Middle East, 14 months ago."

"I'm very sorry to hear that."

"I'm getting over it." Then, in case that sounded callous, "I've come to terms with his death. It takes a while. Working in medicine helps; you're so crazy busy. Long hours, go home, sip wine, set your alarm, sleep. Repeat."

"What was he doing in the Middle East?"

"He was attending a physician's conference on pediatric illnesses. He was committed to helping children." She sighed. "He was a good man. He was supposed to land in Bucharest. It was a terrorist bombing, they told me. Not soon after the plane took off."

"I think I remember that one. Cairo, right?"

"Yes, that's right. I get a telephone call, and that was it."

"So you lost someone too," Sam bleated eagerly. He'd been listening in.

"Yes," she smiled, "I did. Maybe your parents are still alive, eh?"

"No," Sam said, flatly. The kid had spunk, Garner thought.

She turned back to Garner and Zeke. "Of course, you never forget the phone call and the awful news. 'Your husband's plane has dropped from the sky into the ocean. No one has survived. We're so sorry for your loss.' They talk to you about what to do with the remains, if they are ever found. Then you put the phone down, and that's it. Life changed, for good.

"You get on a flight yourself to collect the remains, but there are none. Nothing to speak of, that is, but ash or unrecognizable debris. Which just makes you feel worse, because it rubs in the fact that your spouse is gone for good, is as lifeless as ash. I got together with a good friend, and she accompanied me when I spread the remains in the Alps, where me and Marcel had a holiday once. He was French, but we met in Milan.

"After that, I dedicated myself to needy children. I dedicated myself to my profession, which is helping people in need."

"A noble one," Zeke said. "For sure."

She looked at him and smiled, warming up a bit.

"Right now, I'm filthy. I probably smell. Let's get a shower somewhere."

"You bet," Zeke said.

"Now that you mention it," Garner said. He, Giovanna, and Sam were all grimy with flood mud, and had pieces of leaves and bark stuck to their bodies where the clothes didn't cover. At the very least, they had to be hosed down.

The Rover had now gained quite a bit of altitude. Relief trucks came in the other direction over the winding road. Garner looked back; the part of the desert that once contained a refugee camp of 800,000 now appeared small in the shadow of the San Jacintos. The floodwaters were spread about like a mirage, obscured by the sunlight's harsh reflection off the unyielding Basin.

They drove out of the pass and down into Yucca Valley, entering a quiet but funky downtown strip. They saw an old man in suspenders and a floppy cowboy hat riding a bike, and a young, threadbare looking family pushing a shopping cart, but not too many cars. Lacking any arable soil, Yucca Valley couldn't have received any supplies to replenish the market shelves that must have emptied within 24 hours after Yellowstone's eruption.

This was the high desert, completely lacking in any natural resources to grow food, provide water, and survive. During the best of times, it was quiet, hardscrabble, and on the edge of a dystopian settlement run by hippies, stoners, dreamers, and druggies.

The residents might have fled to the refugee camp, Garner thought, his head resting against the window. He was exhausted.

After they'd driven in silence a couple of miles and saw neither open gas stations, restaurants, or hotels, they came upon the Big Basin Motel. The lot had a few cars and what looked like a water supply truck in the parking lot. Zeke pulled over.

Garner got out of the vehicle and limped across the broken concrete towards an unlit Vacancy sign. He didn't even want to look at the gash on his knee, which had been exposed to floodwaters. Scanning the parking lot, he instantly recognized a Jeep parked off to the side. Or thought he did.

It was covered in mud, but was the same make and model year as the one he'd spent so much time in with Laura and Lance.

CHAPTER 48

The office contained a small modest lobby with an unshaven, emaciated old man behind a counter. When Garner walked in, the man glared at him, a grimace barely stifled. He had a glittery rock n' roll t-shirt on, as if he needed to show proof that he was once young.

"Are you open?" Garner asked. He knew he looked terrible himself, and he wanted to allay any suspicions the man might have about this stranger's motivation.

"We were stuck in the flood down in the desert, and we're looking for a room and a shower. It's obvious we need to freshen up. We have a little boy with us…"

"We have limited services," the man interrupted. His tone was incongruously friendly. "No running water. But I've got a chain shower connected to a half full barrel out back. You can use that. I'll give you a room with that."

"It's a deal."

"I'll say it is. It's free; I won't charge yuh. I understand what's going on, and this is how I'll pitch in."

"That's very kind of you." Garner mustered a smile behind his soiled and bearded face. The man handed him a key.

He had Lance in the back of his mind; he looked around the premises, but didn't see him. He figured the Jeep was a coincidence, but it also reminded him of Laura, left in the back of a van on the side of a Utah highway.

She'd saved his life. Could she be resuscitated or "repaired"? Without a doubt, far more than a human could have been. But she was part human. Or was she? He still felt sadness, and a chaotic mixture of desire and revulsion, considering the smoldering circuit boards he'd seen in her torso.

Yet amputees such as soldiers received automated arms and legs now, so what made her different? She had a human heart, at least in the figurative sense.

He took the key and staggered outside into the sunlight, feeling queasy in a way he attributed to an image he had in his mind, of Laura's shattered body and iris-less eyes, yet the wonderful feel of her in his arms.

He thought of dancing with her to Roy Orbison; meshing his body with hers in a diner booth. She was all human that night.

Laura was part of the unfinished business he had in Utah, not to mention the smashed regions northeast of where he was in California: the dog Tanya in Sandy, Utah; his unaccounted-for family members. The dog was in good hands but somehow he wanted to see her again, like the distant high school friend you walked away from that bad car wreck with.

The way survival binds two souls together.

Kiatsu, Jake, and Abby might still be alive out there, in the desert of ash and bones that stretched for hundreds of miles. That thought began to bloom inside him. He'd searched the lists of casualties and survivors they made available in a registry at the refugee camp, but found nothing.

"We have a room!" he called out across the empty lot. He went to get his backpack and put on a pair of shades. The black clouds had been swept out to sea, and the harsh desert glare had returned. Its windless, arid blue made it seem like the black downpour and the raging storm surge took place only in someone's nightmare.

He craved a shower. He went back into the musty motel. He asked the man behind the desk, "That Jeep out in the parking lot, have you seen or talked to the owner?"

"Yeah. He was some official type of guy, wanted a shower but no room. Lots of people are coming through the motel these days. We're the only one open in Joshua Tree, right now."

"Is he young, about 30, in a dark green uniform?"

"The age is about right, but I don't remember the uniform color."

"Kind of direct in manner, you might say brusque? Bossy?"

"He was friendly and polite enough to me. You looking for somebody Buddy?"

"Just a guy I ran into on the road after the eruption."

"I guess everyone's looking for somebody nowadays. He left. He's probably banging around somewhere close, if his Jeep is still out there."

"Okay, thanks."

He honestly wasn't sure whether he was in trouble with Lance or not. But Lance would likely know what was going on in Utah and Idaho, whether civilization could get back on its feet, and if there were more survivors there. Lance would want to know all about what happened to Laura. Or may be these androids had built-in GPS IDs, allowing them to be tracked?

The thoughts and possibilities swirled around inside his head, like the storm that just clobbered the desert.

He borrowed two towels from the man and wandered out to the shower.

When he saw Giovanna, he said, "Do you want to go first? I have a towel for you."

"Um, not sure," she said tentatively. "Is it private?" Her clothing was covered with dried mud, her black hair was glued to the sides of her face, and flakes of vegetation stuck to her arms.

He shot a quick look at the crude enclosure. A small puddle had formed at its base, but it was no more than the equivalent of a port-o-potty without the roof. It was surrounded by the same hardscrabble desert, only small cactus plants shoved in marginally amidst the rocks and sand.

"It's like camping. I'll wait outside. I won't let anyone near."

"Oh, okay. Thank you. I'll leave the shampoo and soap in there." Already barefoot, she took the towel and wandered over to the enclosure, then unhooked the plastic door and went in.

"Don't you want a change of clothes?" he called after her.

Her voice echoed back, "I don't have one."

"Oh yeah. You know what? I can get at least a tee shirt for you." He'd done one brisk laundry at the refugee camp. It was a reminder of how generally gross he was.

"That's okay…"

He watched the clothing flop over the top edge of the shower stall. He heard a splash as she released the water, then a squeal that was more happy than shocked.

"No one's around, right?" Her voice was muffled from behind the vinyl walls.

"No." But Zeke wandered up to him as he waited in the parking lot.

"Boy that shower must feel good," he said standing in the sun with his wide-brimmed hat and sunglasses. "She is one classy Italian lady, too. Ooo who…"

"Don't get any ideas about Giovanna, okay? She's completely off-limits. Untouchable."

Zeke had both palms in the air, professing his innocence. "I'm a perfect gentlemen. I can offer an opinion, though. She should be a Sophia, that one, and the…" He made an hour-glass shape in the air with his hands. "Tch tch."

"You horny dog. She's a nurse and she's helping out the boy and us. How long have you been away from Amitola?"

"I forget. But coming from you, that untouchable stuff seems funny to me. You're the lady's man, right? What was her name, back in Las Cruces, before I ran into you and Tanya?"

"That was Julie. Poor Julie," he said with a mixture of wistfulness and regret. "I hate when people say that, because it sounds patronizing, but I mean it. She didn't deserve what happened. She was an angel. So is Kiatsu."

"Yeah," Zeke said. "The world is populated by angels, dogs, and wolves. Looking at it that way, we don't deserve to be in the same room. Do you still think Kiatsu…?"

"Yes, I think my wife and kids could still be alive. More so than a month ago, for some reason. I guess hope is a plant that grows."

"So that means you're going back north…"

"You see, I haven't heard otherwise. They had a car; there were three people. They were visible. They'd be on a casualty list if something happened, and I checked the one at the camp. They weren't on it."

He thought Zeke would be thinking, *what if they were burned beyond recognition or otherwise catastrophically injured with their IDs destroyed? What if their bodies were unidentifiable? What if their dental records weren't recovered?*

"They could have been hard to ID, but I still have to

go look for them." He changed the subject.

"I'm hungry. I'm going to look for food after a shower." They saw the door to the shower open and Giovanna emerged with a towel around her neck. She still had grubby pants on but had brushed the dried dirt off, and she was down to a white tee shirt.

"I probably still look messy, but I feel much better."

"No worries honey, you still look like a million bucks," Zeke said. Garner looked at him sideways, then headed off to the shower.

CHAPTER 49

He peeled off his trunks and shirt and removed his hat, which he hung on a nearby hook. He noticed his knee wound was pink, swollen, oozing, and wet. He would have to apply some disinfectant, he thought, from an old crusty tube of Bacitracin he still had in his kit.

He lifted his head up into the sunshine and yanked the metal chain, which poured a cascade of water over his head and torso. He watched some of the dirt and the slime wash off his skin; it gathered into a small gritty pool that clogged near the drain.

Despite Giovanna's squeal, the desert sun had warmed the water, which sat baking in a rusted steel tank outside. It was almost lukewarm. He took a bar of soap and lathered up everywhere but directly on his wounds. A small cracked mirror hung from a stainless steel pipe that connected to the water nozzle. His cheeks and chin looked porous and sand-papery; his eyes were red-rimmed. Hygiene, up till then, had to take a backseat to making it through the next day.

He soaped up his face, then seized a used plastic razor and scraped it roughly along his cheeks, chin, and neck. Then he knocked the black whiskers off the blade in the small pool of grimy water at his feet.

I have to go north through Utah again, he thought, still hacking away at the beard. Zeke will probably go with me. Giovanna will stay with the kid. He raked the razor over his cheeks again, simply for the familiar feeling. He used to shave in the shower every morning.

But he felt like he had no home anymore, as if his fate was to endlessly wander the west to find out what had happened to his family.

He finished shaving, if you could call it that. He rinsed the soap off with another bucket of sun-warmed water, then toweled off and put his trousers back on and came out of the stall.

He was met by the dry whine of flies. The town of Yucca Valley was empty and arid, like an abandoned colony on a hot planet. His stomach growled. Nearby was a sign, nailed crudely onto a wooden post, "Cactus, $2 ea., Pick Your Own."

He laughed to himself, throwing the towel over a shoulder. Zeke leaned wearily against the Rover nearby, idly smoking a joint. When he saw Garner, he took it out of his mouth, glanced at it, as if checking its brand, then lifted it partway into the air, as an offering.

"You're kidding me, right?" Garner asked, only slightly bemused.

"It's not like we have anywhere to go. This is good weed, a buzz to set your head straight. The view is nice."

"I've got to make some plans," Garner said. "Buy some more food and water; get gas. If I smoked pot I'd fall flat on my face and sleep for a week."

"That actually wouldn't be a bad idea," Zeke said.

"Yeah," he half agreed.

It was going to be tough to convince Giovanna that they needed to "borrow" the Land Rover for a much longer time, he thought. A few weeks, at least. Enough time to drive back into Utah.

"Do you have a cell phone?" Garner asked Zeke. "I lost mine in the flood. I need it to check for any messages from my family. I mean, those texts still could have come in, after all that time."

"I lost mine too," Zeke said, exhaling a cloud of pot smoke. The potent aroma filled the baking air. "Good riddance. I hate the damn things," he added scornfully.

He took the joint, and rather too elaborately, as if it was a precise, critical operation, pinched the end of it and returned the roach to a small plastic bag.

"People walk down the street staring into the phones like zombies," he went on. "They walk in front of cars and bash into parking meters. Can't miss a post or a text, God forbid. Amitola wanted me to have one, so she could call me. I turned the little fucker off. The boops and beeps got on my nerves."

"You can turn off sound in your preferences."

"If it isn't that it's another thing. They give you brain cancer."

"There is something to that."

"Now that we don't have technology, we have to rely on our raw wits," Zeke said, failing to mask his pride. "Our talents."

"Isn't the Land Rover technology?"

"Transportation is different," he said, after a clouded pause to ponder the argument. "The wheels are more like a dumb machine, like taking a train in the Old West. Cell phones, all they did is get people addicted."

Garner didn't bother answering. He went over to the Rover and opened up the passenger door to get his map out of the backpack. As if he'd read his mind, Zeke said, "We probably still have enough gas. We only drove from Thousand Palms to Yucca Valley. But it depends where we go from here."

From the other end of the parking lot, Garner heard a car door slam. A man he didn't recognize got into the driver's side of the mud-stained Jeep he'd seen before, while a woman slipped in beside him and shut the door. The engine started.

He'd recognized her immediately. It was Laura. He was sure of it.

CHAPTER 50

The vehicle rolled away and paused in front of vacant Highway 62.

"Hey, Laura!" he yelled, realizing his delusions at the same time. It was like screaming out in a dream. He knew she was dead. A part of him understood that Kiatsu had also been killed. He pursued the car nonetheless, walking quickly, consumed by hope.

The driver turned around and looked at him blankly. He had a disinterested expression, then looked back to the highway as they pulled out. It wasn't Lance.

The woman never looked back. The Jeep slid into the highway and headed north. "Hey stop!" Garner yelled, then halted at the entrance to the road. "That was her, I swear," he said to Zeke over his shoulder. "You remember Lance and Laura?"

"Sure do. That was only a few weeks ago. It's not like I've been stoned the whole time, and forgot everything. I thought you told me Laura was dead?"

"She is. I mean, she was. Lifeless. I had to leave the body by the side of the highway in a van. I tried to resuscitate her. She was in bad shape, unresponsive. I was sure she had died. She had artificial parts that were smashed by bullets."

"And I thought I was the only one who was high…" Zeke muttered to himself.

Garner stood at the edge of some dead grass and sand near the road and watched the Jeep drive away. The directional came on, then the vehicle slowed and made a righthand turn in about a mile and a half onto another straight desert road, heading into Joshua Tree National Park.

"I want to follow them. I want to be sure for myself. We can look for supplies at the same time."

"Suit yourself."

He saw Giovanna holding the boy's hand near the motel entrance. His knee throbbed where the stitches had been put in; he didn't dare to look at it again, but at some point he'd have to ask Giovanna for some help. You can't go where he's been, and keep a wound clean.

He walked up to her across the sun blasted space. The desert was taking over everywhere, as if the people were merely temporary squatters. Giovanna wore a sun hat; the boy shoved a stale sandwich against his mouth and chewed distractedly.

"Where'd you get that?" Garner asked.

"The Land Rover."

"Any more of 'em?"

"No. You can have a bite of mine though!"

"No thanks kid. But that's nice of you."

"They're reconstituting the camp at Joshua Tree," Giovanna said. "In the park."

"How do you know that?"

"The man in the motel told me. He heard on some kind of radio report. The trucks are driving up here, bringing the people, and what's left of the tents and structures."

"They have to move somewhere," he said, wondering how many deaths the flood had caused, out of the 800,000 residents. He was almost inured to the vast casualty numbers tossed about blithely since Yellowstone.

She read his mind. "They have 500 missing, so far."

"That's all?" Five hundred was nothing. It could have been much worse, was the refrain you always heard those days.

"I want to go into Joshua Tree," he said. "I think I know the people in that Jeep. We can take the Rover back there. Is that okay with you? You guys can stay with us."

In some unspoken way, it seemed like Giovanna was in charge now, and that he needed her permission. That was only natural, considering Zeke was at loose ends, interested only in getting high and finding another Harley, so he could start a second rootless desert journey.

"Yes. Where else would I go?" Giovanna said with an air of impatience. "I work with the Red Cross. I'm going nowhere else. And neither is Sam. We will go and help set-up. And you, Brad, where will you end up? After this?"

"Probably northeast again, Utah. I'll search the hospitals. For my family. But first, can you look at my stitches again?"

"Of course. Pull up your pant leg."

She knelt down and lifted up the remaining trouser cloth. She grimaced and wrinkled her nose, as though smelling something unappetizing on the stove, like garlic. He got the impression that it was probably much worse than she made it out to be; she had a smooth professional manner that was aimed at not alarming the patient, but doing what had to be done.

"All the stitches are loose. It's getting infected again. When we reach the park and find a medical tent, I will fix you. You will have to stay quiet for a while and let it heal."

"I don't know how long I can stay around."

She looked up at him thoughtfully, pulling the trouser leg back down with care.

"You're restless, aren't you? Can't stay still?"

"Yeah."

"What eats at you?"

"I don't know exactly. I've been on the move since that damn volcano went off. At any rate, you wouldn't want to spend much time with me," he added after a moment.

"And why is that?"

"I'm radioactive. The kiss of death. First Kiatsu, then Julie, then Laura. Every girl who's with me dies. If Kiatsu did in fact die. And if Laura…"

"That's crazy! You pulled us from the flood." She stood up and crossed her arms, looking out at the desert, where it seemed her memories were set free.

"You know, when I heard Marcel was killed, I felt shock and grief, then guilt. An overwhelming guilt, like it was somehow my fault. You think of all the times you didn't say 'I love you' or express your loyalty. All the arguments and pettiness and selfish attitudes you had, during your marriage. The times you just thought of yourself, and your petty needs and emotions. I wanted to bring him back to life, so I could reverse all the little slights that now never can be healed, because he's gone. It took me a long time to let go of my guilt. Maybe without the medical work, helping others, I never would have. It's not your fault Brad, none of that, with your wife and friends."

He only nodded in silence.

"We should probably get some sleep, while we have a room," she said, quickly shifting to the practical matters.

Zeke and Sam stayed outside and tossed a deflated, discarded football around in the parking lot, while Giovanna and Garner crashed for a few hours in a nondescript room that reminded him of La Casa Grande in New Mexico.

Then they piled into the Land Rover together and

drove the short distance to Joshua Tree National Park.

By the time they got there, the access road was crowded with a convoy of trucks. It made its way slowly, like a retreating army, into the Park, where a few tents had already been reassembled on existing camping sites.

Hundreds of people waited in disconsolate groups, as the trucks disgorged their materiel for the camp. The pristine white desert stretched to the horizon in all directions, interrupted only by the Joshua trees, with branches like arms ending in balls of green needles; and beige boulders and piles of stones that looked like they had rolled down from Olympus.

It didn't take long for Garner to find the Jeep, parked nearby in an empty campsite. He saw the man and woman about 50 meters into the desert, chatting and carrying what looked like sampling instruments. A kind of robotics machine crawled along the desert nearby.

They parked the Land Rover. Garner got out and began walking toward the two people. It was late afternoon. The air was oddly cold, belying the blinding sunshine, as if they were in the sunny arctic and not Southern California. The weather everywhere had turned topsy-turvy.

The dry wind whispered across the sand, with no more of a draft than you'd have from opening a wooden door. His lips went dry and parched as he looked at her. His eyes filled up; he didn't know if he would speechlessly embrace her. He half waved at them as he approached.

The lady was, without a doubt in his mind, Laura. He felt ungainly and awkward as he limped toward them. They watched him dispassionately. Her eyes contained not a hint of recognition.

CHAPTER 51

His knee throbbed and pulsated, as if someone was lightly tapping on it. She had the same face, eyes, hair, and body type, he thought. But this time, Laura looked straight through him, as if he was an inconsequential drifter from the camp, yet another hapless straggler they could ignore.

"Laura?" he said, as he got closer, already confused by this utter lack of regard.

"Laura? No. I'm Jill."

"Who are you?" the man said, in a clipped and annoyed tone that only said, "Go away."

"Brad Garner. I knew you in Utah and Idaho. I swear. Don't you remember me, Laura? We rode together in your Jeep. With Lance. We went all the way to Ketchum, Idaho together. It was just last month. I thought…"

"No, I'm sorry. We've never met. I've never seen you before. You must be mistaken," she said, shaking her head vigorously. Yet a faint glimmer in her eyes fought against the denial, as though she was a bad liar. Or, something had been even hidden from her, and the truth was trying to get out.

His eyes weren't tricking him; she was more than an exact replica, he thought. He even recognized the tone of her voice. That naive, innocent craving to experience anew all things human and female.

"This is crazy, we were in Sun Valley together, at the hospital," he said, his voice rising and insistent. "Those men who shot and injured you. You've survived! It's a miracle! I drove you down into Utah. Don't you remember? The diner, dancing, Sinatra music, and…" *Our passionate lovemaking*, he wanted to say, but he hesitated in front of the stranger. It was the elephant in the room.

A hostile grimace crept over the man's face, an expression almost of jealousy.

"No, I don't remember any of that," she said, turning her head to avoid eye contact. "As I said, I've never met you. Never In my life. I don't know what you're talking about. This Laura, surely you met her some place else."

The other man watched her intently. In response, she shrugged and rolled her eyes, as if to say, "I don't know what this crazy guy is babbling about."

A dizziness came over him. He felt unsteady on his feet. A system began to advance from the north; gray clouds, but not as ominous as the previous storm.

"Do you have an identical twin? I hate to keep pressing the point, but I'm sure it's you, Laura. It's uncanny." He reached out, almost against his will, compelled to lift the shirt and see what had happened to her formally traumatized torso. The broken, smoking circuits; wouldn't he find marks and seams or scars? Signs of repair? Or would it be a flat unblemished stomach? The life had come back in those eyes that had rolled back into their manmade sockets.

The man intercepted his hand with a vice grip like the clasp of a metal handcuff. He suddenly felt empty, denied the truth. The man shoved him backwards aggressively.

"Jill said she doesn't know you," he said with an authority tinged with threat. "That's enough. Go back to where you came from. We have serious work to do. The people in the camp can help you, whatever your problem is."

"I don't believe you. I want to see your stomach, where I tried to staunch the wound," Garner said, in a higher voice that seemed to be getting away from him. "We went through so much together. It's you; I know it is." He could feel the pulsating throb in his knee; the light around the desert was faintly grainy, as if swarming with clusters of tiny black insects.

As he stepped forward, the other man shoved him again, and Garner lurched back and caught the ground with the palm of one hand, preventing himself from collapsing into a heap. He got back on his feet and turned and looked back at Jill. His voice was interrogatory, less desperate. He had to know these things.

"Are you a synthetic?"

They just looked at him blankly, in silence.

"Are both of you androids? Some form of artificial intelligence?"

"You're nuts," the man said, resigned and out of patience. "Out of your mind. Get lost. We'll have you arrested. Or worse."

"Worse? What does that mean? What are you trying to hide?" Artificial intelligence and bad code had become a sort of enemy, ever since it had baited him to sacrifice everything in his journey to Idaho.

He went on: "You're probably not even aware of it. They switch you on and push you out into the world, to do your 'important work.' You're like newborns. What are these machines for, anyways? What exactly is your role, with these agencies you work for?"

"We're testing the survivability of robotics in hostile environments," the man said, as if he was obligated to by his taxpayer-financed salary. "The air is still unbreathable at Yellowstone. Mostly sulfur dioxide, but also some hydrochloric acid gas, and hydrogen sulfide."

"I guess that's where you're headed."

"Maybe."

"Is this a military application? They're developing and testing new synthetics and drones for the battlefield?"

They both watched him with a patronizing smugness. "Good guess," the man finally said. "Nice try."

Garner wiped sweat off his brow, then continued, changing the subject back to Jill. He had something to say. He felt cheated by this rebuff, romantically.

"Laura was a real woman, to me. I guess that means that the designers achieved exactly what they wanted to. They took Laura's basic materials and reissued her into Jill. Isn't that what the experts and the gurus say, we're all destined to be replaced by robots?"

"You're dreaming," Jill said. "He's hallucinating."

"I am." Then he looked at Jill's partner, before he turned to leave. "Check her eyes sometime."

There was no life for him in Jill anymore, only a cold, implacable purpose. In the office world, he'd met humans like that too.

In the distance, he could see hundreds of people filing off the trucks and forming a long line. He saw Zeke, and the boy. The boy was playing with a small dog, throwing a ball for him to chase. He bounced the ball into the desert, then the dog ran off, followed closely by Sam.

CHAPTER 52

Snow swirled in the air, flying heavily like the ash had fallen. The storm was blowing in. The line of people stretched down the road, toward Highway 62. They hugged themselves in the cold, most with ad hoc blankets thrown over their shoulders. It looked like an evacuation, which it largely was. He saw Giovanna, standing in front of one of the newly assembled tents. She'd pulled a government-issued sweatshirt and knit hat on.

"Who are the people in the line?"

"They have diabetes. They are lining up for insulin shots. There are millions of diabetic patients in the western region who haven't been able to get their medicine. Many have died. This is only the beginning."

He nodded and looked around for the boy. "Where's Sam? Have you seen him?"

"He was over there, playing with a dog. Hey listen, I make an inquiry here for a doctor, then we have him look at that wound on your leg. I'm worried about it."

"Don't be. We'll take care of it soon. But thanks."

They could see Zeke, standing on the edge of the desert with a shawl cast over his shoulders, the same one he wore weeks ago when he strode off on the road toward Durango, Colorado. His hands were cupped around his mouth, calling for Sam.

The knee throbbing more noticeably now, and feeling wet through the part of his pant leg covering it, Garner wandered into the desert toward where Sam had run. He saw nothing moving out there, just a long expanse of evenly spaced Joshua trees, sand, and the yellow boulders looking like elephant backs.

He was concerned for the boy; it wasn't a desert you just walked into, expecting to find your way around. It was all of 800,000 acres, and ultimately connected to other deserts like the Mojave.

Another part of himself thought, *we don't need this—the boy running off.*

Zeke looked at him fretfully.

"I don't see him. This isn't good; everything looks the same in Joshua Tree. You walk a mile, you look around, you lose your sense of direction. Suddenly, your ass is wandering aimlessly toward the Mojave." He started walking into the desert to look for Sam, carrying nothing but his shawl, a flint, and a knife. He had no gloves, only that now worn Stetson.

"I'll take that section over there," Garner called out. He was done with Laura, or Jill, whatever she was called, but the whole twisted encounter stuck in his craw.

Zeke called back, "the dog's probably chasing a rabbit. The boy's following him. That dog won't come back. You know, maybe you should stay here, wait for Sam to show up, if he comes from another direction. You ain't walking so good, my friend."

"I can walk; I can't run. We'll cover more ground."

"Okay. You follow that path there. You won't go

wrong, if you stick to the path, because you can just retrace your steps.

"I'm going along those boulders over there. Don't deviate from the route, because as I said, it's like Death Valley here. The tourists wander off, they get lost, they don't come back."

"Gotcha."

They split up, in a vee pattern, Zeke following along a ridge of elephant-backed boulders. Every direction led into empty, endless, now cold desert, with the snow falling gently, like inside a paperweight. The clouds were like cotton; you could see in the distance where it cleared again and the sun beamed through.

Both the truck convoy, the line of shuffling people, and Zeke disappeared from view after he'd walked only ten minutes.

"Sam!" he cried out, limping along. Damn it all, he thought. They hadn't been in Joshua Tree 90 minutes, when the boy runs off after a stray dog, which should never have been loose in the first place. No one is permitted to have a loose dog in a national park, no matter how dire the circumstances.

The snow looked out of place, peppering the tips of the green needles on the trees. It hit the warm rocks, then melted down the sides in rivulets.

His knee was killing him. He didn't think he should go far. Then, as he stared at the snow, he watched the flakes turn black. His view swept the horizon one more time for Sam, but nothing appeared. He turned, now dragging his leg amidst the black snow, around in the direction of the access road and the convoy.

A massive chill came over him, a tingling tide that took over his torso and arms. His heart raced frantically. He raised his arm for a comrade who wasn't there, but nothing in the desert; rocks, sand, decayed wood, leftover ash and bones, could answer or help him. He pitched forward into blackness, and never felt his body strike the trail.

CHAPTER 53

Zeke watched Brad wander about a half mile away. He was scared for the boy. He kept calling out, "Sam, where are you dude?" It was possible the kid had already doubled back beyond Zeke's notice. But doubtful. The sun was going down; the sky was still spitting snowflakes. "Shit," he muttered to himself. "Sam! Make yourself known!" he yelled through cupped hands.

He had his knife and flint but little else, but he wouldn't turn around. Not until the job was done. Zeke knew how to survive in the desert.

He hadn't monitored Garner's progress, but figured Brad had already gone back. Maybe Garner already found the boy? No, they'd be calling out his name right now, the voices carrying across the desert. He didn't even see lights anymore in that direction.

He stopped and listened. The silence was pure and untouched as if it had a supra-dimensional sound of its very own. He kept walking.

"Sam…Sam! Where are you, dammit!"

He heard a howl, then another responding call, from far away. For a brief moment he thought it could be the lost dog, but the sound had the distinct signature of a coyote. He didn't want the boy to encounter, obviously, the pack of coyotes wandering the evening desert.

Things that were white in the desert at night, were luminous. It seemed like he was surrounded by glowing white skulls, but he knew they were only rocks. The snow clouds drifted away, leaving room for a three-quarters moon. The path the Indian took, snowy for the moment and lit by the moon, was also luminous and holy.

The moon appeared to sail with the earth's rotation; a bright, taunting face. "Sam!" he yelled into the silence. He couldn't give up; he wouldn't go back. He was thirsty, so he headed for one of those glowing boulder piles, for which Joshua Tree was famous. Some of the snow would have melted in depressions formed in the rock. He climbed up onto the rocks, careful not to stick his hands too deeply into the crevices. He didn't want to agitate the rattlesnakes. Another reason he wanted to get to the boy; a snake bite would quickly do the kid in. God forbid he finds Sam, but dead.

He clambered around for several minutes, until he eventually found a bowl the eons had scoured into the rock. It had meltwater up to his chin; he thrust his face in and drank greedily, then lifted his head to the moon. He heard nothing but an occasional freshet of wind. This was why people came here in normal times, for the silence, which was now unwelcome.

The moon illuminated the whole desert before him. Yet nothing moved. He watched it for a while; shadows moved, creatures of his imagination. Then he yelled "Sam! Are you out there boy! Say something!" Not even an echo came back, as the desert devoured his voice. He crossed his legs, and in a quiet mournful voice, began to sing an old Ute song his grandmother had taught him.

It sounded like he was singing in an empty church. The desert was a holy place of the Gods, more profound and unsettling than anything men could build.

If he lost the kid, Zeke thought, he himself would be a dead soul wandering the west's dry places.

#   #   #

Garner lay on his back, hands so cold they were bent like claws with fiery tips. He was being roughly carried on both ends, the stretcher holding the weight of his back. Feet crunching on ground, fast paced. Voices, urgent. "Careful! He's in sepsis! Watch where you're going!" Emergency professional types. A slight sway to the carry. They throw a blanket over him. "Feverish; BP 90 over 50; pulse 130," he hears. His own heart pulsates loudly in his ears. When he opens his eyes, great effort!, only those clouds of tiny bugs. He opens his insanely parched mouth, but nothing comes out. He gulps air weakly.

The carriers lift him high, then someone shoves a mask over his face. Another, in a rush, seizes his left arm and inserts a needle. A queasy, helpless sensation of blood and solution flowing. He opens his eyes, but the black insect clouds congeal to black.

CHAPTER 54

Whimpering is how he found the boy, hours later. The dog was gone, but would probably find its way back. Sam wandered aimlessly amidst the Joshua trees, cold and scared but still on the move.

Standing at his perch on the very top of one of those boulder piles, Zeke couldn't miss him. Sam was the only thing moving by starlight for a mile, but for the occasional scrub bush in the wind or jackrabbit. Zeke got to Sam before the coyotes did.

He could hear him from a distance; the crying waxed and waned in rhythm with his walking.

Zeke knew it would take them at least two hours, at Sam's pace, to walk back to the Park access road, so Zeke gave him some water and settled him down. Then he lit a fire using some dead wood, tufts of brittle grass, and the flint in his pocket. He made the fire big, and the boy settled down in front of it and stopped crying. The flames cast long, quivering shadows against the rocks.

He thought about times when they'd hunkered down in the desert in Iraq. Years ago, when he thought of himself as brazen, invincible, and dangerous. Same cold desert air, by the fireside. Then, there was the feeling of a hostile world lurking beyond the flickering shadows. Commonly there was a scent of spilled oil and smoke in the air, but in Joshua Tree the smells were clean, hinting of mesquite and the tart scent of recently burned wood.

The specialty of his unit was ambushes and raiding villages, looking for terrorist cells, the ones who were attacking American convoys. He carried a handgun and a knife then. He was stealthy, lean, and efficient.

He'd let the killer instinct go since the war, but held on to the survival skills.

Zeke stood up; Sam was quiet, seemed comfortable for the moment. Lost in his thoughts. Jackrabbits were all over the place; you could hear them rustling in the underbrush around the campsite. They cast huge warped shadows, with their elongated ears spearing into the darkness.

Zeke left Sam alone for a moment by the fire. He went out in the night and set three traps for rabbits. He was meticulous about it, and within about an hour they had one.

Sam was asleep under the shawl by the fire, when Zeke returned with the animal, a big floppy carcass with long legs. He was glad the kid wasn't awake to see the dead rabbit.

He used the knife to skin the rabbit, then sliced off and dangled, from the tip of the knife, small pieces in the flames. Then he took the leftovers of the skinless body and nestled them up against the fire.

Sam woke up and quietly watched what Zeke was doing, rapt and curious. The meat dripped juices that popped and sizzled in the fire, and parts of the rabbit blackened. Zeke made a little pile of the cooked meat on a rock.

"I wonder why we've been living on old canned soup and stale sandwiches," he said off-handedly. "When we could have been eating rabbit. You like rabbit?"

"No!" Sam said, as if he'd been insulted. "I like rabbits. Not eating rabbits." He rubbed his eyes wearily.

"Okay, there's a distinction there. I'm with you. I know vegetarians, like my wife. But this here rabbit, I found him dead already," he half lied. "That's what I would want to happen to me, you know? If I died, I'd want the eagles to come down and make a meal out of me, rather than rotting away in the desert for no purpose."

"Gross."

Zeke began chewing on a piece; it was the color of dark turkey meat. It seemed like they were talking in a vast amphitheater alone, as though they were the only people around for a hundred miles, which was true in at least two directions. "Delicious. Tastes like duck."

"I like ducks too."

"You don't want to starve, right? It's not like there's a 7 Eleven right around the corner so I can buy you a bag of potato chips and a chocolate shake. Try it." He held out a piece, which Sam took after a long hesitation.

Inspecting it as a foreign object, Sam made a face and took a bite. It became a pleasant surprise for him. "Hmm, I like it."

"You're welcome."

"Thanks."

"We go back at sun-up, in case you're wondering," Zeke said. He kept eating the rabbit, and took his knife and scraped more of the flesh and viscera off the inside of the sizable rabbit skin, so he could use the skin later.

He kept feeding wood into the fire. There was a distinct boundary where the air became cold, but the fire roared along. Sam soon curled up again on the ground. Zeke lay back under the stars–the moon had all but set–and quietly sang the Ute song one time through.

He thought of the orphaned boy losing his whole

family to the Yellowstone pyroclastic flow. He wondered what it was like to witness that event through a boy's eyes; whether the horror would blunt the eventual man's emotions. He wondered what it was like for the parents, as he watched the boy go to sleep, knowing they were about to be immolated. Zeke's grandmother would have asked if they'd had time to sing, before they went off to the afterlife.

As Zeke was falling asleep with his hands clasped behind his head, the boy asked, "What was that song about?"

"That song is about how everything that happens to you in life affects what happens to your soul in the afterlife."

"I don't get it."

"You do good stuff in your life, you know kid?"

"Like when I was lost, you found me?"

"That's right. Then if you're lucky your spirit will be taken by an eagle in the afterlife."

"Better that than a rabbit's."

Zeke had a belly laugh for the first time in a couple of days, then they both lay back in the sand and closed their eyes. "Don't take your shoes off," Zeke said, one eye propped open. "The scorpions might crawl in them."

# # #

Zeke and Sam sauntered into the burgeoning Joshua Tree camp by mid-morning the next day. When people looked up and saw them, they began to clap and yell. Zeke spotted Giovanna outside one of the tents; she began running when she saw the boy.

When she caught and hugged him, Sam appeared embarrassed but otherwise happy, smiling sheepishly. "Oh, I knew you would be found! Don't do that again, okay? Did you know the dog came back?"

"No!" Sam yelled, with a tired, reinvigorated grin. "Can I play with him?"

"No way," Giovanna said.

"Why not?"

"He's sleeping now. No more running away with the dog."

"Brad came back, didn't he?" Zeke asked hopefully.

"In a manner of speaking."

"How do you mean?"

"He left with the EMTs, because of the septicemia. Blood poisoning. The bacteria gets in the blood. It's very dangerous. It can progress to sepsis, which can cause the organs to fail." She placed her hand on her lowered brow; upset, regretful, and almost but not quite in mourning.

"He was unconscious when he left," she said unsteadily. "They took him in one of the few ambulance vans."

"Shit, where'd they go?"

"The EMTs are trying to get him to a hospital in San Diego. It's not too far, but they thought he needed an airlift right away. So they are trying to meet a helicopter in San Bernardino."

"A medevac, oh Jesus. That's bad." Zeke took his hat off and scratched his head, as if hatching new strategies, despite his distance from Brad. "Which hospital in S.D., do you know? My son lives there."

"Sharp Memorial, I think." Then she turned away, and looked in the direction the van went. "I feel really bad. I should have made him stop, and let me clean out and restitch the wound. We delayed it. Delayed it and delayed it."

"It's that guilt again. Don't go down that road," Zeke said. "These are hard times in the west. Everyone's fighting to survive; we're all under the gun. It's no one's fault. Except for maybe Mother Nature."

"I suppose you're right. If we can find a phone, I can see whether he's been admitted to Sharp Memorial. Do you know how we can contact his next of kin?"

"He has no next of kin. They're all gone. Unless his wife and kids are alive, by some miracle." He ran his hand through the shaggy black hair. "Brad, you know, he didn't deserve this. He was just trying to turn something bad that happened to him, into something good."

"Speaking of, we're grateful that you went after and found the boy. That couldn't have been easy out there."

"Piece of cake."

"For you maybe."

"That reminds me, where can I find some food?"

"They are distributing meals over that way in the far tent."

Zeke waved and called to Sam, who was playing in the sand and gravel with some other boys, as though nothing unusual had just happened to him.

"Hey squirt! You come with me. They have a meal tent. Yummy meals. You can get…a piece of cake."

The extended line of people had reformed on the road, leading to the medical tent, where they administered insulin shots. It was a bleak and resigned group of refugees, some carrying babies or with small children in tow, who reminded him of the beleaguered citizens of Ramadi, Iraq, fleeing that city before the violent final liberating battle erupted in 2006.

The only difference being that he didn't hear jet engines, helicopters, and mortar fire over a landscape that looked like the sea floor after the ocean had evaporated.

Joshua Tree, the empty, wondrous desert, was cloaked in a melting white layer, crystalline in the bright sun. He felt he was lucky he had kept himself and Sam warm last night.

He thought he should stay in J.T. and help, like Giovanna. He liked being around her, and her earnest beauty; you could be in worse places than Joshua Tree. But he felt compelled to track down his fatally ill compadre in San Diego.

Brad had no one now. If he passed away, no one

would claim him. After the specified period of time in the morgue, based on some cold-hearted protocol meted out by bureaucrats, they'd cremate him. Down to nothing but an anonymous pile of unaccounted-for ash, they'd pour him on the ground somewhere—a place designated as acceptable for unclaimed urns of ash. Poor Brad's remains would be scarcely different than the trillions of grains of ash originating from Yellowstone's…then Zeke terminated the train of thought, before it became too knee-jerk existential.

Before San Diego, however, he'd have to find a bike.

CHAPTER 55

It was probably morphine. He didn't feel a thing except for his life leaking out of him, like drifting off to sleep, then coming back.

He heard the shrill cry of an ambulance in the hollow depths of the world outside. Then the vehicle stopped, the rear door jarringly latched open, and bright squares of sunlight flared across his closed lids. Not feeling a thing from his arms and legs, he vaguely thought of desert sun.

Laura's face appeared in his day dream, but it was Jill's. She had on the new uniform, but she was Laura for all intents and purposes.

"You were right," she said, staring down at him intently. "I'm Laura. I was embarrassed, because we slept together, back there at the diner. Such things still embarrass me, plus the fact that I was young, naive, and unsure of myself. You were wonderful; know that you were. You showed me the way into romance. I could see why your wife loved you. And what you did, journeying against all odds to

Idaho, was brave, even though you viewed it as foolish and a last resort. A restless solution to your grief and guilt."

"I'm so glad I talked with you and got this off my chest," she said with an affirmative nod of her head. "Yes, you filled a void. You have no idea how empty and full of dread the notion of being Model No. 05674 is. You made me feel human. The world is a cold, damaged place, literally and figuratively, but we, you and me, had our moment under the sun. Now you take care of yourself Brad. I wish you well." He'd wanted to smile, but felt he'd mustered only a grimace, and that again was the morphine or whatever drug they pumped into him.

Some suspiciously unrelated but frenetic activity took place around him, on the edge of his awareness. He was roughly moved along hard ground. He recalled her final words: "I hope they bring you back to life, too."

Airborne. A loud thrumming engine drowned everything else out, just as they fitted a mask over his face and re-inserted something back into his arm. The effect was, laying on his back facing away from a dark sea, then the tide flowing over him.

He slid against his will into the last phone conversation he'd had with Kiatsu, before she'd taken their family to Idaho.

"Can you come with us? It doesn't matter where we meet. We can pick you up at the airport. It will be so fun," Kiatsu said.

"No, I can't."

"Why not?"

"Too busy, that's all."

"You promised Brad. The children are going to be bummed out. Especially Jake. You know you guys were going fishing. Oh, he's going to be really disappointed."

Then you go fishing with him, he thought.

"I have a ton of work. I know that's a lame excuse, but no one else here is taking any time off. We have to keep this new client happy.

It's the nature of the beast."

He paused in front of a window with the cell phone still pressed to an ear, drumming fingers on the back of a chair. He saw the city from above, fast-paced people racing about the streets self-importantly, just like him. This conversation was like waiting for a rainstorm to blow over, knowing he couldn't stop it.

A shyly frustrated pause from her, then: "You're becoming a workaholic. We hardly ever see you. It's gotten worse; the absent father. I thought you were going to spend more time with the kids. Remember, we talked about it?"

"This is what's paying the bills, Kia."

Using her pet name wasn't going to defuse the impasse. "It's out of my hands right now," he said, phone still pasted to his ear while now he walked among the cubicles in the 20th floor city headquarters. The context seemed to give him leverage, an extra authority over his wife.

"Anyways, what would I do at your father's house? I'd come all the way out to Idaho to veg around in a living room, while your dad pours scotch and makes sour comments."

"Low blow Brad." She was quiet for a long awkward moment that seemed that much longer because it was on a phone.

"Sorry. Hey, I'll make it up to you guys. We can go on a fun Columbus Day trip to Manhattan. Or an island. Yeah that's it. We'll go somewhere sunny and beachy."

She audibly exhaled, an unspoken "no" to the proposed alternative.

"Kia?"

"You're not, seeing anyone else now, are you?"

"No, absolutely not! What made you even ask that?"

"Because you're looking for excuses to avoid us, me. You live as if you were independent. You use your job demands as an excuse just to do whatever you want to do."

"Now you're being unfair. Do you want to talk to Maxwell?"

"He's your boss."

"Right."

"What good would that do?"

"He'll back me up on this. I'm not in a position to let things go for a week in Idaho. It would help if you wouldn't put any more pressure on me, honey. I've got all I can handle right now."

This was usually the point when Kiatsu would bring up the possibility of changing his career, but mercifully she didn't.

"Okay Brad, I don't want to argue. The kids will miss you. Will you call tomorrow?"

"You bet I will. Take care honey. I'll make this up to you guys, I swear," he said with a somewhat automatic quality.

"I know you will."

CHAPTER 56

The young girl wandered the hallways of Sharp Memorial Hospital in San Diego, drifting down corridors full of busy, distracted people; curious. It gave her something to do, she thought she might run into another young girl or girls and they could play something together, but the more she saw of this hospital the less she thought that would happen.

No one paid her much mind, or impeded her progress, beyond a kind smile. She even turned a corner unmolested into the busy I.C.U.

She was repelled by the chemical smells but fascinated by the machines, the patients connected to the machines. She walked past the doors which were half open; the atmospheres inside seemed solemn, faintly shameful. She avoided looking at the sick people lying in the beds, sometimes accompanied by people speaking in hushed tones, mostly standing. She kept walking down the hall.

She passed a room and looked through its window, which had cross-hatched wires inside the glass. The names of patients appeared on nameplates attached to the doors. A man with a wild thatch of dark matted hair lay in a bed, partly propped up. His face was covered by a mask with a tube on it. All kinds of crazy tubes and beeping machines were stuck in or surrounded him. But he appeared to be sleeping quietly, to the steady metronomic beat of the heart monitor. She stared at him for several minutes, wondering just how hurt he was, and whether he felt pain at that moment. She thought not, he looked to be in a helpless snooze.

She'd never seen so many helpless grownup people.

A nice female nurse happened by. Her uniform wasn't quite starched "hospital white"; it was a pink bleached white.

"What's your name, honey?" she said.

"Abby."

"And where's your momma or poppa?"

"My mom is in a room way down there…in another hallway. Her burn is getting better."

"Oh that's wonderful! Are you hungry, darling?"

"No," Abby said, after thinking about it. She'd had an ice cream a while back. Then she put her hand, palm first, on the immediate door's nameplate.

"This man's name has the same name as my dad," she told the nurse. "Brad Garner."

CHAPTER 57

Weeks later, flying back to the east coast, the flight path taking them from San Diego, with a connection in Vancouver, over in an arc above southern Idaho and Montana. The Boeing 797 flew well above the clouds and over the same latitude of the now, possibly temporarily, docile epicenter of the Yellowstone volcano.

It was 2026; some of the cities like Casper and Bozeman were still empty, would be for a while. The region was colder and the air directly in the vicinity of Yellowstone still poison. Scientists, soldiers, and sporadic groups of nomads and renegades ruled the region. That much hadn't changed.

About a million and a half people had been trucked, flown, or had migrated themselves to the west coast, southern Arizona, Mexico, Texas, and beyond, but many wanted to go back, when they got the green light. If they ever would. Much of the farmlands and lakes and meadows and deserts nearer Yellowstone remained uninhabitable and contaminated, but grasses, forests, and soils had a way of renewing themselves, given enough time.

The pilot was proud to announce over the sound system that the jet plane was passing just south of the epicenter, as he would if they flew over Paris. His tone of voice was somber in reference to it, however, out of respect to its legions of American victims.

Jake sat in the window seat. Garner reached across him and pulled the window shade all the way up. He leaned over to look, straining to see the ground through wide tears in the clouds. The ground moved gradually beneath them. He saw a blast radius as far as the eye could see, at least fifty miles with all the flattened trees and terrain pointing in a circled pattern.

Where neighborhoods and towns had been was wiped clean, as if by swarms of F5 tornados.

Sometimes the landscape was just an extended black scar where the pyroclastic flows had blasted through, or where lava had flowed. In the middle was a charred, gaping, awful crater several miles in diameter, that wouldn't have been out of place on the moon.

The jet sailed peaceably over the region, as if they were space tourists viewing another planet, until the clouds covered up the view again. A terrestrial wound smothered by a kind of aerial bandage. "Jesus, wasn't that something?" he said, looking at Jake.

"Yeah." Then Jake glanced at him wide-eyed.

"Did you actually go there?" he asked. "When it was going off? We were trying to get the heck out of there."

"No, I never did. Oddly enough, I never went to the epicenter, but I was darn close. You know, I never stopped looking for you."

"I know."

Across the aisle in two more seats were Abby and Kiatsu, who was reading. Abby was plugged into ear phones, watching a movie. He put his head back and shut his eyes, listening to the rush of air from a nozzle above his head. He was thinking of Julie and Zeke and Giovanna, of everyone and everything that had gone down, since Yellowstone launched its magma into the stratosphere.

A man can never know when good luck will come, he thought, a mysterious blessing when he least expects it, after everything has been squandered and lost.

THE END

Printed in Great Britain
by Amazon